Island Murders

by Wanda Canada

Edgewater Press
Wilmington, NC 28411

ISLAND MURDERS

Edgewater Press
Wilmington, NC 28411

First Edgewater Press reprint edition, 2005
First published by Coastal Carolina Press 2001

Book design by Maximum Design & Advertising, Inc.

Library of Congress Cataloging-in-Publication Data
is available.

ISBN-10: 0-9770033-0-2
ISBN-13: 978-0-9770033-0-3

Previously ISBN 1-928556-26-4

Whole copy return only.

Acknowledgements

Special thanks for their endless patience and assistance goes to:
Ellen Rickert, Jean Nance, Kay Schaal, Richard Triebe,
Scott Burkhead, and Nan Graham.
I am much indebted, also, to the talented staff of
Coastal Carolina Press, particularly for the editing expertise
of Emily Colin and Dorothy Gallagher.

To:
John, Mary, Anne, and Catherine

If once a man indulges himself in murder,
very soon he comes to think little of robbing;
and from robbing he comes next to drinking and
Sabbath-breaking; and from that to
incivility and procrastination.

Thomas DeQuincey

Chapter One

A human body in crab-infested waters for any length of time is as gruesome a sight as anyone should see in this lifetime. No one ever wants to look—but they do—and no one ever forgets. Maybe that's as much as I want to say about what it was like to find Dennis Mason, or what was left of him, floating beside my dock at seven on a Monday morning.

My name is Carroll Monroe Davenport, wet female, long of Wilmington, shortly of New York and other parts, lately of the flu, shivering in the early March morning on the southeastern coast of North Carolina. Yes, I know it's a man's name, a family name, but I wasn't consulted at the time.

The wind off the Atlantic was sharp enough to sting, whipping my damp hair and stirring up whitecaps out on the Intracoastal Waterway. A light mist looked like it might blow off before long, but I wasn't too hopeful. The weather had been like that for a week.

After a short, exhausting run, the first since hiding out for days with antibiotics and hot lemon drinks, I was mostly lollygagging on the dock. I shouldn't have been there. It was too cold and too wet, but a serious case of cabin fever set in about the third day, and I had convinced myself it meant I was improving. Good judgment is sometimes not my strongest suit.

Seagulls were begging for a handout, flying in my face, dipping and swooping into the churning tide, pigging out on something they had discovered in water. In summer, gulls won't give me the time of day, but by December, all I have to do is stand at the sliding glass doors and they flock to the yard by the dozens.

I was trying to catch my breath before trudging back up the hill to change and get to the Figure Eight Island job. I owned a small, thriving construction company with my cousin Eddie, who was good with crews, but not so good at the hundreds of aggravating daily details. The finish carpenters hadn't shown up for three days at the Anderson site, the dock crew was running behind, and the landscapers had gone off to Alabama, or far the hell away somewhere, to the stock car races. Our tile men couldn't begin until the finish carpenters got out of the bathrooms, and so on and so on, *ad infinitum.* You get the idea—all the standard reasons why builders begin to drink heavily before they go into bankruptcy. But Eddie and I were more than family, we were friends, and all things considered, we made a pretty good team.

Yesterday, Eddie had called three times, ticked off about one thing or the other, as if I could personally round up all the missing workers, including Duane, one of our job supervisors. I might have mentioned that it was a Sunday or that the company ran mostly on my money, but I knew he was blowing off steam. The completion date was a week away, and we were all tense. I was also aware that Bitsy Anderson, one of the owners, had been on and off the site most of the day, and I was grateful that it was him and not me in my weakened condition. She could be a real pain in a particular spot, and the crew had long-since changed the Bitsy to Bitchy. Inasmuch as I had been on the receiving end of her tongue several times myself, I couldn't say I blamed them. Sooner or later, though, they were sure to forget and use *Bitchy* at the wrong moment.

On the hill behind me sat a wild-eyed contemporary house built of glass and stone, with a world-class view across the Intracoastal Waterway and a mile of tidal marshes and creeks to Figure Eight Island and Rich Inlet—straight on out to the Atlantic Ocean. I live alone except for a surly Amazon parrot named Charlie and Randolph Taylor, a seventy-five year old African American who lives in the cottage at the front of the property with his three-legged keeshond. Randolph came with my mother to the new house to whip the garden into shape and never left. He tends the grounds and the greenhouse with the expertise of a professional horticulturist.

The house, three acres, and construction firm were a legacy from my architect father when he killed himself six years ago. Long before that, when I was fourteen, my mother took the Sunfish out and drowned somewhere between the dock and Rich Inlet. I was with my father when he found her, so I know about drownings and tidal scavengers.

There are other deaths I seldom talk about, and when people ask, I just say that in my thirty years I've had enough excitement to last me a lifetime.

I finally leaned over the dock railing to see what all the commotion was about and found the gulls feasting on little bits and pieces surrounding an oblong mass floating half under the surface of the water.

A shiver of horror ran up my spine as the mist turned to light drizzle. A dog barked somewhere far off, the sound coming sharp and clear in the quiet morning. I climbed down to the floating dock for a closer look, stepping over unexpected smears of blood, knowing with cold dread what the submerged lump of clothing must be. And because chances were good that a fast-moving tide could carry the body halfway to Wrightsville Beach before help arrived, I snagged the bundle with a boat hook and tied it, hook and all, to a piling.

For most of my life, I've lived on the water near Wilmington and I knew what to expect, but when the body suddenly flipped face-up, if you want to call it that, I added even more pollution to the coastal waters of the great state of North Carolina.

When I stopped shaking, I went back up the hill and called 911.

The sheriff must have been somewhere in the northern part of the county, because I had only a few minutes to slip into warmer clothes and dry my hair before the doorbell rang. Stan Council stepped into the front hall with two wet, icy-handed deputies, one of whom looked to be about seventeen, the other in his mid-twenties. Stan wiped his big feet carefully, glaring at the others to make sure they did likewise, and then gave me a hug. He's a big man, a former defensive lineman for the Chicago Bears, so you know you've been hugged when Stan does it.

"How you doing, girl?" Water dripped off the back of his

hat and ran down his jacket.

I said, "If I could shake the after-effects of this flu, I wouldn't complain about anything, Stan. How about some hot coffee before you deal with another problem? The three of you look half-frozen."

Stan shook his head. "Best get on with it. It's shaping up to be one of those god-awful Monday mornings." Behind him, the youngest deputy glanced with longing toward the warm kitchen.

They opted to stand in the hallway, dodging the low chandelier, while I explained what I had found. When I hinted that I thought the body might be Dennis Mason, Stan's weary look disappeared. He drew himself up sharply to his full six-foot eight-inch, three hundred pounds of black southern sheriff.

"Dennis Mason? How can you tell?" he said.

"Well, obviously I can't be sure. I hope I'm wrong, but you know that Burberry coat he's been wearing since he came back from Scotland last year? You must have seen it—kind of an olive-green waxed cloth—not something you see much of around here. He wore it everywhere all winter, especially on his boat. Claimed it was wind-proof and water-proof..."

Quick looks circulated among the three of them. Stan removed his hat and rubbed at the back of his neck. I hadn't seen him in about three months, and it seemed to me there were more gray hairs visible and deeper lines in his face. It occurred to me that he had been up all night.

You have to understand a few things about Stan Council-other than that he's built like Rosey Grier. As a pro football player, he was a local hero in Wilmington long before our

Michael Jordan became famous. Once I heard him tell the press that he ended his long career because his knees hurt, that he came back to Wilmington because he just plain wanted to come home, and besides which, Chicago was the coldest damned place he'd ever been. He's held office for fifteen years, and in the last two elections, no one has bothered to run against him. Being opposed to Stan Council in New Hanover County is like being against Christmas. To be a black Democratic sheriff in a southern white Republican town can't be easy. To be revered is a miracle.

A strong bond existed between Stan and my father, stretching back to Vietnam. When I was a kid, they fished, played poker, and laughed like men intent on making up for lost time, with Randolph forming a threesome. On our frequent fishing trips, they would rock the boat with bellows of hilarity and eye-popping tales, yet they always made sure the biggest fish got caught by a spindly little girl in pigtails. After my mother drowned, it was never the same, but I still love fishing and poker.

"Well, no sense putting it off," Stan ordered. "Let's get it over with, boys, while we've still got a body."

I grabbed a warmer jacket and caught up with them just before they reached the pier. The sun remained hidden, but the rain had let up somewhat. I could smell the marsh muck at low tide and maybe a hint of something else seventy-five yards ahead.

Along the bulkhead, Randolph had long since forked over the composted garden. The banana tree was still a heap of dead leaves, but what looked like radishes and potatoes were already inches tall behind the butterfly daffodils. With a little faith and a lot of imagination, I could even smell spring.

The body was waiting, caught against the cross bracing, with the dark water lapping greedily and the flash of blue crab just beneath the surface. Three grim-faced men pulled it in to the edge of the floating dock. One of the "boys" gagged twice and then got it together.

Stan said, "Goddamn!"

Once was enough for me. I stayed topside under the shelter, filled with disquiet and a kind of unseemly, primitive fascination.

Dennis Mason was a year behind Eddie and me in school, the kind of kid who would be called "at risk" today, the product of an ugly divorce, an over-protective mother and a long family history of failed fortunes. In a small town like Wilmington, everyone knew he was into marijuana and beer by the age of thirteen, finally dropping out of school six months before graduation. In later years, he spent a lot of time in his boat, and we often ran into him at waterside restaurants. He was a loner, except when he was drinking.

Within a half hour, eleven men were clustered on the pier, the floating dock or down in the marsh grass. They cursed vehemently when the *Captain Moffitt* and his double barge churned by, sucking and swirling the water first out and then back again.

I gave up and went back to the house for hot coffee and more dry clothes.

Halfway up the hill, the youngest deputy came alongside me. "Sheriff Council says you shouldn't go anywhere, that he'll want to talk to you again in a few minutes."

"No problem," I said. "Tell him I'll be inside where it's warmer."

As I stepped on the porch, I noticed the wind had risen enough to nudge the rocking chairs into motion. I thought it was fitting that the wind chimes in my four-hundred-year-old live oak had begun playing repetitious, mournful music. Through the greenhouse glass a hundred feet away, I could see Randolph tending the orchids near the entrance.

The answering machine was blinking in the kitchen, indicating that two messages had come in while I'd been on the dock. I pushed the play button, then the stop as Randolph burst wild-eyed through the back door shouting, his voice hoarse with panic.

"Carroll! Carroll! You better come quick. Come quick to the greenhouse." He slammed out again as fast as he had arrived.

"Randolph...?" But he was gone, and outside on the crest of the hill, I could already hear him bellowing for the sheriff.

I grabbed my jacket, slipped on my shoes without tying them, and rushed outside where all hell seemed to be breaking.

Catching up with Randolph, I said, "What is it? Tell me what's wrong."

Instead of answering, he whirled in a rapid about-face and began flailing his arms toward the front driveway, agitated beyond measure. "Oh, good Lord, have mercy on us all. Whatever you do, don't let Eleanor come near the greenhouse." He was breathing hard and struggling to keep his voice down.

"Randolph, what in the hell...?"

In the direction he was pointing, my eighty-five-year-old grandmother was getting out of her aging Cadillac which she had parked in the circular area near the garage, blocking two official cars.

Randolph hissed, "Don't ask! Just stop her! Quick!"

I moved hurriedly along the brick path toward the driveway, glancing back just in time to see Stan and Randolph rush into the greenhouse. In the process, I banged my ankle against an ivy-filled concrete planter.

"Well, shit," I said in disgust, forgetting that my grandmother's hearing still rivaled that of a twenty-year old. With as natural a smile as I could muster, I kissed her cheek, not fooling her for a minute. She looked from me to the activity in the greenhouse and back again, keen eyes missing nothing.

I took her basket of gardening tools and said, "I didn't know you were coming."

"You just forgot," she said, in the same tone of voice with which she often reminded me that her own mind was still sharp, thank you very much.

In appearance, she was as fragile as old crystal, but she was as strong emotionally as anyone I'd ever known, with that deep and abiding certainty that each succeeding tragedy is never the worst that can happen. She was also a woman who dearly loved excitement.

Instead of a quizzing, I received a scolding. "I can't believe you're out here half frozen, child, and you just getting over the flu. You'll have pneumonia next, and I'll have to move in permanently to make sure you take care of yourself."

"I would pack your bags in a heartbeat," I said. Indeed, nothing would have suited me better, and if Randolph's wife, Lucille, hadn't been there to watch over her like a mother hen, I would have long since put more than a little pressure on her to do just that.

"Perhaps when I'm ninety-five and slow down a little. But for now, though, why don't you come inside and tell me over a cup of tea just why there are six county vehicles parked out front and why the sheriff is in your greenhouse."

Before I quite knew how she managed it, she had maneuvered us both through the front door and into the kitchen, where she began to run water in the kettle.

I gave her a hurried rundown on the dock situation, trying not to shock her aging heart with lurid descriptions, while she interrupted little except to say *"oh dear"* and *"my goodness"* once or twice.

When I finished, she simply said, "It will kill his mother if it's Dennis...Lula lives her life for that boy. I hope you're wrong."

"Listen to me seriously now, Gran. Something else has happened in the greenhouse. Whatever it is, Randolph doesn't think you should see it, but I have to know what's going on. Will you promise you'll stay here where it's warm while I go find out—maybe fix us a sandwich to go with the tea? I'll give you a full report as quick as I can."

She looked at me long and hard, the smallest flicker of fear or premonition at the back of her eyes. "I've made it a point through the years to always trust Randolph's judgment."

Patting my hand, she made a shooing motion. "And if vandals have ruined the orchids, I'll shoot them myself."

I left her standing at the kitchen window with the binoculars, still in her coat, watching the activity on the dock.

Once outside, I could see through the greenhouse glass that Randolph had prudently moved the dendrobium orchids and the freesias away from the entrance so they wouldn't get knocked over.

"I'm sorry, you can't go in, ma'am." The same young deputy was busy stringing yellow police tape across the entrance and around the building.

Randolph, standing near the back wall with Stan, looked up and hurried out. "It's bad, Carroll...real bad." He swallowed. "Stan says it's Eddie...that it looks like his throat's been cut. And there's blood everywhere in the back of the greenhouse...everywhere!"

"Eddie? Our Eddie?" I could hear my voice go high with shock. Nausea swept me, and I swear I felt my face grow cold. Suddenly, the warm moist air from the greenhouse was filled with the sickening smell of freesia blossoms and blood.

I closed my eyes.

"Sit!" Stan said in his booming official voice, pushing me toward a wooden bench outside. "Put your head down and take a deep breath. Now, don't you fall apart on me. I've got no time for fainting and hysterics. Randolph, you old fool, after everything she's been through, you can't just throw it in her face like that. What's the matter with you?"

Randolph collapsed on the bench beside me, tears rolling down his face. "I didn't know at first. I didn't know it was

Eddie. I'm sorry, Carroll."

I hugged him tight for strength. His wiry old body was trembling as much as mine. I took a deep breath and then another, while Stan stood over us.

"I'm all right, Randolph. Stan knows I won't fall apart. Is it really Eddie?"

Stan nodded. "I wish I could say different."

In a burst of anguish, I blurted, "But he has a wife and a little girl. My God! What's happening here?"

Stan stared down at the dock, then back to the rear of the greenhouse, his face as grim as I could remember seeing it. "I haven't a clue," he said, "but I'm sure as hell going to find out."

Chapter Two

By one-thirty I was on my sixth stomach-cramping cup of coffee, but I still couldn't eat. Little bits of flesh floated around in the back of my mind, and I could still smell blood mingled with the greenhouse dirt.

Around eleven o'clock, a helicopter had landed on the level grassy area near the bulkhead, producing enough vibration to rattle windows and cause Charlie to make weird, non-parrot noises, like a chicken warning of hawks. If the garden had been further along in the season, the corn would have been laid flat. Only one man alighted—a tall civilian with sandy hair in a brown leather jacket, white shirt, and red tie. He received a slap on the back from the sheriff who spent five minutes in serious conversation with him. At one point, they both looked up the hill toward the house. Binoculars were always handy on the water, and Gran made full use of them, tutting her indignation when the downdraft whipped the daffodils.

At one time, I counted seventeen people on the scene, both in and out of uniform. Except for three still in the greenhouse, they had all come and gone, leaving deep ruts by the drive and trampled marsh grass below the bulkhead.

With permission from Stan, Randolph went to hose down the floating dock and the nasty smears on the side of the Boston Whaler. I watched him through the kitchen sliding doors, standing with the hose in his hand, staring off toward Rich Inlet.

Around two o'clock, Stan left on the chopper alone.

I called the job site on Figure Eight Island and broke the unhappy news to a stunned crew, or at least the two who had shown up for work. Jinks, a twenty-five-year-old with a useless degree in sociology, answered the phone.

After three years of mostly temporary jobs, he had ditched his chosen field and gotten a contractor's license. I'd been lucky to find him, even though I knew it wouldn't be long before he traded his unkempt beard and foot-long ponytail for a business of his own. He had the right perfectionist attitude about his work and a calmer hand with the clients than I did.

Best of all, Jinks had taken Randolph's dropout nephew, Davis, under his wing, teaching him the trade for the last few months and personally picking him up and delivering him home each workday. I hired Davis as a favor to Randolph, who had assigned himself the task of *whipping the boy into shape*, as he called it. Mostly we worried about Davis getting caught with gang members again after a run-in with the Wilmington Police, which involved a short joyride in a car not their own—better known as car theft—and a very long night in jail.

A lot of people had gone to bat for Davis, including the arresting officer and a savvy black female judge, all of which only seemed to increase his surliness. We were left with only Randolph's hard-knocks strategy, which was to work him until he was ready to drop so he wouldn't have enough energy to get into trouble—not an easy maneuver when the subject is fifteen and six feet tall.

Over the years, Davis had built up a backlog of anger toward a number of people in his life, not the least of which were a missing father and a mother who cared more about her drug habit and a never-ending stream of enabling male friends than she did for her son. Now, for the first time, things seemed to be working for him. I told Jinks to take Davis and go home for the day, and to please see if he could find the elusive Duane and tell him what had happened.

Duane, by far the most experienced of the three and technically the supervisor, was also the most undependable. If the boys were reliable informants, he had lately been hanging out at Barnaby Bill's Bar near the downtown waterfront. I hoped not. The one thing I didn't need was a worker three stories high—in more ways than one—on whatever drug was currently being imported into Wilmington via South American ships in port.

"Have the landscapers shown up, Jinks?" I said.

"Looks like they *were* here. Maybe. That big old dirt pile has been moved, but I can't see much else got done. They must have come late yesterday 'cause I was here by seven-thirty this morning. Nobody else has been around except Ms. Anderson, spitting hell as usual. And yeah, Eddie's wife—she's been calling and calling. What do I tell her next time?"

"I'm on my way to her house now, so just clear out and don't answer the phone. Oh, and Jinks, warn the boys not to talk to reporters. Have them call me, or better yet, Sheriff

Council. And everybody be back on the job tomorrow morning. Closing is set for a week from now, and we both know there'll be hell to pay with the Andersons if it isn't ready on time. I should also know about the funeral arrangements in the morning."

The light on the answering machine was still blinking. I had forgotten about the messages. I pushed the play button and listened with escalating heartbreak to the two from Eddie's pregnant wife.

"Carroll, it's Alex about eight o'clock. Do you know where Eddie is? We had a fight last night and he didn't come home. I think I'm beginning to get worried, because it was just an argument really, and I... Call me if you get this message."

"Carroll, it's Alex again. Now I don't know whether to be worried or pissed. The guys at the job say Eddie hasn't been there at all this morning, even though it's almost ten o'clock. I don't know what to think... I don't know what to do, or who else to...so just call, OK?" Four-year-old Tully was crying in the background.

It was enough to squeeze the hardest heart.

I reset the machine and rested my aching head on the countertop. The chair creaked beside me. My grandmother's eyes were red around the outer edges.

"You heard, Gran?" I said. "I'm not sure I have the courage to call her back."

She rubbed the goosebumps along my forearm. "My dear, we have to be strong about this. That child is going to need us most desperately...and Alexandra...I can only imagine what she must be going through." Her voice cracked. "And that poor unborn baby on its way..."

She was no stronger than I was. Only more accustomed to the pain of eighty-five years of losing loved ones. I thought of Eddie just before his parents' funeral, crying out over and over, *It isn't fair, it isn't fair.*

I wiped my eyes on my sleeve. "Who would do such a thing, Gran? I've been racking my brain for some reason Eddie would be in my greenhouse—unless he was coming to see me. But in the middle of the night? And it's impossible not to think that somehow I should have heard him, helped him. Anything, except let him bleed to death all alone in the greenhouse."

What I didn't say to Gran was that I was appalled by the half-formed suspicion that Eddie had avoided banging on my door because he hadn't wanted to put me in danger, too.

She closed her eyes. "Stan will find out. I know his tenacity, and he won't stop probing until he knows who killed him. But it won't bring Eddie back, and Alexandra will need all of us to get through this. Stan called her brother so she'd have someone with her when he made his official visit, but men are never very good at this sort of thing. I understand her mother is somewhere in Europe with a fourth husband?"

"Fifth," I said.

She waved a hand as if to say *three, four, five, it doesn't matter.* "I'll be surprised if Alex even knows how to reach her. The two of you are as close as sisters, and it's you she'll turn to."

"Right this minute, Gran, I don't see how I could be any

comfort to her. I don't know if I can do it."

"Oh, yes you can. You went through the worst that can ever happen in New York, and with your daddy and Sylvia." Her voice broke when she said my mother's name.

How hard it must be to live so long and lose so many. And now, her only grandson, the last male in the family.

"Anyway," she went on, "I never knew, Carroll, how you got through it, up there so long in the hospital—but you did—and it made you strong somehow. I could see it in your eyes when you came home."

I said, "Because you sat by my bed, day in and day out, for weeks. That's how I survived it."

"You're the very image of your mother, beautiful both inside and outside, and as surely as I know anything, I know you have the compassion and heart to help Alexandra and my only great-grandchildren when they need you the most."

I granted her the nostalgic pride of a loving grandmother, but while my mirror reflected the same blonde hair, stature, and attractive face, it never bestowed the luster and joy that graced everything my mother did and that made her truly beautiful.

I said, "For a woman of such advanced years, you can fight pretty dirty. But you're right, as usual. It must have been a man who first claimed women are supposed to be at their best in times of adversity. Whoever it was, I guess we'd better go prove him right. Do you want to go home or stay here and rest?"

She rose unsteadily. "Oh, no, I've rested enough. I'm going with you, young lady. You'll need my moral support."

"You're right about that, too."

Eddie's house was a two-story brick colonial with a bright yellow door, set well back off Mimosa Street behind live oaks hanging with Spanish moss, just a block away from where the famous trolley once ran all the way to Wrightsville Beach. The blue and red of Tully's new swing set was just visible over the brick wall around the backyard.

Before we could knock, Alexandra's brother, Simpson, looking stunned and uncertain, swung the door open and led us into the living room.

"Lord, it's awful," he said. "She didn't say a word while the sheriff was here, and now she's laying on the bed, white as a sheet, not crying or anything. It's like she's just frozen up and wants to scream or something and can't. I don't know what to do. Thank God you're here."

"You go on up," Gran said to me. "I'll help Simpson take care of Tully."

Simpson shook his head. "Tully isn't here, Mrs. Monroe. Goldie came and got her just before you arrived. I didn't know what to say to a four-year-old—whether to explain to her or not—and Alexandra just went up the stairs like a zombie and closed the bedroom door. I tell you when that child started banging on the door with her little hands and screaming for her mama...well, I just ran next door for Goldie. I couldn't think of anything else."

Gran let him help her off with her coat. "Simpson, you did exactly the right thing. Now though, I think you look like you could use a good stiff drink while Carroll goes upstairs. And if you would be so kind, I'll have a little brandy while you tell me whether we ought to call Doctor Matthews and where your mother might be reached."

I went up, knocked softly on the door, and entered without waiting for an answer. When I pulled a chair up to the bed and took her hand, Alex opened her eyes. Simpson's diagnosis wasn't far off. She was in shock, I thought, but mostly in despair.

She was wearing navy blue sweats, which hid her pregnant state, but made her fine-boned face look even paler. The flame-colored hair was swept back with a rubber band like a teenager's, her feet were bare, her lifeless hands as cold as ice floes. I had seen critically injured animals with that same dazed look in their eyes.

"Carroll?" she whispered.

"I'm here, Alex." I pulled the spread up around her and tucked it beneath her feet as her teeth began to chatter.

She gripped my hand in sudden fear. "Where's Tully?"

"She's all right. Goldie took her next door." I rubbed her hands with vigor, trying to bring some warmth.

After a deep relieved breath, she closed her eyes again. Her hands still clutched mine spasmodically.

The eyes flew open. "Carroll? I can't... I don't know what to..."

"Shhhh," I said. "Don't try to talk. You're in shock, I think."

She turned her head away. "You don't understand. It's my fault."

"Oh, Alex, no! Don't think that."

"It is...it is. All my fault."

"Shhhh," I said again. I wanted to assure her that every-thing would be all right, that we'd help her get through it, that time would ease the pain, but each platitude on the tip of my tongue sounded stupider that the last. I couldn't find the right words, because I knew from experience that her life would go spiraling downhill and never be the same again. Some help I was.

"Don't leave," she begged.

"Let me just call Simpson to bring you something to help get you warm...hold on."

It was only a matter of a few steps to the hall railing and a hurried call for Simpson to bring the sweetest drink in the liquor cabinet. The tears had already started falling when I stepped back into the room, followed by great, wrenching wailing while I held her, rocking her like I would have rocked four-year-old Tully.

How long she cried, I had no idea, but it wore her out. I was vaguely aware that Simpson was in the room at one point with a glass that he left on the night table. Her shivering and shallow breathing began to frighten me. For the first time, I noticed the open window beyond the bed.

I said, "Alex? Can you take a few sips? You're half fro-zen, and I'm really getting worried. Please, Alex?"

Slowly but surely, she began to stop sobbing. I got her to take one sip of what smelled like Kahlua and then another.

"Drink all of it," I said. "You need it."

I got it down her eventually, spread another blanket over her, and closed the window. When I went to get a warm washcloth, I was startled by my own image in the bathroom mirror. My face, too, was streaked with tears. I wiped both our faces with damp cloths and loosened her ponytail. She was asleep before I took away the empty glass, worn out.

As I was closing the door, Lily Puss, the champagne Persian, darted into the room and curled up on Eddie's side of the bed. I left her there.

Downstairs, Simpson had the phone off the hook and my grandmother's feet up on the sofa, a pillow under her head and a green afghan across her legs. Her eyes were closed. He was in the kitchen with a cell phone making hushed calls about Eddie's death.

I had never much cared for Alex's brother. When we were children, he had whiny, tattletale ways, and as an adult had developed a serious banker attitude. But he was doing the best he could right now to watch over three generations of women. I thought I might have to revise my opinion. No one needed me, so I went out the back door and cut through the side shrubbery to Goldie's house.

When I returned to Wilmington after wandering the globe for two years, Goldie was one of the first people I met at a boring party I hadn't wanted to attend in the first place. She was new in Wilmington, recently married to the son of one of our wealthiest families, and struggling with what passes for society in a small southern town.

Always outspoken, the first thing she said to me was, "So tell me about New York and your nervous breakdown." If I remember correctly, I bristled and shot back, "Only if you tell me why you married a shithead like Richard Howe."

She replied, "I'm beginning to wonder about that myself." And we both laughed, calling it the ultimate icebreaker. Later on, of course, we shared all our disquieting stories, but by then, Richard was mayor of Wilmington and she was in the process of divorcing *The Dick*, as she called him. She was also fast becoming a shamefully successful real estate broker, selling only high-end properties. Her ability to out-cuss a merchant marine often got Goldie Goldman in trouble. But then, I'd had that problem myself from time to time.

Nothing had ever been out of place for long at Goldie's house—except her husband—and the divorce had been a worthy remedy. She had naturally blonde hair, a body and smile that women envied, even gourmet cooking skills. She was the perfect wife for a politician, yet he'd seemed surprised when she wouldn't let him walk all over her with his five-hundred-dollar Italian shoes and his women. I thought Richard Howe was the biggest fool in town.

Without bothering to knock, I walked into the kitchen, calling out as I had a hundred times before.

"Keep your voice down," Goldie whispered, coming in from the hallway. "Tully's in the den watching cartoons, and I want to talk to you before she knows you're here. Come in and tell me what in the world happened. I didn't understand much of anything because I needed to get Tully out of there *but* fast. Is Eddie really dead?"

"Really," I said, my eyes moistening.

Food was always Goldie's answer. Over hot tea and crackers with paté—trust Goldie to have paté—I went back over the whole story as best I could, skipping a full description of what might turn out to be Dennis Mason. We peered into the den from time to time to be sure Tully was still out of earshot.

"Was Eddie shot?" asked Goldie.

"According to Randolph, who found him, it appears his throat was cut." The visualization of that simple statement hung in the room like a funeral film.

Goldie carefully folded a napkin around the remains of her cracker and moved it away. There were tears in her eyes. "I don't have the words to express how much I hurt for all of you. I am so sorry—for Alex, for Tully, for you. And for me, too. Eddie was a great guy to have for a friend and neighbor."

I said, "Don't cry, please. You'll get me started again."

She wiped her eyes. "Don't count on it."

"Goldie, does it sometimes seem to you the whole world is going crazy?"

She said with vehemence, "Going to hell is more like it. God, I can't believe this! That little girl's daddy is gone forever—poof—just like that." She poured her cold tea down the sink. "It just makes me so damned mad that you can't walk down the street anymore without looking over your shoulder. Where's it all going to end? Worst of all, what's it going to be like for little kids like Tully in a few years?"

We sat in silence, two intelligent, modern women without a clue between us, until Tully herself came in to say the cartoons were getting scary.

She didn't know the half of it.

If you ever lose faith in Mother Nature's ability to achieve

perfection, take a close look at a small, loving child one day.
Hands, feet, shining hair and eyes will give a lift to even the
crabbiest old dog. Personally, I thought Tully was way, way
above the average child, with the looks of a Victorian Shirley
Temple and the noodle of a brain surgeon in the making.
But what did I know about children? Nor was I likely to find
out with one of my own.

Tully was small for her age and dressed like a doll child
in blue-flowered, jumpsuit pantaloons with a round collar
of white eyelet ruffles. On her feet were tiny little unscuffed
patent leather shoes. She was one of those children who never
seem to get dirty, except at my house, where I let her putter
in the dirt and roll down the hill with Randolph's three-legged
Max. More often than not, she went home smelling like com-
post, shrimp bait, and dog.

Crawling in my lap, she snuggled Alex's fire-kissed curls
up under my chin and asked with adult seriousness, "Auntie
Carroll, is my daddy dead?"

Paralyzed, I didn't know how to answer, and Goldie appeared equally useless. What would be the right thing to say
to a four-year-old? Daddy's gone to heaven? Or gone to live
with the birds and the butterflies? God took Daddy to help
him build houses? Anything except, *Some son-of-a-bitch slit
Daddy's throat and left him to bleed to death in Auntie Carroll's
greenhouse.*

Before I could answer, with typical small-child behavior, she changed topics on me. "And Auntie Carroll, you know
what?"

"What, darling?"

"I'm gonna have a baby...a boy baby!"

This I could handle. "I know, sweetheart. Or maybe it will be a girl baby. Did you think of that?"

"Oh, no," she declared solemnly. "I saw a picture, and Mommy's doctor said it was a boy baby. He's kind of funny-looking, though. And Auntie Carroll...?"

Oh, God, here it comes again, I thought. "What, darling?"

"Is my mommy gonna die, too?"

"Oh, sweetie, no. Of course not. You see..."

"But she was crying, and Goldie said she was sick."

"Tully... Tully, listen to me. Do you know where your heart is?" When she placed her little hand over her chest, I went on, "Well, Mommy's heart is hurting her, and it makes her feel very, very sad. Plus, she has a little baby in her tummy and that makes her tired and sleepy. Do you understand? Goldie? Help me out here."

"Hey," Goldie said. "I bet some cookies would make Mommy feel better. What do you think, Tully? Would you help me bake her some chocolate chip cookies?"

"Can I break the eggs?"

"Sure. Why not?"

How little it took to distract a four-year old from death.

The telephone rang. While Goldie answered, I sat Tully on the countertop beside the refrigerator and began pulling out eggs and butter.

I heard Goldie exclaim in a raised voice. "In a pig's eye! I won't do it! And if you dare show up on this street with TV cameras, I will personally come out and slap you silly.

Wouldn't *that* look just great on the evening news?" She slammed down the phone with force.

For maybe five whole seconds I controlled my curiosity. "Come on...what? Who in the world was that?"

She rolled her eyes. "It was Richard, of course, wanting to know if I could get him in to see Alex for a few minutes so he could express his sympathy. As if he were the original Mr. Feelings. My ex-husband running for Lieutenant Governor is more like it. Just who the hell does he think he's kidding?"

"He is the mayor, after all, but I must admit it seems a bit odd and ill-mannered to want to come over so soon."

"Typical Richard Howe," Goldie said bitterly. "Trust me, he never does anything without a reason. Two long years of being married to him taught me that—plus a lot of other things. I can attest to the fact that he is definitely not the sympathy type."

"What's *sympatie*, Goldie?" Tully said.

"Sympathy, my little chicken, is what we're going to put in these cookies so your mommy will feel better. Now let's put the eggs back in the carton until we're ready to break them, otherwise they may go splat all over the floor. Can you find the chocolate chips for us?"

My chair scraped on the floor as I got up. "I need to leave, anyway. Gran is next door with Simpson, and she's had about all she can take. If you can keep changing the subject, it might be better to let Alex do the explaining."

She grimaced. "Don't worry. I wouldn't know how anyway. Call me tonight and touch base about funeral arrangements."

"Right," I said. "OK, Tully...big kiss for Auntie Carroll. Save me some cookies, will you?" I left them searching for chocolate chips and scrambling to keep the eggs from rolling off the counter.

Back next door, Simpson confessed to mixing one of Goldie's sleeping pills with the Kahlua and Alex was still out, her eyes scrunched up in pain. With any luck, she would sleep until morning. I could imagine Simpson's distress if I tried to explain about drugs and fetuses, so I gave him my mobile number and drove Gran home to the tender religious care of Lucille, knowing that would irritate her enough to keep her temporarily distracted.

It seemed to me, when I left her on her doorstep, that her good-bye hug was a little tighter than usual.

In the car, I checked for new messages on my home answering machine. There were two. I made a mental note to return a call from Sam Vitelli, my father-in-law in New York, and then phoned one Detective Wilson Paige at the sheriff's office, who wanted to know how soon I could come in for a few questions. Since I was already on Market Street, just three blocks away, I said now was as good a time as any—which only goes to show that I can be as stupid as the next person without even setting my mind to it.

Chapter Three

The sheriff's department, at the corner of Fourth and Princess, is located in what has to be the most repulsive building in the state of North Carolina—a monument to design by committee. It stretches a full city block all the way to historic Market Street, where elegant homes and churches built as early as the seventeen-hundreds must cringe at its high-tech brick walls dripping with leach stains. Through the years, Wilmingtonians have made a game of suggesting cures. Short of tearing it down, my personal favorite advocated planting kudzu and waiting one full growing season.

I asked for Detective Paige and studied the drug paraphernalia display board until a gray-haired volunteer escorted me through a side hallway and into an undersized room with a scratched metal desk and four chairs left over from the sixties. Someone had read the research on calming colors and painted the room a pale shade of pink. I hoped they hadn't spent real taxpayer dollars on a decorator.

In spite of New Hanover County's law against smoking in public buildings, an overflowing ashtray sat in the middle of the desk. I moved it out in the hallway and left the door open.

It was fifteen minutes before Detective Paige decided to make an appearance, an unlit cigarette in his hand and more in his shirt pocket. He was about my height, with little piglet eyes, greased hair and an apparent partner. I disliked him on sight.

"Carroll Davenport? My name's Detective Wilson Paige and this here's Satterwhite."

I shook hands, wondering if Satterwhite was the man from the helicopter that I had watched through binoculars that morning. I couldn't be certain. A leather jacket hung casually from his fingers, the red tie was loosened, and the sleeves of his white shirt were folded back twice on his forearms. He nodded without speaking.

Paige said, "Sit down, please, Ms. Davenport. Sheriff Council had to go up to Raleigh for a governor's meeting and wanted me to run over a few things with you. I assume that's no problem?" He motioned toward a chair as he took a cigarette lighter from his pocket. The good-looking Satterwhite moved his chair to a corner of the room as an observer, wincing as he sat.

I said, "Not unless you intend to actually light that cigarette, in which case, we might have to do this interview in the park across the street."

Without expression, he put both the cigarette and the lighter in his trouser pocket and began to pace back and forth in front of the desk. I added *no sense of humor* to my initial observation. I thought I saw Satterwhite's mouth twitch.

"What we have here...what we have us here is a real serious problem," Paige announced as he flipped open a file folder. "Both men had severe trauma to the back of the head. Both men were on your property. And from the amount of blood present, Monroe apparently died in your greenhouse, although we found two different blood types on the dock." He paused for effect.

I steeled myself to the picture he was painting and said a silent prayer that Eddie had been unconscious. I wasn't ready to deal with the thought that he might have suffered terrible pain or had time to regret everything he was losing.

"Strange that you didn't hear anything that night. A man might tend to make a hell of a noise when he knows he's about to die, wouldn't you think?"

My lungs didn't seem to be filling with enough air. I looked away from the pink wall and refocused on Paige. "That troubles me, too, but the greenhouse is a hundred feet from the house, and there are lots of intensified noises off the water at night-horns, music, barges, dredges, even cruise ships. You learn to sleep through it all."

He nodded as he were having difficulty believing it, and after a moment said, "Anyway, we'll know soon whether the blood on your floating dock was from both our victims."

I thought he had placed unnecessary emphasis on *your* property, *your* greenhouse, *your* dock.

He continued. "Where was I? Oh, yeah..."

I interrupted him. "Was there identification on the drowned man? Was it Dennis Mason?"

"Can't say yet." He began to pace again. "So far, it looks maybe like a robbery. Watches, rings and wallets were missing. We found a boat, *The Sundowner*, near Rich Inlet about an hour ago."

Dennis's boat. I knew the name.

"Blood in the boat, of course." Paige consulted his notes. "And vomit." He looked down at me. "Was your cousin a drinking man, Ms. Davenport?"

I hesitated. "He wasn't an alcoholic, if that's what you're asking. He would never have come to work drunk or drinking, for instance. He knew his limit."

"What about at parties, or out with the boys? You know what I mean?"

I thought before answering. "We grew up together, Detective. Once he would tie one on with the best of you—but not for years now. He had a wife he loved dearly, a four-year-old daughter, and a baby on the way. He took all that very, very seriously...right from the beginning."

"You're saying he wasn't a boozer. What about drugs?"

"No way."

"OK, so he wasn't a boozer and he wasn't a user." He snorted with amusement at his rhyme. I gritted my teeth, liking him less and less, becoming aware of an anger that had been building all day.

"Now, Ms. Davenport..."

"What?"

"Could he have been involved with drugs in some other way? Could you be involved with drugs?"

I waited a full ten count, I swear I did, but now he had frosted me. "Are you going somewhere with this, Detective, or are you just trying to tick me off?"

He threw up his hands. "It's my job to check, Ms. Davenport...just doing what the taxpayers pay me to do. But I'm having a little trouble understanding the scenario. Monroe was with Dennis Mason, a known alcoholic and a drug user. Some say he was even more than that. We think it looks strange, that's all, the two of them apparently out in the boat together late at night. Simmer down, now. No offense was intended."

Really? I held my tongue, but only by biting it. Satterwhite was leaning his chair back against the wall, eyes almost closed, just watching.

Paige pulled a sheet of paper from the folder. "Right. Now then, you say you found the body around seven-thirty? What were you doing down on the dock? You told Sheriff Council you'd had the flu?"

"Yes to seven-thirty. And I usually go down to the dock with coffee after running, as a kind of a cooling-down period. Yes, I am getting over the flu, and no, it wasn't very smart to be running or on the dock in the rain, but I'd been cooped up for days." I shrugged. "I couldn't stand it any longer."

He questioned me carefully about the names of my neighbors, whether they had regular visitors that I knew about, unusual dock activity, whether I had heard any noises in the night. Things like that. I answered as well as I could.

"Who else lives on your property? Any regular overnight visitors for you?"

"I live in the main house alone, Detective. No regular overnight guests, by which I assume you mean male friends. My grandmother sometimes spends the night, but I think you can safely mark her off your list since she's eighty-five. Otherwise, there's Randolph Taylor, in his seventies, who lives in the guest cottage. His wife, Lucille, visits once in a while, but never overnight. There's also Davis Taylor, their great-nephew, who stays whenever he chooses. He works for the construction company and helps out on the property from time to time."

"Tell me about the great-nephew. Is he the gang member who was arrested for car theft?"

"One night in jail straightened him out. You can safely mark him off your list. He's a good kid."

"Nobody else?" he asked sharply.

I wondered if he thought I was going to name every friend who had ever vacationed with me. With a bite to my voice, I said, "Oh, and there's Tully. Eddie's four-year-old spends the night often."

His jaw tightened. "Why doesn't Mrs. Taylor spend the night with her husband?"

"You'll have to ask that yourself, Detective, but don't count on getting an answer from either of them." Lucille would tear a strip off him if he tried. "Family rumor claims she filled him full of buckshot one night after catching him in bed with another woman. We don't know for sure, and they aren't talking, but it could explain why he walks with a limp."

"When was this?"

I almost smiled. "Nineteen fifty-four, I think. Somewhere around the time of Hurricane Hazel."

He stopped pacing and gave me his *I'm the investigator here, so don't give me any crap* look. "Do I understand one of your men didn't show up for work today?"

"Duane Wilder?"

"Nobody seems to have seen hide nor hair of him since he was last seen with your cousin on the island late yesterday. Don't you find that odd under the circumstances?"

"Not with Duane. Surely he isn't a suspect? He's worked with us since we started the company."

"They ever have words?"

"Some," I said. "Nothing serious." Usually it was Eddie chewing Duane out for showing up late or not at all. We had discussed firing him a dozen times, but good supervisors were hard to find in a building boom. I couldn't see Duane killing anyone.

He shifted in a different direction. "You and the deceased were business partners, right?"

"Yes," I said. "More than four years now."

Paige paused in front of me so that I had to crane my neck to look up at him. "Since you came back to town?"

"Not right away. After six months or so."

He said casually, "Any problems getting along? Any fights? Business problems? Was there any sexual activity between the two of you?"

"Detective, for God's sakes. He was my cousin and a friend—like a brother. I was *not* having an affair with him. The very idea is...would have been repulsive."

"OK, OK! Stranger things have happened in my career. What about the other questions. Fights, business problems?"

I took a deep breath. "The only business problem we had was from too much business, and no, we didn't fight. We grumbled, said what we thought, and let it go. That way, we never built up enough steam to fight. Even as kids, we got along well."

"Money problems?"

"I doubt it," I said. "He lived a reasonable lifestyle, drew a percentage of the profits from the company, plus he had a small private income. Besides, if he needed money, he would have gone to my grandmother or come to me. He never did."

"Could his *small private income* have involved drugs?"

"No. It did not. It came from his parents' estate."

The good detective said, straight-faced, "A lotta people dying in your family. How about you?"

"How about me what?"

"Are you having money problems?" he said impatiently.

"Trust me, Detective, I *do not* have money problems. Or maybe I do, but not the way you mean." I looked down at my worn jeans and sweat shirt. Mud was smeared on old boots, hiding the scuffs, and the out-dated jacket flung across the back of my chair was the only dry one I had been able to find. I didn't exactly reek of money, old or new. Besides, where I came from it wasn't nice to be able to tell a Jones from a Vanderbilt. We seldom flaunted it.

He stopped. "What does that mean?"

"I guess, Detective, it means I have too much money."

He snorted once more, as if to say there was no such thing.

"More rich people declare bankruptcy than poor people, and sometimes they kill their kin. Money does strange things—big money the strangest of all." He studied his file again. "A lot of your money came from your dead husband's estate? Is that correct, Ms. Davenport? Or should I say Mrs.

Vitelli? Three-quarters of a million dollars in insurance, I believe. You want to tell me about that?"

"Davenport will do, and is legally correct. You've done your homework, Detective." I could match the frost in his voice. Not for anything would I tell this insufferable man what I had done with Daniel's insurance money.

He waved the file folder under my nose. "NYPD faxed me the file on Vitelli's murder. Got it about an hour ago and found it very interesting reading. For instance, it hints that you were a suspect at the time. Were you? Did *you* kill your husband?"

I said nothing, merely stared at him for a few seconds while disturbing pictures flashed through my mind. In spite of all my careful control about that day in New York, I could feel my hands begin to tighten. I put them carefully into my jeans pockets and took a deep breath.

Once upon a time, in my other life, a famous and very expensive New York psychiatrist suggested I conquer anger by turning it into love and overcome fear by turning it into anger.

"Let me put it this way." I spoke in a voice that would have frozen ice cubes. "My father-in-law is Sam Vitelli. I'm sure you'll find him mentioned in your file because I understand he has some involvement with organized crime in the New York area. He believes that he knows who killed his son and why. There was a woman involved, as well as drug territories, neither of which I knew anything about until I found out the hard way. Altogether, twenty-seven bullets entered his body—one less than his age. I saw what kind of damage they caused and so did Sam. Do you think for one minute I'd be alive if he thought I had anything at all to do with his only son's murder?"

"Ms. Davenport...?"

"Excuse me, but I'm not finished. You can't have read the file or you wouldn't ask such a dumb-ass question."

"Ms. Davenport, you are required to answer. I repeat, did you kill your husband? It seems that there was some question about whether your own wounds could have been self-inflicted. Is that correct?"

My boiling point had been reached. "First of all, Detective, I'm not required to answer any of your ludicrous questions. Secondly, you are seconds away from having me walk out that door, unless you're prepared to arrest and charge me with your jacked-up, half-witted speculations. And if so, you better be damned sure you know what you're doing unless you want to go back to driving a beer truck or whatever the hell you did before. I'm of the opinion that the sheriff is likely to kick your butt into the Cape Fear River."

It didn't seem likely that many people fired back at Paige. His ears turned the color of cooked shrimp. "Now hold on just a damned minute. I read the goddamn file, and you're treading on very thin ice, lady. I can throw your ass in the tank overnight and see if you feel like answering questions after spending eight hours with whores and drunks."

I got to my feet, seething, and grabbed my jacket.

Paige shoved the telephone my way and snarled, "You want to make your one phone call to a lawyer, go ahead."

I looked him in the eye. Among his many other failings,

he probably wasn't much of a poker player. "You're bluffing, Detective, and I'm tired and hungry and not in the mood to be bullied by a fool. If the sheriff wants to send someone reasonable to question me, I'll be at home. But make it well before nine o'clock, because it's been a bitch of a day and I'm turning in early."

Behind me, Satterwhite cleared his throat as the front legs of his chair hit the floor. "May I have a word with you, Detective?"

"Right now?"

"*Right now,*" he said. "Ms. Davenport, please be kind enough to sit back down while I consult with my colleague in the hall."

I swear I saw a twinkle in his eye. Maybe Paige saw it too. If anything, he appeared to grow even more furious as he stalked out of the room.

I've always had a weakness for polite men, or maybe it was the hairy forearms. Whatever it was, I didn't sit back down, but pulled on my jacket, ready to leave the moment they returned.

"Two more minutes," I said. "After that, I'm out of here."

"Fair enough," Satterwhite said.

He was back in less than my limit, after no more than a murmur of raised voices in the hall. I was sitting stiffly on the edge of the desk, itching to give the back of my tongue to the next conspiracy-theory nitwit who dared open his mouth.

With a straight face, Satterwhite said, "Well, that went smoothly, I thought. You know, I could almost feel sorry for the man."

Now, I can recognize an attempt at humor as well as the next person, but I wasn't kidding when I said I wasn't in the mood. "Is this where we play the bad-cop, good-cop routine?" I said wearily. "And who the hell are you, anyway?"

"Satterwhite...Benjamin Satterwhite. Ben if you will."

"No, I mean *who* are you?"

"A friend of Sheriff Council's."

Hello. That was helpful. "Well, what can *you* tell me?" I snapped. "I've lost a cousin and a business partner. Dennis Mason I can deal with, although being eaten by crabs is a hell of a way to go. Eddie is another story. We were the only cousins close to the same age in the family, and from the age of six months we could almost read each other's minds. I can't believe he was mixed up in anything shady. I would have known, his wife would have known, the whole damned town would have known. He couldn't keep secrets."

Satterwhite looked at the ceiling. "They've been watching Dennis Mason for months. He was an active participant in graveyard pickups around Wilmington."

"What, pray, are graveyard pickups?"

"I mean the drugs come in at night by helicopter and get shoved overboard into the marshes, creeks and inlets. There's a lot of territory out there—miles of empty waterways accessible only by small boats. Who's going to suspect? A lone fisherman in the middle of the night checking crab pots, flounder gigging? Who cares? All you see is the blinking red light of the helicopter, which doesn't even slow down, and later on the running lights of a lone boat."

Helicopters are a common occurrence here at night. I

had always assumed they were military craft, heading to or from the Sunny Point installation further down the Cape Fear River, or the Coast Guard flying grid searches for missing boaters. I could sit in my living room at night and watch a small boat come roaring down the Intracoastal Waterway, run up the creeks and back out again in a matter of minutes. You had to suspect drugs were involved, but I had never connected the helicopters.

I said, "How would they find the bundles in the dark?"

"High frequency signals in the load, or we suspect they may sometimes plant signals in the creeks to help the choppers know where to drop the goods. These are not imbeciles we're dealing with—and money is not an object."

"All right," I said. "I'm finding this information both fascinating and depressing, but I'm not clear on what Detective Paige was hinting. Does he think I'm running a drug ring, or that I murdered both Eddie and Dennis? Sheriff Council has known me since I was a baby, and he's well aware that I don't need the money. And God knows, I don't need any more thrills in my lifetime. So what would be the point? And speaking of points, why would he bring up something that happened more than six years ago in New York? It was a crime so brutal and horrifying that no police officer in his right mind would believe I was a suspect for more than five minutes."

"But they did," he said. "And you were."

He was serious. I studied his face, the set of his jaw, the steadiness of his stare. I took a deep breath. "You must be getting wrong information from someone. The police in New York, a Detective Tremont, if I remember, questioned me twice in the hospital. There were other things—more important things—to worry about at the time. I assumed they had to cover all the bases, rule out the jealous wife motive, and then get on with the business of finding the real killers. But they never did. I checked with Tremont about a year ago."

"Paige can be a horse's ass; I've worked with him before. But, he's right about one thing. You're still on the list of suspects with NYPD. According to them, you moved a notch higher when you left the country four months after the murders and stayed away for two years. Look at it from Paige's angle." He ticked the items off on his fingers. "You went to northern Malaysia, a prime corridor for heroin movement, where you remained for almost a year. Then you traveled extensively in a dozen different countries with no apparent means of support for another year after that."

"For heavens' sake..."

He went on. "You moved back to Wilmington, North Carolina, where you settled back into your home overlooking prime graveyard pick-up marshes. You still travel a lot. And last, but not least, heroin traffic in this port city increased almost immediately."

How, I wondered, could basic information go so wrong and people arrive at so many half-witted conclusions? I was dumbfounded.

All I could think to say was, "I was twenty-three years old, eight months pregnant, and hospitalized for more than three months with a nervous breakdown. And they imagine I did all that?"

"Understand, it's one possible scenario. Your original injuries were real enough for the first week of hospitalization. The next three months in a private hospital are highly suspect in their minds, and listed as a probable ruse to keep from being questioned. And then you simply disappeared."

"I didn't disappear, for God's sake. Half the people in Wilmington knew where I was—at least generally. Two dozen or more had an address and phone number. Didn't Tremont ask?"

He offered a stick of gum, his mouth twisted wryly. "They did, indeed, starting with your grandmother, who pinned their ears back. Said you'd had enough problems and to leave you alone. That pretty much covers what other friends said, too. Some in stronger words, including Sheriff Council. So you can see how it looks."

Ordinarily, I'm an easygoing sort of person. As Granddaddy Monroe used to say, most things aren't important enough to get all that worked up about, and nobody will give a good goddamn anyway in a hundred years or so. I seldom get angry enough to explode. Today looked like an exception.

All of a sudden, the word "*tired*" didn't begin to describe the way I felt. Falling-down exhausted was more like it, and not in a state of mind to rein in my tongue. It was time to leave.

"No," I said, "I don't see how it looks, and I'm sure as hell not in the mood to try to see it from the viewpoint of a bunch of loose cannons. Now, your two minutes are long gone and so am I. And so help me, if you try to stop me, I will sue the pants off both of you." I jerked the door open, almost plowing headfirst into Detective Paige.

"Ms. Davenport, you can't..."

"Go to hell, Detective," I snapped, and kept moving. At the exit door, Satterwhite materialized to hold it for me. He had an odd three-quarters tilt to his mouth. Was the son-of-a-bitch actually laughing at me?

"I'll walk you out," he said.

"What is so amusing?" I asked through gritted teeth. And to hell with you, too, I thought.

"The look on Paige's face. I've been itching to take a swipe at that smug, self-righteous attitude since I've known him. I enjoyed watching you do it for me. Now, which direction to your car?"

"Why?"

"I'm walking you to it. Since it's getting dark, or haven't you noticed?"

"A southern gentleman?"

"No ma'am. A Maine gentleman, or so my mother believes. Besides which, I was hoping for a ride back to Figure Eight Island."

I stopped dead in the middle of the sidewalk and looked him up and down. "You *cannot* be serious!"

"I am, indeed."

I placed both hands on my hips aggressively. "Look, I still don't even know which part you're playing in this comedy of horrors. Give me one good reason why I should be your taxi service."

"Benjamin Satterwhite." He thrust out his hand. "Agent Satterwhite, FBI out of Charlotte, on a week's medical leave starting this morning."

I stared at his hand, open-mouthed, feeling the wrath work its way up from my toes. "Why didn't you just say so to begin with? And while you were at it, you could have given just a teensy little explanation about why the FBI is involved. That was you in the helicopter this morning, wasn't it? Well, hell...!"

I didn't wait for an answer. Nothing irritates me more than to be laughed at or treated like a goose-brain. What's more, the patronizing son-of-a-bitch was actually smirking. I turned and stalked off up the street with Satterwhite's footsteps close behind.

To cap it all off, there was a ticket tucked under the windshield wiper. I stuffed it in my pocket and said, "Just get in the damned Jeep and don't say a word!"

"Yes ma'am."

With the key in the ignition, I warned him, "I'm too tired for any more questions. So help me, I'll dump your backside on the closest corner if you start."

I turned up Fourth Street and spotted Detective Paige getting under the wheel of a new white Lexus. What a pity he wasn't crossing the street.

My anger carried me in silence all the way out Market Street halfway to Figure Eight Island before I cooled off. Satterwhite had his seat back and his eyes closed, looking gray around the mouth. I felt the same way myself.

I said, "What happened to you?"

"Bullets," he said. "Not so good for the kidneys."

It surprised me that I was the kind of person who would

say, deadpan, "What a shame."

He cracked one eye. "Close enough."

"Close enough to what?"

"To an apology," he grunted.

I was going to ruin the enamel on my teeth. "It's been a hell of a day from the beginning. Plus I'm just getting over the flu, and I don't feel like anything except collapsing. So give me a break before we have another body on our hands. I'm going by a job site first and then straight home to sleep for twelve solid hours, then I promise I'll help any way I can. Just keep Paige away from me."

A sigh from the other seat. "Sounds too good to be true. I haven't had a full night's sleep for weeks. And then a friend loans me his cottage at Figure Eight Island for a month, and what happens? Stan Council tracks me down before I even get here, and now the office wants me on assignment out-of-state within a week."

"How did you rate a chopper?"

"Simple expediency. I was at the airport and Stan needed it to get to Raleigh on time for a law enforcement meeting with the governor."

"Are you really a friend of Stan Council?"

"Not anymore."

In other circumstances, I would probably have laughed. "Why don't I trust you?"

"That's a good question, lady. Who do you trust?"

"Stan Council," I said. "And believe me, that is the only point in your favor at this moment. Certainly not Detective Paige. The man has a computer chip loose somewhere."

"Good thinking. But on the other hand, Paige is of the opinion that Sheriff Council's judgment is flawed where you're concerned."

"Well, too damn bad for him."

"A word of warning. A pissed-off investigating officer can make a dangerous enemy. Don't antagonize him too often."

"I'll keep it in mind," I said.

By the time we turned off US 17, I could barely hold my head up. At the turn for Edgewater Club Road, I assumed the bright glow on the horizon was the moon rising. But only for a moment.

"Looks like a forest fire," said Satterwhite.

"No," I said. "There are no woods that far east. It's a house fire—a bad one."

At the Figure Eight bridge, the guard said, "Don't know which house, Ms. Davenport, but the fire trucks went through about twenty minutes ago, heading down to the south end." He waved us through.

On the causeway stretch, I said, "OK, which direction, Satterwhite? Only two ways to go, north or south."

"Past the club house and then left on Beach Road North— the Morehouse cottage."

I hesitated. "Mind if we check out the fire first? I've got friends scattered all around the island. Besides which..."

"What?"

I shook my head. "Just an uneasy feeling. I'll sleep better if I check on a job site."

Chapter Four

From South Beach Road, I could tell the fire was at the Anderson site. The closer we got, the worse it looked.

"Oh, my God!" I groaned. "What next?"

The fire was so intense we had to park half a block away. Porters Neck Volunteer firemen were on the scene, doing their best, but the wind was gusting more than thirty knots, and I knew right away that only a total optimist would have thought they could put out the flames.

Satterwhite opened his door. "*This* is your job site?"

There are people who think a fire is exciting, but I'm not one of them. The words *primeval* and *terrifying* work better for me. I got out of the Jeep, ignoring Satterwhite, walked as close as possible, and just stood there appalled for the next ten minutes, watching it burn—every carefully crafted crook and crevice of seven months' work. Without warning, the north wall collapsed in a combustion of flames and flying cinders. I had to turn my face away.

Silly, to be so in love with a house.

Jinks from my construction crew was standing beside one of the four trucks in serious conversation with a fireman. When he spotted me, the two of them walked over.

With a quick glance at Satterwhite behind me, Jinks laid an arm across my shoulder. "Leon at the Yacht Club called

me when he couldn't reach you. I want you to hear something from Johnny Powell."

Johnny had been in my class from the ninth grade on,
but as adults we didn't move in the same circles. Besides, I
might not have acknowledged the governor if he'd been
dressed in the same hat and gear.

"Hi, Johnny," I said. "Sorry I didn't recognize you. Thanks
for coming out and trying. Any idea what happened?"

"Yeah, that's what I wanted to talk to you about. When
we first arrived, all the men could smell the gasoline. It was
obvious the fire had a strong start in at least three different
places, and then the wind picked up and we just couldn't hold
it. I tell you this, it's a damn good thing there were no other
houses at this end of the road or we might have lost them all."

I knew he had to be thinking about a Bald Head Island
fire a few years back, when a wind-driven fire burned thirty-
five condos in the same number of minutes, spreading so fast
the firemen couldn't get their hoses out of the way in time.
Fire was always a problem on islands.

"Anyway," Johnny said, "the arson team will be here first
thing in the morning. I just thought you would want to know."

I said, "Thanks for being straight with me," and watched
him walk back to the hoses. There didn't seem much point in
pouring water on a total loss, but they could never assume
the wind wouldn't shift again.

"Jinks?" I said.

He knew what I was asking. "Absolutely not, Carroll.
There were no gasoline cans anywhere on the site, plus Duane
never even showed up today, and he's the only one who

smokes. The tile crew came in at three, but I checked up when they left. No joints, no cigarettes, no nothing. Anyway, I don't think Johnny Powell is thinking about cigarettes."

I had to ask. "What about Davis?"

"Sure, he was there. But you know he doesn't smoke. That boy is too tight-fisted to buy himself a Coke, much less a pack of cigarettes. Says he's saving up for a car. He's been working like a Trojan."

"Thanks, Jinks. Will you stay? I don't think I want to see the end of this, and I need to get home before I fall down. There's nothing we can do here tomorrow, so keep trying to find Duane. With or without him, you and Davis get over to Forest Hills Drive and start ripping out. I'll be there as early as I can."

He cast another suspicious look at the silent Satterwhite, gave a mock salute, and disappeared into the crowd of on-lookers.

I said, "You ready to go, Satterwhite? I've got to get out of here while I can still stand up."

"Whenever you are."

I was getting into the Jeep, my back turned, when something flew past my left shoulder and shattered against the frame of the driver's door. I threw up an arm to protect my face, my first thought that something had exploded in the burning house.

Satterwhite had faster reactions. He whirled in a trained crouch behind me, a blur of motion, reaching under his jacket for his gun, seeming surprised that he came up empty-handed. He stepped ahead of me.

A voice screeched out of the shadows as a woman rushed forward. "You bitch...you stupid bitch! You let your idiot crew burn my house down! I told you they were smoking on the job, but no, Miss High and Mighty couldn't be bothered to supervise. I'm supposed to move in on March 16th. Now what do I do? Tell me that?"

Her face was a study in fury and streaked soot.

"Who the hell are you?" barked Satterwhite.

"Get out of my way, you fucking piece of trash."

"Bitsy Anderson, one of the owners," I said to his back. "Either drunk or crazy. It's hard to tell which a lot of the time."

She planted herself three feet away, her platinum hair wild with disarray, in blatant contrast to the pink sequined dress she wore. Her face was contorted with a rage made up of half rotten temper and half booze.

Bitsy ordered him again, "Get out of my goddamned way!"

I looked at the dent in the Jeep. "It's all right, Satterwhite. I can handle her."

And maybe I could have, too, but I was not in my most placating mood. He moved aside.

It was a mistake on my part. "Calm down, Bitsy. We're all sorrier than we can say, but there is no way yet to tell what happened. Johnny Powell thinks they smelled gasoline. If true, that would make it arson, although they won't know until their team comes in tomorrow." I spotted her husband approaching. "George? Is that you?"

George Anderson stepped out from behind the Jeep and

took Bitsy by the arm. "That's enough now, Bitsy."

She turned on him, too. "Get your fucking hands off of me. Didn't you hear what she just said? Arson?" As quickly as she dispatched her husband, she turned back to her main target. "Arson!" she spat the words at me. "You probably set the fire yourself. With that sneaky Eddie dead, you burned it for the insurance money to get at me. You vindictive cow. I ought to have you arrested!"

"Bitsy..." George tried to put his arm around her.

She shrugged it off. "Shut up, George. You never wanted this house in the first place."

I measured my words carefully. "Go home and get some sleep. It's a huge disappointment to all of us, but the house is insured to the hilt. I'm sure you'll not lose any money. We can talk tomorrow and see where we go from here."

She threw herself directly in front of me. "Don't tell me what to do, you arrogant slut. I'll go home when I'm good and ready. Not when you tell me to. Do you understand me? *Do you understand?*"

Around us, residents and a few firemen had gathered to watch the show. Every word would be all over town by tomorrow night.

Well, hell, I had to have some pride.

"Suit yourself," I said, turning away.

Bitsy advanced as fast as a spitting cat, slapping me hard across the mouth with her open hand, knocking me back onto the front seat of the Jeep. Just as rapidly, she was on top of me, lashing out with her fists while I protected my face with my arms. I was stunned.

It was over in less than a minute. Satterwhite jammed her against the rear door and pinned both hands behind her back.

"Lady," he said in a voice loud enough to penetrate her fury, "you touch her again and I'm going to slug you one. Not only that, but I'm going to make sure you cool off in jail. Now, are you sober enough to understand that bit of information?"

George shouted angrily into the fray, pulling at Satterwhite's arm. When that didn't work, he elbowed him twice in the small of the back. I heard Satterwhite's sharp intake of breath before he went down on one knee, momentarily losing his grip on Bitsy. And then Jinks was there pulling George away.

"Who the hell are you to threaten my wife with jail?" George shouted.

Satterwhite spoke through his teeth. "If this is your wife, then I suggest you take her home to sober up, and both of you better pray Ms. Davenport doesn't press charges. Last time I checked, assault was a criminal offense. You'd do well to remember that."

Bitsy screamed, "You son-of-a-bitch."

I was back on my feet by then—dazed, but back on my feet. "Let her go, Satterwhite. George, just look around you. Take her on home now. You don't want this broadcast all over the county."

Horrified, he gave one incensed glance at the crowd of onlookers. Probably most of the island residents had come to watch the fire.

Bitsy began to cry. She took one last swing at either me or Satterwhite, I couldn't tell which, stumbled and fell sprawling in the dirt.

"Damn you, you'll be sorry for burning my house," she said. "I'll make you sorry." George helped her to her feet, and with his steadying arm, she lurched across the road. I watched until they drove away in a black Mercedes.

"A cat fight." I shook my head ruefully. "In the middle of the road on Figure Eight Island. She will never live it down."

"You've made another enemy," Satterwhite said, leaning against the side of the jeep, looking pinched around the mouth.

"Not really. If she'd been born male, she would have been the schoolyard bully. As it is, she takes her bad temper out on just about anybody who can't help her along socially. Alcohol just makes her meaner and less refined in her tactics."

"I'd still watch my back," he said. "Anytime..."

"Satterwhite," I interrupted him, fatigue rolling back over me like a forty- foot wave. "If I don't start home this instant, I'm not going to make it."

"Hell," he said straightening up. "I'm long past ready. I'm just trying to figure out how I'm going to get myself into the damned Jeep."

"I hope you make it soon or you'll have to either walk home or sleep where you drop. I'd feel bad, I really would, but I'm leaving all the same. Do you need some help?"

"No," he grunted. "I'll make it." And did, folding his long torso into the passenger seat with gritted teeth. "One Twenty Seven Beach Road North."

"Only two miles, but not guaranteed to be bump-free. Do you need a doctor? I'm not totally heartless, you know. I assume this is the medical thing you mentioned?"

"Yeah, two forty-fives about three weeks ago. They nicked a kidney and messed around with some other stuff. The doctor finally told me things weren't healing properly because I was worn out and run down. The truth is, I'm lucky to be sitting here groaning about it."

"Listen, Satterwhite. Seriously. I'm grateful you pulled her off me and sorry the table turned over on you. I mean it."

"Forget it," he said.

When we arrived at his cottage, I backed into the driveway so the passenger side would be closest to the front door. "Can you make it on your own?"

"No problem," he said, but I noticed he held onto the top of the door with both hands while getting out.

He leaned his head back in doorway. "Oh, yeah, Davenport?"

"What?"

"You owe me."

"Probably," I said.

"Dinner?"

"Maybe sometime. Assuming we both survive the night." He nodded, and I waited until he fumbled with the unfamiliar key and closed the door behind him.

I turned the jeep toward home, more than five miles away, where I barely had energy to remove my jacket and shoes before collapsing across the bed with my mouth throbbing.

The owls had begun their nightly chorus in the live oak

outside my window, and as I fell into blankness, I thought I might like to stay that way for a week.

For whatever reason—probably too much death and stress—in the middle of a comatose sleep, I began to dream in rambling images, each sharper than the one before. There was my grandfather in his ornate mahogany coffin with tufts of grass growing around the edges of white silk. Then my mother floating face up in Rich Inlet, her long blonde hair like fluorescent seaweed, without a single fleshy crab rip anywhere on her beautiful face.

In a swirl, my mother turned into Eddie, with a yawning red mouth of a wound where his chin should have been. Through it all, I could hear Tully crying in the background.

You'd have thought that would be enough gore for my mind to supply in one night, but it had other memory tricks in its dark recesses. A younger me in maternity clothes, with a bag of groceries on the stairs of the New York brownstone. The stereo was playing Bach, which meant Daniel was home, but it was much too loud for old Mrs. Reisner upstairs. Someone had painted my front door blood red. I struggled with the groceries and the tricky lock.

Inside, the music was concert-loud and coming from the bedroom. I went down the hall calling for Daniel to turn it down, the bag of groceries still clutched in my arms as I pushed the bedroom door slowly, slowly open. The dream went into overdrive, long-familiar images speeding by like scenes from a horror film. The bag of groceries crashed to the floor. Mayonnaise rolled across the room and broke against the blood-splattered baseboard, mixing with feathers on the carpet. Daniel's face and bare chest were covered with blood, stark against the padded headboard punctured with strange ripped holes extending along one side and down the wall. At the foot of the bed, a woman lay half off the mattress, blood still pooling across her breasts and dripping down one out-stretched arm.

Rapid shadows and motion filled the room. Once again, I felt the searing, ripping pain in my abdomen and heard screaming that seemed to rise up and up, above even the Bach in the background.

I woke, panic-stricken, in my own house and in my own bed, convinced as always that I was in the brownstone, that the shadowed figures were still present. Only half-awake, I switched on the lamp by the bed and followed the ritual of going from room to room until the house was ablaze with light, every door and window locked tight, every curtain drawn.

Like I said, too much stress and death. I knew from ex-perience there would be no going back to sleep any time soon. My watch said it was one-twenty. I took a long hot shower, washing the smoke from my hair, and made a pot of strong coffee that I drank with cream and sugar. Even so, my hands were still unsteady when Goldie called at two thirty-five to tell me Alex had lost the baby.

Chapter Five

Hospitals are desolate places at night. Corridors become uninhabited tunnels of dimmed lights and cracked doorways. And night waiting rooms, for the most part, are hushed and solemn testimonials to the frailty of the human spirit.

In just such a waiting room at New Hanover Medical Center, Goldie and Simpson Hardwick were slumped on opposite ends of a dull gray sofa on the fourth floor. Goldie was smoking, in spite of a bold sign that declared this to be a smoke-free building.

They rose wearily when they saw me. It was obvious Goldie had been crying, and while I doubted that the stoic Simpson would actually break down, he had lost his competent look. I gave them both a hard embrace and asked about Alex.

"We're waiting for the doctor now," said Goldie. She stubbed out her cigarette in a potted ficus that had seen better days. "I can't remember his name."

"Harris," said Simpson.

I breathed easier. "Ray Harris is one of the best OB/GYNs in the state, so she's in good hands. Now, will one of you please tell me what happened."

"Everything moved so fast," Simpson said. "Goldie went up to check on Alex about midnight and found her bleeding and doubled over with pain. We didn't wait for the ambulance. I just carried her to the car and rushed her here while Goldie got Mrs. Louba from next door to stay with Tully."

Goldie collapsed back on the sofa. Tonight she wore a shapeless purple sweater over wrinkled slacks, her hair uncombed. A far cry from the sophisticated realtor.

She said, "We might as well sit. It could be a while yet."

"Not me," said Simpson. "I'm going downstairs to grab some coffee before I fall asleep. How about you two?"

"Yes, please," I said, "with cream and sugar." If I kept this up, I was going to burn a hole in my stomach and gain ten pounds.

Goldie shook her head. "Any more caffeine and I'll be bouncing all over the ceiling."

There was an odd little pause from out of nowhere as Simpson looked at Goldie. Then he turned and walked away, his leather soles making eerie scratching sounds down the night hall. She watched him until he turned the corner.

Sometimes, even in the middle of a crisis, good things happen to deserving people. I almost missed it.

She said, "Carroll, I know that look. Don't say a word about it, please. Most of the time, Simpson doesn't know I'm alive."

"Sorry," I said. "I'm just wondering what planet I've been living on that I didn't see this before now."

Goldie twisted a frayed thread on her sweater. "Forget about me. What are we going to do about Alex? She was hysterical when she realized something was happening to the baby, screaming more because of that, I think, than the pain."

She shuddered. "I never want to experience anything near it again as long as I live."

I said, "I wish I'd been there." And meant it, on the theory that whenever bad things happen, it's always easier with people who love you. Eons before feminism raised its two-sided head, women were just always there, in a long chain of unbroken aid and comfort that wasn't about to change any time soon.

Ray Harris and Simpson showed up from different directions at the same time, before I could tell Goldie that there wasn't a chance in hell we would be able to do much for Alex. That it was an emotional pain that only dimmed with time, never really disappearing, and that when we were old, old women, it would still be a hard scar that wouldn't heal.

"Mr. Monroe?" Dr. Harris asked Simpson.

"No, I'm Simpson Hardwick, her brother. How is she?"

"She's asking for her husband. Is he here?"

"Oh, God," Goldie wailed.

Harris looked from one to the other. "What did I say?"

We let Simpson do the explaining. "Her husband was found murdered less than twenty-four hours ago. She's been in a state of shock since she got the news. We're assuming that's what brought on the miscarriage."

Doctors don't react much to death and suffering. This one was no exception. Ray Harris wore a clean and starched white coat with four identical pens lined up in a neat little row, just barely touching each other in his pocket. Other than rubbing both hands across the back of his neck, he showed no emotion.

"I've been in the hospital since Sunday evening, so I

haven't heard much of anything. That explains a lot about her depression, although God knows she has enough reason with the baby. We've left a message for her regular doctor, but I understand he's fishing down in the Keys and won't be back until Saturday. We've done what we can, but her blood pressure is low enough for us to want to watch her for a while. Her emotional condition, of course, is a whole other story."

"When can we see her?" asked Goldie.

"They'll be putting her in a room soon, but don't stay more than a few minutes. She pretty well exhausted herself, and sleep is about the only healing thing for her right now. We've sedated her and will increase the dosage when she's in her room. Once she goes home, though, she'll need a great deal of comfort and support, but I don't expect I need to tell you that. Does she have a mother?"

"Sometimes," Simpson said with asperity. "But these two women are her best friends."

"I'm Carroll Davenport," I said, shaking his hand. "And this is Goldie Goldman. We'll do everything we can to make it easier for her."

He looked the three of us up and down, measuring whatever compassionate qualities we had left in the middle of the night. "I'll tell you what she *doesn't* need, and that's a lot of assurances that she's young and can have more children someday. The process differs from woman to woman, but under these circumstances, I would think her grief will be more than doubled. Let her mourn and be depressed. Just don't let her sink into deep depression, and don't leave her alone too much or let her exhaust herself with the funeral and visitors. Above all, she would benefit most from lots of rest, and from the company of women who understand. Have either one of you ever lost a child?"

"No," said Goldie.

"Yes," I said.

Harris nodded. "Then you know what I'm talking about. I'll leave her in your good hands. Check the nurses' station in a couple of minutes for her room number, and remember, stay just a short time with her tonight. Then, go home and get some sleep. The three of you look like hell."

I had to ask. "*Will* she be able to have more children? At some point soon she'll want to know that."

"I don't see why not. Now get some sleep—doctor's orders."

Simpson walked with him as far as the nurses' station. When he returned, Goldie was crying softly on the sofa. He sat down and put an arm around her shoulders. In the silence, we could hear the overhead clock change the minute hand with a click and the far-off sound of squeaking crepe-soled shoes.

Minutes later, we filed soberly into the room, where a nurse was just leaving with an empty syringe on a small tray. Alex was three-quarters out of it already, not awake enough to respond to our sympathetic hugs and useless phrases, although she gripped my hand with more strength than I would have thought her capable.

"We love you kid," Simpson whispered when we left, but I thought she was asleep long before she heard him, looking paler than anyone I could remember seeing who wasn't already dead. Her red hair was the only bit of color in the stark room.

In the hall I said, "It's four-thirty. Why don't the two of you go home and snatch a couple of hours of sleep? It doesn't look like she'll wake up any time soon."

"I don't know," Simpson said reluctantly.

Goldie took his hand. "Come on. I'll give you a glass of milk and a sweet roll for being such a great brother. If you don't want to go to bed, you can at least put your feet up in Richard's recliner that I was too cussed to let him have in the settlement. I think Carroll is right. We're all exhausted— maybe you most of all."

I added my reassurance. "You'll be five minutes from the hospital. I'll even leave our telephone numbers at the nurses station."

"All right, all right." He threw up his hands. "I guess that's the best thing to do, but I sure hate like hell to leave her." He sighed. "Come on then, Carroll, we'll walk you to your car."

"Don't worry about me, I'm parked illegally just a few steps from the door. Besides, I want to talk to the nurse before I go. Now both of you, get on out of here."

Even then, they turned and looked back twice before they reached the elevators—nice people who deserved each other. I guess I should have warned him. Once he tasted Goldie's homemade sweet rolls, he was going to seriously regret bachelorhood.

I'm not sure I could have explained the nagging unease that left me so reluctant to leave Alex that I was willing to mislead Simpson and Goldie, but I knew they wouldn't go if they thought I was staying. Not exactly lying, but close enough to give me a twinge. So true to my word, I talked to the young nurse on duty, who assured me she would let Alex sleep through early morning rituals. Then I settled in for a long wait in the room's only comfortable chair.

Alex neither opened her eyes nor moved for the first forty-five minutes. She lay ghostlike and lifeless, reminding me of a fallen winter-white camellia. She would find her way again, but I knew that she was never going to be the same. Eddie, Eddie, I thought, who would ever have believed it would end this way?

I sat on, watching the IV drip slowly in the darkened room, listening to her steady breathing.

The day before their wedding, a shaken Eddie sat on my dock and sheepishly confessed that he was scared witless Alex would back out at the last minute. I laughed at his fears. She was even more smitten than he was. I went so far as to bet him a year's salary she wouldn't cut and run.

With my eyes closed, I could still see his bare feet propped on the rail, as serious as an old man, the breeze ruffling his hair. His murder was going to leave a shattering hole in all our lives.

Eddie was only one of the family doggedly opposed to my marrying Daniel Vitelli. He described Daniel with words like domineering, self-centered, combative, and when he called him a Mafia baby, I cut off all contact. My father and Gran received much the same treatment. Daniel was handsome, funny and exciting, and he took over my life in a way I never intend to let happen again. I closed my eyes to every caution flag—his friends who joked about call girls and shakedowns, his mood-swings, the expensive, frenzied lifestyle—and married him in a lonely civil ceremony that seemed romantic and daring at twenty-one.

Love is not only blind. It is often deaf, dumb, and stupid in the bargain. Daniel was not the only one who had been careless with his future. In the process, I lost a baby, a husband, a father, and a faith in relationships that might well last me a lifetime.

When I think about it, I can't help but find it remarkable that the only good thing to come out of it all was the link with Sam and Isabella.

Gran sent Eddie to New York to bring me home from the hospital, where he was alternately furious and comforting when I wouldn't go, stubbornly pointing out the reasons I was better off in Wilmington with family and friends. I couldn't explain why I wanted to hide somewhere, to get on a plane and never stop. Most of all, I didn't say that I wasn't yet ready to walk back into the house where my father had just put a shotgun in his mouth. In the end, he drove me to Kennedy Airport himself, swearing that Gran and Lucille would each kill him when he arrived home without me.

After six months, he tried a second time, flying to the east coast of Malaysia. I fixed him up with a blonde Australian math teacher. He stayed a week and went home tanned and fit from jogging on the beach, vowing to reassure Gran that I was safe, if not sane, and running around half-naked among the natives.

A sound—maybe the swish of the door—woke me. It took me several seconds to become aware of a man dressed in scrub greens and surgical mask moving a pillow from the extra bed to where Alex lay fast asleep.

I blinked, finally realizing two things—that he was unaware I was sitting in the dim corner, and that the pillow was descending toward her face.

Chapter Six

"Hey!" I shouted, loud enough to wake every patient on the fourth floor. "What the hell are you doing?"

He whirled at the sound of my voice, dropped the pillow, and bolted from the room. Without thinking of the consequences, I chased after him.

"Help!" I yelled to a startled nurse entering a room across the hall. "Call security!"

He brushed against her as he sprinted for the exit stairs, knocking a medicine tray out of her hands. She gave a squeal of fright as capsules and syringes hit the floor rolling.

I was twenty feet behind him when he sprinted left and instead of taking the stairs, made for an elevator just opening near the nurses' station. I was close enough to hear him pounding the buttons with his fist. The doors began to close. I slid my foot in the opening, the doors bounced back, and I was facing an ugly little black gun pointed straight at me. Like a dog chasing an eighteen-wheeler, I hadn't given a thought about what to do if I actually caught up with him.

Smart move, Davenport.

Was I about to be gunned down in plenty of time to make the noon television news—faithfully viewed by Gran and Lucille? Caught on film, courtesy of security cameras.

He had a week's growth of beard and was in his late forties, six feet and thin, except for an extra fifty pounds around his belly. Where the mask had slipped, I could see bulbous lips. And overall, he had the rough, mean look of a man who would be instantly suspect in a dark alley.

"Get back," he snarled. "Right now! Move!"

An elderly man in robe and slippers, the only other person in sight, froze in position.

"Why?" I said. "Why try to kill Alex?"

"Fuck you, you interfering bitch."

He raised the gun six inches and aimed it, as far as I could tell, straight at my heart. I couldn't breathe.

"Mind your own goddamned business or I'll know where to find you. Now back up! All the way to the corner! Keep going! You, too!" He pointed the gun at the old man, who gave a sharp gasp and slid to the floor. The door closed.

I followed in the second elevator, to the main lobby and out onto the sidewalk, in time to see a burgundy Mustang tear out of a handicapped space and head toward Seventeenth Street. I thought the plate was from North Carolina, but couldn't be sure. All I got were the first three letters, *RLT*.

Back upstairs, there was bedlam. A dozen people were caring for the stunned patient, still motionless on the cold floor. Wanting to get back to Alex fast, I advised a sleepy-looking security guard to contact the police with the license plate information.

"Hold on," he said. "You can't leave."

"I'll be in 422. Send the police in when they get here."

In Alex's room, the hall scene repeated itself. She was still groggy from the drugs, but moving fast toward hysteria.

Two nurses hovered near the foot of the bed, one of them middle-aged with a lifetime of sour experience written on her bony face. The younger one was the nurse who got pushed aside in the hallway.

A second guard stood beside Alex, a two-way radio in one hand and a notebook in the other.

"Who are you?" he barked.

Alex held a hand out. I went over to the opposite side and held it. Her skin felt dry and cold.

"I'm Carroll Davenport. I was in the room with Ms. Monroe when someone tried to put a pillow over her head. He panicked and ran when he realized I was here. I followed him as far as the front walk. He drove off toward the main road, and then I couldn't see which way he went."

"No shit?" he said. "Are you sure? I mean, excuse me, Ms. Davenport, but could it have been an orderly or one of the doctors?"

"I don't understand," said Alex. Beneath my fingers on her wrist, the pulse was racing. Her eyes flicked between us, silently urging our agreement. "There must be some mistake."

"I wish there were," I said. "He pulled a gun on me at the elevator."

"Jeez," the guard said. "Why would anyone do that?"

"Excuse me!" With impatience, the senior nurse waved me out of the way. "I need to attend to my patient. She's had just about enough excitement, thank you, so the two of you go discuss all the gory details you want—in the hall. Come back in five minutes." She flipped the curtain irritably, closing out the three of us.

"We better do as she says." The younger nurse spoke for the first time in a slight British accent. When the door swung shut, she continued. "I saw him, too, Joe. He came tearing out of Mrs. Monroe's room like a bat out of you know where, nearly knocking me down. You had better call the police."

I said, "There was another guard at the elevator who was calling when I left. What you really need to do...Joe, is it?"

"Joe Cheshire, yes ma'am."

"Well, Joe, I'm sure the police will be here fast. What we need you to do is stand guard outside this door. *Nobody*, and I do mean nobody, should go in the room except Dr. Harris or these two nurses until the police arrive. You might also find somebody on your radio who can alert Sheriff Council."

He was confused. "The city police won't like that, ma'am. It's their jurisdiction."

"That's true, but this woman's husband was murdered in the county yesterday. The attempt on her life may be connected, and Stan Council will want to know about it fast."

Cheshire nodded twice as if he suddenly had a grasp of what was going on. "It was on the news last night. I won't budge from this door."

I turned to the nurse. "I need to make three quick phone calls. Can you find me a directory and a phone where I can have some privacy?" Behind me, I heard the static from Joe Cheshire's radio as he made his contacts.

"Follow me," the nurse said, and showed me into a small, windowless office where the desk was cluttered with papers, books and used styrofoam coffee cups, then searched through drawers to find a phone directory.

"Sorry," she shrugged at the mess. "It's Nurse Merriman's desk. Just dial *nine* to get an outside line." She hesitated. "Will you be long? I'll catch hell if she finds out I let anybody in her office."

"No problem. I'll say I came in on my own. Her bark is bound to be worse than her bite."

She rolled her eyes. "Prove it to me some day. As far as I'm concerned, she's a right bloody old dragon."

I made the quick calls. One to a private security firm I'd used before, one to Simpson, and one at the last minute to the sheriff's office.

When I returned to Room 422, Alex was standing alone in the middle of the floor with an open blue robe over her hospital gown, looking ready to collapse at any second. Nurse Merriman with the sour face was on the phone. I caught the tail end of her conversation.

"She insists on leaving even though her blood pressure hasn't stabilized. Please inform Dr. Harris right away."

"Alex?" I said. "What's going on?"

Her mouth was set in a fixed grimace, the skin around her lips white with pain or fear. Or both. It was obvious that she was struggling to stay on her feet.

There was drugged panic in her eyes and the pitch of her voice. "I have to go...to get home. Tully is all alone at the house with old Mrs. Louba." She collapsed in a straight-backed chair. "Help me, Carroll. I can't find my shoes..." Tears began to roll down her cheeks.

Between us, Nurse Merriman and I got her back into bed.

I found her shoes.

"What's her blood pressure reading?" I asked.

Nurse Merriman hesitated. "We can't give out..."

"For pity's sake! All I have to do is look at her chart."

"Ninety over sixty, but..."

I pressed her. "What does that mean exactly?"

"It means," she said with exasperation, "that she's lost a lot of blood and is disoriented from her medication. She could pass out and fall. We can't be held responsible for what happens if she leaves in this condition."

"Are we talking life-threatening or what?"

She stiffened. "Not unless the bleeding starts again, but I must tell you..."

"I'm leaving," Alex said with a sudden show of determination, "whether anyone likes it or not, and you can't stop me. I'm not a prisoner in your damned hospital!"

The anger had to be a good sign.

Our dragon put her hands on her hips. "Honey, you aren't going anywhere in your condition. Look at you, you can barely lift your feet."

"Listen, Nurse Merriman," I said. "Someone just tried to kill this woman, and frankly, I'm not inclined to argue with her for several reasons. Number one, this much agitation can't be good for her; and number two, it seems obvious that she'd be safer at home with an armed guard, a nurse, and fewer strangers running in and out of her room. Now, if I were you, I'd be helping her get dressed before she decides on number three, which is to sue this hospital."

That did the trick.

Fury puckered her face even more than sourness. "Well! I can see you people are very determined. However, we *must* check her out with the proper paperwork." She scowled at me from the doorway. "And since you have obviously put yourself in charge, *try* not to let her fall off the bed and break her neck while I'm gone." She flounced from the room, righteous anger in every white-shoed step.

When the door closed, I leaned over Alex, who had her head back against the pillows. She really was two-thirds out of it.

"Alex? Are you sure you can make it?"

She nodded slowly without opening her eyes. "I've got to get home to Tully."

"All right," I said, "home it is. I'm willing to go along with this, but when we do it, I'm not taking any chances. There will be a private security guard here within fifteen or twenty minutes. We're not budging from this building without him. Can you still hear me, Alex?"

Her eyes snapped open. "I'm not deaf!"

"Good. Now listen carefully. Tully is with Simpson and Goldie, and Mrs. Louba is spending the night. I've already alerted Simpson. He says Tully is safe and fast asleep."

Her hands unclenched as the message penetrated; a little color crept back into her face. She nodded once, twice, trying hard not to cry again. "I think I saw him, you know...with the pillow, but I was so sleepy..."

I said, "Don't think about it. We can both identify him, so he won't dare have the nerve to come back. Right now, let's concentrate on getting you home to Tully in one piece.

Is that still what you want?"

"Yes, but..."

"No buts. Just take a deep breath and relax until our guard gets here. Then we'll be gone in a flash."

And we did just that. Alex lay quietly for another twenty minutes until her protection arrived, just before Joe Cheshire's radio crackled that the Wilmington Police were downstairs talking with hospital security.

"We're not waiting," I said, and gave him phone numbers and information to pass on about where we could be reached later.

After that, we made a furtive, five-man procession through the darkened corridors, with Nurse Merriman insistent on pushing the wheelchair herself. They waited with Joe Cheshire while my hired muscle, a former Raleigh police officer named Bobby Valentine with biceps the size of cantaloupes, went with me to bring the Jeep around to the back entrance.

It was going on six-thirty, not yet dawn. Fog lay thick and intimidating across the parking lot. Normally I loved fog, but I could feel my scalp crawl with unknown expectations until we found the Jeep.

Between us we got Alex stretched out in the rear seat with my jacket as a pillow and Nurse Merriman hovering every second, like a mother bird with a downed nestling. I softened toward her somewhat, until she shoved paperwork and a small bottle of pills toward me at the last minute.

As I scribbled my name on several forms, she said, "Someone has to take the responsibility, and it isn't going to be me."

Relieved at last of any job-threatening complications, she wheeled the chair away through the double doors without looking back.

We took the shortcut down to Canterbury Road and Live Oak across Oleander. If we were being followed, I couldn't spot a suspicious car. Without incident, we pulled into Alex's driveway in less than ten minutes.

True to his name, Valentine simply carried Alex into the house and up the stairs. Simpson and Goldie stood side by side, discreetly dressed in robes. When I raised one eyebrow behind the men, Goldie had the grace to blush.

By the time we got Alex tucked in bed with another pill, it was a little after seven. Over coffee in the kitchen, I gave the whole group—including Valentine and Mrs. Louba—as detailed an account as I could. They pelted me with questions, except for Valentine, who got up and immediately began testing windows and locking doors. I was glad to see he was treating the situation with the seriousness it deserved.

At last, I held up my hands. "Enough! I don't know any more, except that he had mean weasel eyes, he was ugly, and Alex is scared out of her wits. Whatever you do, don't let her out of bed and try to keep her calm. Valentine seems to know his business, but all of you should be careful. I'll be in and out of the Jeep if the police try to reach me. Which reminds me, Simpson, as much as I hate to bring up the subject, has the time been set for Eddie's funeral?"

"Not yet. We're still waiting to hear when the coroner will let us have the body. Sheriff Council implied that might happen today or tomorrow. If so, we're set to go ahead with services on Thursday. Friday at the latest."

"Christ!" Goldie said. "I just remembered. Friday is the thirteenth."

Chapter Seven

By the time I got away from Eddie's house, the sun was breaking through the clouds. I made a call to David Brannigan, whose crew was framing a difficult contemporary at Wrightsville Beach for me. He didn't answer, so I left a message to call if he needed anything. But I knew he wouldn't. I had worked with David before, and there was no better framer in the eastern part of the state.

I then swung by to get Jinks and Davis going on the renovation project a few blocks away on Forest Hills Drive. It was a forty-year-old brick ranch needing little more than a roof, kitchen, heating, electrical, and a healthy dose of sex appeal. As Eddie had said, it would be an easy turn-around. We had been waiting until the Figure Eight job was finished before getting underway. It was the kind of project we liked—an outdated house that would glow with appreciation at a minimum investment. A sow's ear into a silk purse. Sometimes the money was almost embarrassing.

Jinks's beat-up Ford pickup was already in the drive. For once, the gun rack in the back window seemed like a good idea—maybe one I should try myself. But I thought the Jeep might be so mortified it would refuse to leave the garage.

I found him in the den, arguing half-heartedly with Davis about where to start, the banter more subdued than usual.

Davis turned around. "Morning, Carroll."

At least he looked at me. Most of the time he gazed at the ceiling, the walls, the floor—anywhere but where he should. Friends assured me it was a typical teenage tactic intended to drive you crazy. Sometimes it worked.

Jinks said, "How you holding up, boss?"

"Could be better," I said, which should have qualified for understatement of the year.

Jinks buckled his tool belt. "We went by the trailer again for Duane, but his motorcycle wasn't there and Tiffany never answered the door. Could be the two of them just took off somewhere."

"That doesn't much sound like Duane," I said.

"Maybe not, but that Tiffany could talk him into just about anything."

I walked back toward the kitchen. "Well then, it looks like you guys are the entire crew today. I know you can handle it, so let's take a quick walk-through and get ourselves organized."

Jinks teased, "Davis is itching to get to the sledgehammer part. Right, Davis?"

"Yeah," said Davis, a hint of grin showing. Lately, you could go a whole day without getting even that much. In the last six months, he had gone from fun kid to a wearying mix of six-foot teenage belligerence, deliberate bad grammar, and dreadlocks. Once in a while, we got a glimpse of the old Davis trying to break out, but never knowing whether good kid or bad kid would show up for work was hard on our nerves. Addicted to reggae music, he wore earphones while he worked, which lent him a weird kind of psychotic jerk as he shuffled through his work. The earphones drove Randolph wild.

I touched him lightly on the shoulder. "Maybe when we tear down the shed out back. In the kitchen, though, if I catch you taking cabinets down from plaster walls with a sledge-hammer, they'll be calling you *Two-Toes Taylor*, if you get my drift."

He jerked away. The slightest twitch at the side of his mouth told me *good kid* was on the payroll today. For the moment.

I said, "However, using a crowbar is almost as cool. If you work hard, Jinks might let you do the wall at the end of the living room all by your lonesome."

Jinks winked. "I don't know, Carroll. I'd hate to miss out on that much fun."

"You guys..." Davis moaned.

"Well," Jinks said, "it worked for Tom Sawyer."

I regrouped. "So let's start with the scutwork first by tearing out the carpet. But no macho stuff, either one of you, when you're carrying them to the dumpster. We don't need back injuries on top of everything else right now, so man-handle it as a team. In the bathrooms, we'll keep the basic cabinets and just remove the doors. It's here in the kitchen that we need to take everything out with care. No crowbars, either, if you can help it. That means you, Davis, my man. Plaster repairs will set us back a week or more. What else? Oh, yes. If you'll move all the appliances out on the back porch, we'll get Habitat for Humanity to pick them up—the cabinets, too, if they come out in sections. Don't forget all the basics. Tape the vents and wear a breathing mask. You know the drill..."

"Keep it neat, keep it sweet," they said in unison.

"Very funny," I said. "Any questions?"

"Nah. It's a piece of cake," Jinks said. "We'll be out of this baby in no time."

"And just to be on the smart side, Jinks, I think you better lock this one up tight tonight. Keep the key in your pocket instead of under the doormat."

"You think...?"

"No, I don't think we're likely to have a repeat of last night, but I'm not taking chances, either. A determined arsonist won't be put off by a locked door, but we'll at least make him crawl through the damned broken window."

With a last warning to stay alert, I left them to get on with the job. Davis caught up with me halfway down the drive.

"Not another advance?" I said, smiling to reassure him that we might let him live long enough to reach eighteen.

"Naw, not that. I just wanted you to know I didn't smoke no cigarettes in the Anderson house, Scout's honor."

"I believe you, Davis."

He hesitated.

"Something else on your mind?"

"Well, yeah," he said. "Jinks and me, we sure are gonna miss Eddie." He turned with hunched shoulders and shuffling feet. "I wanted you to know, that's all."

I humbly blessed his screwed-up little heart, and let him get as far as the back door. "Hey, Davis! Were you really a

Boy Scout?"

"Yeah," he grinned. "For about two weeks."

I drove back out Market Street in a steady stream of traffic heading north. On Middle Sound Loop, most of the cars disappeared, and the countryside settled down into spotty subdivisions, trailer parks, and the occasional horse farm. It never ceased to amaze me that some of the highest and best ground along the coast was still occupied by mobile homes.

The locals swear that during Hurricane Hazel in 1954, the tidal surge rose halfway up the hill behind my house, that there was nothing visible—no marsh, no Figure Eight Island, no nothing—except enraged ocean as far as the eye could see. You can still read the high water markers at Wrightsville Beach. Back then, people were too smart to build expensive houses where they would be destroyed by hurricanes. Unlike now. But, a few years from now, these same mobile home sites would be worth a million dollars each. I had bet on it. Whenever I could make the right deal.

All along the east side of the road, dirt drives ran back through thick pines to the Intracoastal Waterway. Shortly past Johnson's Marine, I turned down a rough track with a battered *Private Road* sign at the entrance. Vandals, or maybe ticked-off neighbors, had used the sign for shotgun practice. One corner was blasted away.

I drove with care, wax myrtles and last year's blackberry vines scraping at the sides of the Jeep. Fifty yards back I reached a clearing that held a ten-dollar trailer with a million-dollar panorama. Scattered around the property were varying sizes of trash piles—old sofas and chairs, box springs, laundry appliances—all assembled in orderly batches like one would rake leaves into heaps around the lawn. Duane had been cleaning up the place.

I passed a fire-blackened cinderblock chimney standing in drunken testament to better days, pulled around to the water side, and parked beside a green Chevy pickup with a muddy license plate. There was more mud covering the motorcycle in the truck bed. Neither one belonged to Duane.

Tiffany answered my intermittent knocking dressed in a thin blue nylon wrap, yesterday's mascara smeared under her eyes. Her hair, dyed jet black and kinky permed, hung below her shoulders. I wondered how in God's name she ever got a brush through it. Duane said she was twenty-three, but the road miles on her face looked more like thirty-five to me.

"He ain't here," she said before I could open my mouth. The screen door remained closed.

"Do you know where I can find him, Tiffany?"

"How the hell should I know? But if you do find him, you can tell him for me that he ain't coming back here except to clear out his shit. And if that ain't soon, I'm gonna throw it out in the mud."

Maybe that explained the trash around the place.

With a straight face, I said, "When did you last see him?" Tiffany squinted as if she needed glasses. "Who cares? Maybe Sunday morning or afternoon. Anyways, he never showed up Sunday night at all. Never called, never showed, and I'll be damned if I'll put up with that."

I said, "Help me out here, Tiffany. Where would he be

likely to go? His mother's phone has been disconnected, and I don't have time to drive all the way down to Long Beach."

"Wouldn't do you no good. She moved back to Memphis, anyway. Duane said he was gonna meet somebody on Figure Eight, but he's just as likely to be gone off to his mama's. And good riddance to both of them, I say."

A door slammed inside the trailer. A voice, booming and cigarette-cracked, shouted, "Who the hell keeps hammering on the goddamned door?"

"It's nobody!" Tiffany yelled back.

"Yeah?" he snarled, appearing in the doorway. "Well, nobody sure is making a fucking lot of goddamned noise!"

Tiffany said, "It's Duane's boss looking for him, cause he ain't showed up for work."

Down one side of the fleshy male face pushed up against the screen, fresh abrasions ran from temple to chin. I saw more than I wanted of abundant belly, dirty feet, and bad teeth before he shouted through the door. He wasn't as big as Stan, but not far from it. Beer had not been kind to his physique.

"Duane ain't here, and decent people are trying to get some sleep without all this banging and yakety-damn-yak! So piss off!"

Who the hell was this oversized jerk? "Excuse me," I said. "But I was having a conversation with Tiffany."

"What?"

"I simply need some information from Tiffany."

"Oh, yeah? Well, she ain't talking to you no more. *Now* you're talking to *me*, and I say you should get the fuck gone from here before I lose my temper!"

"No need to get all tizzified," I said, with as much patience as I felt he deserved. "If he shows up, can you tell him...?"

"Please," said Tiffany nervously. "You'd better go. We don't know nothing about where Duane is."

He shoved her aside roughly and unlocked the screen. "Fuck you! Now get the hell away from my door."

My grandmother, so properly southern, would be mortified to know what kind of habits I picked up while living in New York City. "Go fuck yourself," I said. "And by the way, I know for a fact that Duane pays the rent." Because I had loaned him the last rent payment myself.

"Not any more!" he spat, and slammed the door so hard the trailer rocked. A scrawny, half-grown yellow cat shot out from under the foundation and raced for the nearest trash pile.

I went down the rickety wooden stairs, pondering his use of the phrase *decent people*. I figured everything was relative, but by heaven, there had to be some exceptions, and he was one of them. I power-locked the doors in the Jeep before making a wide sweeping turn. To hell with the two of them and Duane thrown in to boot. Damned if he would get his job back this time.

At the far end of the turn, I had a clear view through the live oaks, across the waterway and marshes, all the way to Figure Eight Island. I braked and sat with the motor idling. Not only could I see the island, but I was close enough to the burned house to see cars parked beside it at the end of Kingfisher Lane. With a pair of standard binoculars, I could have identified the figures standing by the vehicles—one of whom would be the county fire marshal.

As the crow flies, I was close enough to wave; but I was no crow, and had to backtrack to US 17 in a huge circle almost eleven miles long. Martin Farrell was ready to leave when I got to the site. He shook my hand, an amiable man nearing retirement, with a full head of gray hair and Paul Newman eyes. His wife of forty years played bridge with my grandmother every Thursday morning.

He started with Eddie, shaking his head. "I wouldn't have thought Eddie had an enemy in the world. How's your grandma taking it?"

"We're still stunned, I think, and having a tough time realizing he isn't coming back."

He nodded several times and after a suitable pause said, "Well, Carroll, it was a hell of a fire. On the bright side, you're not gonna have to bother with all the final inspections for a Certificate of Occupancy on this one."

"You're all heart. Give me the bad news, Martin."

He turned toward the fire-blackened ruin with a resigned gesture. Only the south wall was left standing. Three stories of charred brick, crumbled in places and empty on the inside. The rolled brick steps to the front door were buried under burned timbers and collapsed roof structures from the upper and lower porches. Over it all, the pungent odor of wet charcoal and ashes permeated everything. The sight brought a lump to my throat.

There are few things sadder than a burned-out hull of a house.

"It's like Johnny Powell figured last night," Martin said. "Traces of gasoline in four different locations, lots of stacks of scrap lumber from the dumpster to help it burn. With the strong wind we had out of the south last night, she must have gone up like Fourth of July fireworks."

I rubbed my forehead. "I was hoping Johnny might have been mistaken."

"Not Johnny. He's been at it too long not to recognize the smell of a gasoline job. What about you, Carroll? You been making enemies or something, courting somebody's husband or maybe running short of money?"

"Something," I said. "Damned if I know what to think. I've racked my brains and can't come up with anyone who would be ticked off enough to do something like this. It was a beautiful house, an adaptation of one of my father's old designs. I was so cocky about it, you know, like maybe he could see it somehow."

"Jack would have been proud." He cleared his throat and continued. "Most of the doors and windows were open, which fueled the fire with plenty of oxygen and kept it roaring. We found paint cans in two of the bedrooms. Were the painters here that day?"

I shook my head. "No, and the house was close enough to being occupied that we kept it locked at night. It's hard to tell now, but what we built was a classic Bahamian house, with front and back porches up and down and a wide central hall-way running through each floor. It was a tropical house, built for maximum air movement. If all the double doors and even half of the windows were open..."

Martin said, "It never had a chance. You know you'll need to get in touch with your insurance agent...get him out here before you mess with anything."

"Yes," I said. "I'll do that, thanks."

At the edge of the lot next door, one of the men shouted, "Hey, Martin. You want to come take a look at this?"

I ducked under the yellow tape and went with him. Two investigators were bent over scorched weeds.

"What have you got, Vick?"

"Looks like a telephoto lens, or what used to be one. Expensive, too. A funny thing to find in a vacant lot." He pointed to a piece of long charred barrel, partially melted, that might have once been camera equipment.

"I wouldn't touch it," I said. "It may be connected to a murder investigation. This looks like one that belonged to Eddie."

Martin said, "There won't be any fingerprints left on this baby. Vick, go get something to put it in."

I studied the tall weeds in the immediate area. "By chance, you haven't found a camera, have you?"

"Not yet, and if it was in the house, we could miss it altogether."

"Let me know if you find one."

When Vick went off to the truck, Martin turned serious. "Somebody meant business here. If I were you, I'd keep a close watch on my other belongings—like my car, my house, any other jobs I've got going. You know what I mean?"

"Yeah, Martin," I said. "I'm afraid I do."

Chapter Eight

Figure Eight's Yacht Club wasn't yet open, but the bartender, Leon Sherman, was there restocking liquor stores and let me in. He was ex-military, from the close-cut crop of hair to the spit-polish on his shoes. Even at this early hour, he wore a starched white shirt with a green tie.

"Sure," he said. "I'll try to answer your questions, if you don't mind me working at the same time." He gestured out the window toward two female foursomes on the tennis courts. "Good time to talk—before the ladies finish the game. They're famous for having a powerful thirst afterwards. Fuels the vocal cords for good gossip. How about you? Anything to drink?"

"If that's a fresh pot of coffee behind you, I'll settle for a cup. I'm trying to make up for lack of sleep this morning."

"Coming right up. Made it myself not more than ten minutes ago. Cream and sugar?"

"Both, thanks." I was finding fat and sugar comforting these days. Too comforting.

He poured two cups, took a quick sip of his own, then bent over the cartons on the floor, removing bottles of liquor. "Hell of a thing about Eddie. I liked the guy—same as most everybody. I figure this is about him, so just spit out whatever questions you have. I'll help if I can, and no hard feelings otherwise. Agreed?"

"Agreed. I understand Eddie was here Sunday night?"

Leon waited until he stopped rattling bottles. "Sure was. He came in around seven-thirty or eight, and sat at the far end of the bar, looking like most men who drop in here after a fight with their wives—a combination of pissed, depressed, and ashamed. I didn't pay much attention because the Whittaker reception was going full force in the other room and champagne wasn't strong enough to suit a lot of them. Eddie stayed about an hour or so and left looking like a man who had made up his mind about something. I assumed it was to go home and apologize to the little woman."

"What time would that have been?"

He shrugged. "Nine, nine-thirty. Same as I told the sheriff. Couldn't have been much later, because I clocked myself out about nine-forty five."

"Did he say anything, talk to anyone?"

"Sure he did. Probably a dozen or more people went by to say hello. I figured that's what made him feel better."

"Can you remember who?"

"Well, you've got me there. Like I told the sheriff, I was knee-deep in orders most of the evening because of the reception. I guess I just wasn't paying enough attention. The only person I remember clearly was Dennis Mason."

"No one else?"

He shook his head. "Something about their expressions made me think they were having words or I might not have even noticed. Not fighting words, mind you. Just something about the way they looked."

"Could you hear what it was about?"

He straightened and reached for his coffee. "Too noisy, what with the crowd at the bar and music from the other room."

"Anyone else on duty that night who might have spoken with him?"

Leon frowned. "Didn't think of that. Ramon was mostly helping with the reception and took over after I left, but I'm not sure I saw him talk to Eddie."

"Would you know if the police questioned Ramon?"

He shrugged. "Probably. 'Course I can't say for certain, but he'll be in here around eleven-thirty for the lunch bunch. Might be worth your while to talk to him yourself."

"Maybe I'll do that." I slid off the stool. "At any rate, I appreciate your time, Leon."

"Never too busy to talk to a beautiful woman. Just sorry about the reason. Sorrier than I know how to express, anyhow. Hell of a thing to happen to a man in his prime."

I left him with his boxes and exited by the front door as the gaggle of tennis players came in laughing.

I was only wasting my time, asking the same questions as Stan, with none of his training or experience. No one who knew Eddie would imagine him being involved in anything that could get him murdered. Dennis Mason was another story, but try as I might, I couldn't find the hook that put the two of them together or how Alex and my burned house fit. A sensible person would have left it alone, especially one who had enough on her plate.

Someone thought otherwise. As the heavy door swung

shut behind me, I had full view of the Jeep, smack in front of the entrance, looking pathetic with four flat tires.

Chapter Nine

I cussed all the cuss words I could think of, with a few in foreign languages thrown in for good measure. Furious, I stalked around the Jeep twice before I went back inside to use the pay phone because my cell phone chose that moment to demand a recharge.

There wasn't much point in calling my Nationwide agent, since I kept a thousand-dollar deductible on my insurance. I called Hanover Tire instead. They promised to bring four new Michelins as fast as possible, but exactly what that meant in actual hours or minutes, they refused to clarify.

I went back outside and looked up and down the main road, still angry enough to spit. There were no thugs or vandals anywhere to be seen, no maniacs hiding in the bushes or the marsh. Nothing but seagulls circling overhead and the far-off call of a crow.

I wanted to kick something.

If nothing else, a good aerobic workout would clear my head and cool me off. With the keys under the driver's floor mat and a note under the windshield for Hanover Tire, I slung my bag over a shoulder and started walking, kicking stones and seashells along the road shoulder, scattering a flock of cormorants warming their feet on the overhead wires.

It wasn't until I had walked as far as the main intersection that I realized where I was headed. By then I was, if not exactly tranquil, then at least level-headed again.

Sunshine, warm in my face, had begun chasing in and out of the clouds by the time I rang the bell at One Twenty Seven. All the shades were drawn, and there wasn't a car or a person in sight up or down the street. What did I expect? It was a summertime island, after all, with only a handful of full-time residents. The rest of the year, except for weekends, it was an exclusive, deserted ghost town.

I rang the bell again, and when no one answered, I peered through the garage window at a dark green car, then walked around back to where Satterwhite sat reading in a sheltered corner of the deck. He had a fuzzy pink blanket doubled across his legs, and for some perverse reason, I found the sight immeasurably cheering. He watched in silence as my footsteps resounded on the wooden planks and I sat down on the other lounger.

"Very fetching," I said. "It takes a confident man to wear pink."

He grinned. "Short of stripping the beds, it was the only one I could find." He slipped his watch off and shook it. "Has my watch stopped? Is it dinnertime already?"

"Don't I wish! That would mean this day was almost over before it could get any worse. But, what am I saying? It couldn't *possibly* get worse, and I'll have to take a raincheck on dinner."

"I figured as much."

"Meaning...?"

"That you seem like the kind of woman who gives

rainchecks."

I couldn't argue with that one, so I let it pass without even bothering to bristle. He had a way of concentrating on what I was saying which I found annoying and a little unnerving. In the strong light, I could see that his eyes were a sharp, clear green, an unusual combination with sandy hair. It took me a moment to drop back into the conversation.

"You'll freeze out here," I said, although I was flushed from my walk. I had even unzipped my jacket. The sun had stayed out long enough to warm me to the skin.

He was reading a worn hardcover copy of Charles Kuralt's *Life On The Road*. He closed it on his thumb and waited. "I'll live."

In the middle of a long silence, I said, "I suppose you're wondering what I'm doing here."

"Something like that."

I hesitated. "The truth is, I'm not sure. I was at the club questioning the bartender, and when I came out, the Jeep had four flat tires. Cut, I think. I was so mad, I just started walking, and well...hell... I don't know why I'm here... Just forget it. You look rested and less likely to keel over in the first strong breeze this morning. That's a good sign."

"I can't say the same for you. You look like the devil. Bad night?"

"You could say that," I sighed. "And more."

"So, say it."

The trouble was, I didn't know where to begin. I walked over to the railing and stood looking west across the winter marsh at the glint of sun on water, at the reflection off the windows of my house in the distance beyond the Intracoastal Waterway. I could see the masts of two weather-brave sailboats waiting for the Figure Eight bridge to open.

I said, "Did you know that wild ponies roamed the island in the eighteen-hundreds? I would like to have seen that."

Satterwhite didn't speak.

I rubbed at my forehead. Without turning around, I said, "I think I'm beginning to get spooked. There are too many bizarre things happening. Dennis and Eddie, the fire last night, and then Eddie's pregnant widow lost the baby in the small hours of the morning. Bad enough, you would think, but then someone tried to smother Alex in the hospital, and the tires..."

"Whoa! Back up! You lost me in there somewhere. Alex is Eddie's widow?"

I nodded.

"How do you know somebody tried to kill her?"

"I was in the room at the time, half asleep, until I caught him putting a pillow over her face."

His eyebrows went up. "Half asleep?"

"But not when he pulled a gun on me after I chased him to the elevator." I had his full attention now.

"Shit!" he said.

I shivered in a sudden gust of wind, like a premonition or a ghost walking over my grave. It's never wise to tempt fate by proclaiming that your troubles can't get any worse.

Satterwhite got up with a slight grimace. "Let's get inside before we both have a relapse. I don't know about you, but I've got better things to do than be an invalid again, and

I'd as soon be dragged out to sea as wind up back in the hospital."

In the kitchen, he rinsed the coffee pot and made coffee with the ease that comes from doing it for yourself. He took off his jacket and slung it across a chair. I didn't ask why he was wearing a shoulder holster and gun, and he didn't offer an explanation.

The phone rang and he said, "Get that for me, would you? My hands are wet."

I picked it up. "Hello," I said, but there was one of those awkward silences on the other end, until a husky female voice commanded, "Let me speak to Agent Satterwhite."

"Hold on a second." I held the phone out to him and watched him shake his head and mouth the words *take a message.*

"Sorry," I said, "but he can't come to the phone right now. Give me a number and I'll have him call you back."

"Who is this?" she snapped.

I've always hated when some stranger on a phone demands my name. I could have said that it was none of her business. Instead, I said, "Who are *you*?" and got a sharp bark of irritation in my ear.

She said, "All right. Just give him a message from Lorna, and get every word down exactly. Tell him..."

"Excuse me..."

"What?"

"I'm not the secretary here."

"Hah!" she said. "I'll bet not. You just tell him that he'd better stop dodging my phone calls and let me hear from him soon. And you can damned well remind him that he's supposed to be recuperating instead of fooling around in bed with some bimbo. He's got exactly one week to get well and back on the job or he can kiss his ass goodbye. Now, have you got that, Miss?"

"Yes, *thank you*. I'll tell him you called." I replaced the phone.

He was watching. "Your cheeks are red. I think I can guess who that was."

"Lorna," I said. "Whoever that is. She seems to think you might be...ah...fooling around, so to speak, instead of re-cuperating. I gather she would like for you to stop it at once, get well and return to work within the week in order to save a certain section of your rear anatomy. And, oh yes, she wants you to return her phone calls."

"Not a chance," he said.

"Can she cost you your job?"

"The boss lady can, indeed, and with a vengeance that makes brave men cringe. But I've also been with the Bureau seventeen years, and she knows I wouldn't bat an eye if she fired me. So she won't."

"Well, if it happens," I said as a joke, "I can always use a new construction supervisor."

"An appealing thought. I'll keep it foremost in mind-right after a couple of years sailing around the Caribbean." He poured the coffee with his back turned. "Now, tell me what you did when he pointed the gun at you?"

"He yelled for me to stop, so naturally I stopped," I said slowly, remembering. "He got on the elevator, and I followed him like a fool. Fortunately, he drove away before I could get myself killed." I took the coffee with a less-than-steady hand and sat at the table.

"Wilmington police jurisdiction? To which you duly reported everything?"

"Through a security guard at least," I said. "It's been a busy morning."

"If I were you, I'd check in with Stan again. He'll be assuming attempted murder is an important piece of the puzzle, and looking to you for more information. When we finish, I'll run you home, but for now, start at the beginning, and don't leave anything out."

"All right," I said, and did my best to remember the details, picking up speed as I went. Still, I was surprised that it took only a few minutes, and in that time he never interrupted or took his eyes off my face.

He said, "They'll need a full description. You might be thinking of facial characteristics, hair and clothing colors, shoes—things you weren't even aware you were seeing. It's better done immediately, but I can't argue with getting Alex into a safer environment. You did good, though, to get a description of the car and a partial plate reading. That may help."

"It doesn't seem real. None of it does." My fingers were turning the untouched cup of coffee in circles. It had a bright blue BMW logo.

In a softened voice, he said, "You took quite a chance running after a man bent on murder."

To my embarrassment, I had to blink hard. "It was an

instinctive thing to do. I was appalled, indignant, mad as a fool. I never gave a thought to the consequences. She was a friend who had just lost a baby and a husband, and I remember thinking, *how dare he*?"

"Careful you don't wind up a dearly-departed friend," he said. "It might be wise to remember that his actions make him sound like a man who is no stranger to violence. The fact that you can identify him should worry you a great deal—enough to keep you from running around the countryside by yourself, if you get my meaning."

"Maybe I'm the one who needs a bodyguard?" I joked, but my revulsion must have been clear.

"There are worse things—like being dead, for instance. I'm beginning to like you, Davenport, so much so that I'd hate to wake up tomorrow morning and read in the newspaper that you'd become food for the fishes or had that beautiful throat slashed or..."

"You've made your point," I stood up and reached for my jacket. "Now, if you're ready, you're going to have to drive me home. I'm too spooked to walk back to the jeep."

He didn't move. "I'm dead serious."

"So am I."

"Good," he said. "It could keep you alive."

He drove me back by the Figure Eight Club in a dark green Buick with tan leather seats. There was no sign of the Hanover Tire truck or that it had been there with replacement tires.

"I think I'll take a look," Satterwhite said, and walked around the jeep, inspecting all four tires. "Cut, like you thought. Not a sissy job to accomplish on Michelin radials."

I nodded. "It did occur to me to wonder about Bitsy Anderson, but it seems out of character for her to get her hands dirty. Somehow, I can't picture her running around town slashing tires."

"Just don't bet your life on it."

Going across the bridge, I said, "Here's what I'm beginning to think. Maybe both Eddie and Dennis saw something or knew something they weren't supposed to. Or one knew and the other was just in the wrong place at the wrong time. And now, some unknown person thinks Eddie told Alex something she doesn't yet know she knows..."

"Or doesn't want to know."

"Don't start the drug stuff again. I won't believe that for a minute, and I'd stake my life Eddie wasn't involved in anything illegal-or even immoral for that matter."

Satterwhite waved to the guard as we passed through the gate. "Detective Paige is more than a little convinced the two murders have something to do with drug drops. Seems reasonable to me."

"When Alex is up to it, I'll have a long talk with her, but I can't believe she knows anything."

"When you do, ask her if she can spot anything out of place, maybe something she doesn't think should belong to..."

"Eddie's truck," I said.

"What?"

"Where is Eddie's truck? I never thought to ask Paige or Alex. Nobody mentioned his truck, and I forgot about it. It wasn't at the job site or I would have seen it this morning, nor was it at his house. Surely they've searched for something as important as his vehicle."

"If it was anybody other than Paige, I'd be more confident. Could be Stan went up to Raleigh figuring Paige had a handle on things, and the truck fell through the cracks. As soon as we get you home, I'll check in with Stan."

By then, we were at Porters Neck Road. He asked, "Which way? Remember I came and went by chopper."

"Turn to the right."

In a minute we were at the "T" intersection and turning left on Bald Eagle Lane.

"Are there?" he said.

"Are there what?"

"Bald eagles?"

I said, "When I was a kid, yes. But they disappeared with the golf courses and subdivisions. I thought there would be no more in my lifetime, but now there's a pair nesting along Futch Creek, a mile further north. I've seen them a few times over the marshes."

When we reached my driveway, Randolph's dog, Max, met us near the entrance, barking with uncustomary fierceness.

I rolled down the window and shouted, "Get of the way, Max!"

He stood his ground.

"Just drive around on the grass. He doesn't recognize the car."

Satterwhite smiled. "First time I've run into a three-legged guard dog."

"He's nervous," I said. "Too many strangers have been

around, and this is the day Randolph volunteers at a homeless shelter."

We pulled up near the house and got out. Max had moved closer to Randolph's cottage, and was still doing his barking, guarding thing. For such a little dog, he was making a horrendous racket. That in itself was unusual for Max, since Randolph had seen to his rigorous training in the niceties of dogdom—not to dig in the flower beds, not to bark, and the most important one of all—where all good doggies should go for their bodily functions.

"He'll stop as soon as we get inside," I said.

Satterwhite grunted. "I think you've had company." He pointed at the front door standing wide open, the jamb splintered.

The air was suddenly much colder.

"Damn it all," I said.

He removed his gun from the holster. "Stay out here while I make sure the house is empty."

"Not on your life!"

"Shit," he said. "Then stay behind me."

I wasn't about to object.

The foyer appeared untouched. I could almost have believed that Randolph had left the door open accidentally, but there was no denying the havoc in the living room. Cushions were thrown off the sofas, drawers were open, chests emptied, pictures askew.

Someone had been in the fireplace and left a trail of soot tracked across the hearth rug and an ugly black handprint on the white mantel. I picked up a heavy poker as we passed the fireplace. Satterwhite looked around, saw my weapon and rolled his eyes. We went in a slow search from room to room, looking in closets, under beds. Or rather, Satterwhite searched while I hovered in doorways.

Charlie was huddled on the top perch of his cage, untouched as far as I could tell, but subdued, his feathers puffed up like a sparrow's on an icy day. There were two green tail feathers on the bottom of his cage.

The kitchen and den were the worst. Both doors stood open on the refrigerator, the contents of the freezer strewn about the floor amid broken dishes, glassware and spilled food. Pots and pans had been thrown out of the lower cabinets. Spaghetti sauce was smeared like thick blood across the wooden floor.

"Holy Mother!" I said, staggered by the cleanup needed in the kitchen alone. Satterwhite checked the garage without me. When he re-entered the kitchen, he put his gun back into the holster with a scowl.

"Could be worse," he said.

"How? Just tell me how?"

"Well, take a good look around you. Vandals would have caused much more damage to the walls, the windows, the cabinets, you name it. They would have broken everything possible—things you didn't even know you had—just for the hell of it."

In the middle of the room, I turned in a slow circle. He was right. For instance, not everything was thrown out of cabinets; no glass doors were broken. The floor mess lay where it had been thrown. I shuddered at the thought of tomato sauce drying on the walls or, God forbid, the ceiling.

"Searching for something," Satterwhite announced.

"What, for heaven's sake?"

"When we figure that out, we'll be a step closer to finding out who," Satterwhite said. "Now, here's what I want you to do. Take three deep breaths to clear your head. We're going to walk you slowly back through each room to see if you can spot anything missing. Since this room is the worst, we'll save it until the last. Ready?"

"Satterwhite..."

"Ready?"

"As I'll ever be, I guess."

We started in the dining room, which looked much worse than it had on the first trip through.

Satterwhite said, "Close your eyes and try to visualize what it looked like before."

This time I didn't protest.

"Now open them and tell me what's missing."

An end wall nearest the kitchen held built-in shelves fitted with glass doors. Much of the china lay on the floor in pieces, jumbled up with crystal glassware. I picked up two pieces of a dinner plate, fitted them together. "My mother's," I said, feeling the tears gathering behind my eyes.

"There'll be plenty of time to cry later, Davenport, "he said gruffly. "For now, keep your mind clear and tell me how many million-dollar paintings are missing."

"Go to hell."

"That's better. Now tell me. And don't touch anything else."

The paintings were crooked, but still in place, only one of them worth more than ten thousand dollars—except in memories—like the one of my mother at the age of seven. The gilt mirror hung over the sideboard as usual, the drawers and doors below crookedly open. On the mahogany surface, a pair of sterling candelabras from the early nineteenth century sat untouched. Silver flatware lay jumbled in a drawer and scattered on the Heriz rug that had graced my grandmother's sitting room for fifty years.

Satterwhite interrupted my reverie. "What do you think?"

"I would have to do a count, but it seems fairly certain they weren't silver thieves. As far as I can tell, nothing is missing in this room."

We moved to the main living area, which had fared better and would be simple to set right.

I longed to straighten the overturned lamps, the cushions; pick up a cracked Chinese bowl from the floor. "Maybe nothing's missing here, either."

"You've been lucky. Much of the time, we're talking slashed upholstery, broken chairs..."

"Remind me to send someone a thank-you note," I said sourly.

"Right," he said. "Now, the den."

On the first quick pass, I had seen enough to know the den was a bigger mess than any room except the kitchen. For sure, it hadn't gotten any better in the last few minutes. This was the room I used as an office, as my father had, and where I spent much of my time on business and pleasure. It was a big room, the dimensions almost eighteen by thirty feet, with bookshelves or cabinets everywhere, even over windows and doorways. A creekstone fireplace, in the middle of the west wall, was flanked by matching gun cabinets whose doors were wide open. The entire east wall was constructed of oversized glass doors.

Files, papers, architectural plans, and books were tossed everywhere. Days would be required to straighten them back into some kind of order. At the end of the room, my father's old English partners desk had been turned on its side, some of its drawers dumped on the rug. The room smelled of leather, fireplace ashes, and the faintest hint of body odor. From the doorway I said, "Four slots are empty in the gun racks."

"What kind?" asked Satterwhite.

"Rifles, I think. My father was the collector, not me." I walked over and looked into the lower drawers beneath the racks. "Handguns and ammunition were kept in these two drawers. It seems like there should be more than this, but I'd have to look at the insurance list to be sure. The cabinets were always kept locked. I haven't looked in them in years."

"Anything else?"

I looked slowly around the room—at the television and stereo equipment, the broken Waterford vase, the crushed camellias on the bluestone hearth—back at the gun cabinet.

"I was wrong," I said. "Only three of them were rifles. One of them was a shotgun—a Browning."

"You're sure?"

I turned abruptly and walked away from him, out of the room and down the hall.

He came after me. "What's wrong?"

"I'm sure." I steadied myself against the wall. "It was the one my father used to kill himself. I can't...I can't tell if anything else is missing in there."

"Good God," he said. "Why would you keep such a thing?"

"Stan Council made the decision. I wasn't here, remember? I was busy luxuriating in a nervous breakdown in New York at the time, and nobody bothered to ask me. If they *had*, I would have told them to throw it the hell somewhere in the middle of the ocean."

He nodded at the rage in my voice. "A good place—for something like that."

"It's been a long time. You'd think..." I took a deep breath. "Sorry. Let's just finish this, please."

I stood in the doorways of the three extra bedrooms, one after the other, looking at similar chaos, my mind elsewhere. They held little of value except for the antique furniture. It wasn't until we reached the master bedroom that I became aware Satterwhite was holding my arm. A sudden longing for physical closeness surprised me, somehow saddened me. I pulled my arm gently away.

By now I was becoming almost used to the chaos of emptied drawers, overturned mattresses, torn-apart closets. My room reeked of spilled perfume, which had ruined the dresser top. In the bathroom, a frilly bra was laid out in the tub, straight and precise across a plumped pillow, the flesh-colored lace somehow as threatening as a death note.

I froze. The room was so quiet, I could hear Satterwhite's

breathing, overlaid by the sound of Max still barking in the distance.

"That damned dog," said Satterwhite.

And I began to come out of my trance.

"Randolph!" I said. "Oh, my God!" I turned and bolted back through the house and out the front door, my heart pounding like a pile driver.

Chapter Ten

It was a hundred-and-fifty-foot race to Randolph's gray shingled cottage, but it seemed to take me a lifetime. The door was open, and just inside, I could see something lying on the floor. Ten feet before I rushed up the stairs, Satterwhite grabbed me roughly from behind.

"Get the hell back! I mean it this time!" He drew his gun again, paused briefly just inside the door, stepped over something, and moved quickly through the living room.

I ignored him, because Randolph lay face down a few feet inside the entrance. Blood had matted in his grizzled hair and run down along the side of his face to form a small puddle by his right ear. I couldn't tell if he was dead. When Satterwhite returned, I was on my knees beside him, desperate to find a pulse.

"Call an ambulance," I said.

"Where's the phone?"

For a moment, I went blank and couldn't remember where Randolph kept his telephone.

"In the kitchen...the wall by the doorway," I said, and then shouted out the address behind him. I found what I thought might be a faint pulse, but couldn't be certain because my own heart was beating so hard. I snatched an old coverlet off the sofa and spread it with care across him. There was nothing I could do but keep him warm and hold his hand.

I knew I was crying, convinced that he was dead or very close to it. Satterwhite was back in no time, and I felt a swell of relief that there was someone with me who wouldn't fall apart in an emergency.

I said, "See if *you* can find a pulse. I can't tell if I'm feeling his or my own."

Satterwhite knelt down, put two fingers along the side of Randolph's neck. "There's a pulse, no doubt about it, a fairly strong one, too. When I met him this morning, he seemed like a pretty tough old guy for his age, so you can let up on yourself a little." He felt over Randolph's arms and legs as if he knew what he was doing, then gently inspected the bloody mess on his head.

"I'll never forgive myself if he dies. I thought he was gone for the day. If I had looked back as we drove in, I would have seen his front door open or the car around the side of the cottage. I should have connected Max's barking...I never gave him a thought."

"You did," Satterwhite said. "You told me he was volunteering at some homeless shelter today."

I shivered, feeling like I had as a kid when I lost something valuable out of sheer carelessness. Every material thing in my life could be replaced, but if I lived to be a thousand, there would never be another Randolph.

I tried to focus. "It looks like an awful wound to me, and he's unconscious. I don't know what to do."

"Remember, head wounds always look worse than they actually are." At the look on my face, he added, "Look, don't beat yourself up over this until we find out his condition."

"Easy for you to say," I flared. "This man has been a friend all my life. He taught me to read, to tie my shoes, to fish. Half the things I know, I learned from..."

"Davenport?"

"What?"

"If you can get hold of yourself, there must be someone else you need to call. Does he have a family member who can meet him at the hospital?"

I took a breath and got to my feet. "His wife. Will you stay with him while I phone Lucille?"

"Go on. I won't leave him. Just remember not to touch anything except the telephone."

In the kitchen I leaned my head against the wall and did a slow ten count to calm myself before I dialed my grandmother's number. At least I had enough sense not to cause Lucille to have a wreck on the way to the hospital. I intended to explain everything to her in a calm, rational, low-key manner.

When she answered after the second ring, I chose instead to lie like a cowardly dog.

"Mrs. Monroe's residence."

"Lucille, it's Carroll. Listen, Randolph has had a little accident and he needs you to meet him at the hospital with his insurance information."

"Oh, my Lord have mercy! Is he hurt bad?"

"No, no. There's nothing for you to panic about. He just can't find his insurance card, that's all."

"You wouldn't lie to me, would you, Carroll?"

I willed myself to breathe. "You know I'd be afraid to,

Lucille."

She said tartly, "What did that old fool do to himself this time? Cut off a finger?"

The summer before, Randolph had accidentally plunged a garden scythe into his forearm, resulting in a lot of blood and a quick trip to the medical center. A month later, he tripped and sprained his right wrist. I thought he needed his eyeglasses changed. So did he, until Lucille made an appointment with the ophthalmologist and needled him to keep it. After that, he dug his heels in and refused to budge. Far be it from me to figure out old and complicated relationships.

I said, "No, nothing like that, but he may need a few stitches."

She heaved a put-upon sigh. "My peach cobbler has ten more minutes before it's finished. I won't leave a second before then, and I've got flour all over me for heaven's sake..."

"Just throw your coat on and don't worry about it. And Lucille, I think it would be better if you didn't tell Gran about this. She's had enough to worry her. I'll meet you at the emergency entrance as quickly as you can get there."

"But, I thought you said..."

"Gotta run, Lucille. Randolph's waiting." I hung up on her, feeling guiltier than hell. In the living room, Satterwhite glanced up, no doubt wondering if I was planning to bite his head off again.

I got back on my knees beside Randolph. "How is he?"

"His pulse is steady, and the bleeding has stopped. Any further diagnosis will have to be left to the experts, but I'm thinking he has a concussion or he wouldn't have been out so long."

I pushed the hair off my face. "You've obviously had more experience at this sort of thing than I have. Isn't there something we should be doing?"

"Just stay calm. We haven't moved him, and he's covered with a blanket. Now all we can do is wait."

So I waited, and stared at the German wall clock and the same level of destructive chaos in Randolph's house that I had found in my own. All his wonderful books, so important in his life, were dumped from the shelves. His cherished night-blooming cereus was uprooted and thrown out of its pot, the huge fat buds crushed in a mess of dirt and greenery.

We waited more long minutes, until we heard distant sirens on Porters Neck Road.

Satterwhite looked at his watch and nodded. "Good response time. Can you hang in there if I go out to the entrance and flag down the truck?"

"Go!" I said.

Without his presence, the room felt hushed and empty, except for the movement of Randolph's red plaid shirt, rising and falling with each slow breath. To me he looked pale, close to death even. I couldn't bear to think that anything might happen to him.

All my concentration was on Randolph, on the sirens growing louder along Bald Eagle Lane, and on Max, who was still barking near the front steps. I never sensed another presence in the room until, at the last moment, hair tingled on the back of my neck, just before a large fist knocked me sprawling against the wall.

Chapter Eleven

In my dazed state, I had a swift impression of someone big rushing across the room. I must have instinctively turned my head just enough to keep the blow from snapping my neck, but the impact still left me stunned. Satterwhite started in from the porch at the same time the intruder plunged through the open door. He slammed a huge shoulder into Satterwhite's chest at a hard run, knocking him off the front porch and down the brick steps.

I labored to my feet, trying to pull some breath back into my lungs. Little yellow and black spots danced in front of my eyes as I clutched the railing and half-slid, half-stumbled to where Satterwhite was attempting to rise, his teeth clenched in pain.

He said, "Son-of-a-bitch! Where the hell was he hiding in there?"

I heard the *thunk-thunk* of heavy doors closing, and then two paramedics were bending over Satterwhite, who was still on his knees. He slapped away a blood pressure cuff and waved them toward the house. "Forget about the two of us. Get to the elderly man in the front room." They ran into the house. To me, Satterwhite asked, "Which way did the bastard run?" I pointed toward the trees, part of a three-hundred foot section of dense woods tangled over with smilax, grape vines, and poison ivy. "That way. But neither of us will be chasing him through there."

"Like hell I won't!" He half rose to his feet, an intense grimace of pain on his face. He sank back with a grunt. "Goddamn it."

"Satterwhite, shut up. He's half again your size. You're not going anywhere." My teeth were chattering from cold, shock and fear. It didn't help that I was sitting on wet ground that had seeped through the seat of my jeans, and I couldn't remember how I'd gotten there.

I rose, feeling dizzy and nauseous. The side of my face ached from temple to jaw. I would have a devil of a bruise by morning. "Can you get up?" I asked Satterwhite.

"Maybe," he said, but did it like an old man with bad rheumatism, straightening with difficulty and biting off a couple of expletives. "Satisfied?"

I turned my back and struggled up the stairs where the two paramedics were busy with Randolph. They fastened a neck brace, slid him onto a board and loaded him on the stretcher. I hovered anxiously, my hands clenched together.

"All right, let's get him out of here," one of them said.

Satterwhite said to me, "Go with him. I'll lock things up."

I weighed the lack of color in his face. "What about you? You need to be checked out, too."

"I'll live. Now get on out of here."

I didn't need to be told twice, and ran toward the truck's double doors as they were closing. The driver grabbed me by the arm and said, "In the front, Miss. Mike's gonna have his hands full as it is."

In the cab, I buckled up with clumsy fingers, not surprised at the unsteadiness of my hands, and tried to see what
was happening with Randolph in the back. The paramedic
called Mike looked fresh-faced and young enough to be just
out of school. I had no idea whether he was doing what
needed to be done, whether he was well-trained or brand new
on the job. He had placed an oxygen mask over Randolph's
face and fitted him with a blood pressure cuff.

Beside me, the driver took note of my anxiety. "Don't
worry. Mike knows his stuff, and he's older than he looks."

"Thanks," I said, and faced forward, suddenly finding that
the wild ride was both too slow and too fast. Our speed turned
the trip into a dizzying flight around thoughtless drivers, construction lanes, and red lights. Randolph lay motionless. I
said a silent prayer that we would make it in time—and once
or twice that we would make it to the emergency room at all.
My watch was either not moving or was broken. I couldn't
tell which.

Lucille arrived five minutes after Randolph disappeared
into the bowels of bureaucracy. I was watching from the emergency room door, hoping to meet her outside the building, and
was a few feet away when her car door opened. She took
one look at my expression, her face crumpling, and put both
hands over her mouth. Behind her hands she made a high
muffled keen.

Like Randolph, Lucille was in her seventies, thin and wiry
the way some women are all their lives, full of frenetic energy

in spite of her graying hair and withering dark skin. She reminded me a lot of Charlie, who never seemed to be able to decide whether he should make sweet, grateful bird tunes or try to bite off one of my fingers. We had lived with a wary truce since I was a teenager.

She stiffened when I put an arm around her shoulders, pointing an accusing finger. "You lied to me, didn't you? He's dead! I know he's dead! I would never have thought you would lie to me." She began to cry, her face a fierce mask of anger and resignation.

"No, no, Lucille. He isn't dead. Truly he isn't. I didn't want to frighten you so much that you killed yourself on the way here, that's all."

I could have been talking to myself.

In a raised voice I said, "Listen to me now, Lucille. *He is not dead.*"

She said something under muffled sobs, but she didn't stop. If Randolph died, she would never forgive me. Of that much, I was certain.

"Come on now, Lucille, dry your eyes, and let's go see what we can find out. The doctors have probably had time to look at him by now. You wouldn't want Randolph to think he's upset you, would you?" I tried to smile.

She sniffed and glared at me, then wiped her eyes on a pink flowered apron streaked with flour and peach stains. With jerky motions, she took it off and flung it onto the front seat, recovered her purse, and locked the door with care. With a shaky breath, she said simply, "I'm ready."

I took her by the arm, but she snatched it away, walking

ramrod-stiff beside me into the building. A harried admit-
ting person said we'd have to take a seat until they called us.
Lucille began to protest.

Pulling her away, I said, "Let's give them a few more minutes, Lucille. Then we'll try again. Most likely, they aren't
finished examining him. Come on, now. Try to relax."

I steered her to the back of the room where there was a
little more privacy, away from a small crowd of noisy family,
equally worried about one of their own.

By then she was ready to look me in the eye without spitting. "Tell me what happened to him. Is he hurt bad?"

"Somebody broke into both houses this morning. I don't
know how Randolph wound up in the middle. The paramedics think he may have a broken arm, but they're more
worried about a head injury. He was unconscious when we
found him."

Lucille's words quivered. "Did he come to?"

"No," I said honestly. I wouldn't lie to her again.

"Oh, Jesus, Jesus, Jesus!" She began to rock back and
forth, her eyes closed, mouth moving in silent prayer.

For an interminable time, we sat frozen, listening to the
incessant *whooshing* of automatic doors as anxious people
came and went. Occasionally, a name was called out, but never
mine or Lucille's. I got up and approached the front desk
again.

"Any word yet on Randolph Taylor?"

A weary nurse, crisp and clean as a novice, looked me up
and down and then back at my bruised face. "Are you re-
lated?"

I shook my head. "No. I came in with him, but his wife is here now. At her age, it would help a lot if she could have some kind of reassurance about his condition."

Maybe she hadn't been there long enough to have lost all compassion, or maybe she was having a good day. For whatever reason, she said, "I'll see what I can find out."

She was back in a matter of minutes. "Mr. Taylor has been taken for a CAT scan. After that he'll be moved to ICU. It will still be a while before you can see him."

"Can you estimate how long?"

Her look said I had pushed my one favor to the limit. "It could be an hour or more. It depends on whether they're stacked up at the CAT."

"Thank you," I said. "It isn't what we wanted to hear, but at least we know what's happening. We'd be grateful if you could let us know the minute they move him upstairs."

"I'll do my best."

I turned back toward Lucille.

"Just a minute, Miss."

"Yes?"

The nurse looked at her paperwork. "Someone who came in with Mr. Taylor promised us an insurance card. Was that you? Is your name Davenport?"

"Sorry," I said. "Give me a minute and I'll have it." It seemed like a week since I had asked Lucille to bring the card. Lucille was on her feet when I returned, looking more than anxious, looking apprehensive and wound tight. I repeated what the nurse had said. She seemed incapable of doing more than nodding.

I put her oversized canvas bag in her hands. "If you have it with you, they need his insurance card."

She fumbled in the bag until she found it, and then walked with me to the front desk.

When they were finished, I said, "Are you going to be all right, Lucille?"

A straightening of the shoulders was her only reaction.

"Let's take a walk before we go crazy just sitting here," I suggested. "Not for long. Just to stretch our legs and get away from the tension in this room. You're going to be mad at me for years to come, but for now, let me at least try to help. Fifteen minutes. What do you say?"

To my surprise, she nodded and said, "And you can call Davis."

"I should have thought of him myself. He'll want to be here with you and Randolph. Also, a good jolt might be just the thing for his rebellious young heart."

We found a pay phone and I called the job site in Forest Hills. When Jinks answered, I told him to drive Davis to the emergency room *post haste*, and that I would explain when they got there.

I borrowed more change from Lucille and phoned my Nationwide agent, who said he would try to find the adjuster and get him to hot-foot it out to the house to take a look. When I told him where the keys were hidden, he said sourly that he wished his clients wouldn't make it so damned easy for burglars. So it served him right that he got to hear about an additional loss. The torched house on Figure Eight would set Nationwide back a minimum of seven hundred grand.

After that, I lured Lucille as far as the cafeteria for three bites of lemon pie and a hot sugared tea to take back. She had lost a little of her paralysis. Enough, anyway, to embrace Davis when we got back to the waiting room. He obviously had something that I was lacking. With Jinks to back him up, he could handle Lucille's emotional outbursts.

Once again, I explained everything, and didn't argue when Lucille told Davis bluntly that Randolph could die. There may have still been rebellion in his heart, but it wasn't showing in a crisis. He even got to hold Lucille's hand. Jinks stayed on for moral support.

It was more than an hour before we were finally allowed to see Randolph in ICU on the same floor. Lucille and I went in the room first.

Randolph lay behind a pale blue curtain, unmoving, his eyes closed. There was a thick white bandage on the side of his head and a cast on his left arm. He looked shrunken and frail. Lucille went to his side and gripped his good hand. On the other side of the bed, a nurse was busy adjusting an IV drip.

"How is he?" I said.

Without losing her concentration, she said, "He opened his eyes twice when they rolled him in, but I understand he's still drifting in and out for the most part. Dr. Bradshaw will be along in a few minutes, and I'm sure he'll be able to answer all your questions."

From the foot of the bed, I watched Randolph's chest movements with a lump as large as a lemon in my throat.

As soon as the door closed behind the nurse, I picked up

Randolph's chart. Other than a blood pressure reading of one hundred forty five over ninety, the scribbled abbreviations were hopeless to decipher.

Lucille began talking to Randolph in a low crooning voice, indistinguishable words of comfort and intimacy that pointed out their need for privacy. I tiptoed out of the room. Davis, looking uncertain, crept into the room and took my place.

In the hallway, Dr. Bradshaw, formal and competent in his white coat, was just beginning his explanation to Stan Council—and to my grandmother, who had appeared out of nowhere.

Bradshaw began again for me. "As I was saying, Mr. Taylor has a concussion from trauma to the side of the head. He was conscious and talking earlier, pretty cranky actually. A good sign. But we don't like to take chances with head injuries, especially when the patient has been unconscious. We'll want to watch him closely for a while to make sure there's no subdural hematoma. Aside from the head injury, he also has a simple fracture of the left forearm. We've put a cast on it, and if all goes well, he should go home in a couple of days."

There was a short relief-filled silence before Stan said, "Doc, what can you tell us about the knock on the head? Was he hit or was the injury from the fall?"

Bradshaw shook his head. "There is no way to know for sure. It's likely he'll be able to tell you himself, although it may take a few days before everything is clear in his mind."

"Just give me your best guess."

Dr. Bradshaw frowned in the manner of a man who disliked guessing at his answers. "The severity of the injury seems inconsistent with those found in a normal fall. However, it would be impossible to accurately determine exactly what kind of..."

Stan interrupted. "In plain words, someone gave him a hell of a whack on the head with something other than the palm of his hand?"

Bradshaw frowned. "We could also say in plain words that your Mr. Taylor is a damned lucky man, so do him a favor and don't stay very long."

Stan shook his hand. "Thanks, Doc."

When he was gone, I looked at my grandmother. Her face was several shades lighter than normal, and I said, "Do you want to sit down somewhere, Gran?"

She turned on me with a determined blaze of anger in her eyes, my bruised face gaining me no sympathy. "No, young lady, I do not need to sit down. *Nor* do I need to be treated like a doddering old fool twice in one day by my only grand-daughter, who had the unmitigated gall to advise Lucille not to tell me. If something like that should *ever* happen again before I reach one hundred years of age, you are likely to find out precisely just how upset I can get. And now, if you will excuse me, I would like to go in to see one of my oldest and dearest friends."

With that, my own *nearest and dearest* turned her back on me and swept into Randolph's room. If I had ever won-dered, there was no longer any need to ask which side of the family was responsible for my temper genes.

"Whoa!" said Stan, a grin on his face. "Couldn't have put it better myself."

"Stan, I don't need..."

"Stop right there, girl. You need a couple of lectures from somebody, and you might as well get started with me."

"I don't know what..."

"You know exactly what I'm talking about, and it is not your grandma. Now I, too, am going to spend three minutes with an old friend, and when I come out, you better still be standing in this very spot. We're gonna have ourselves a little chat. Do I make myself perfectly clear?"

I could have been fifteen again, getting chewed out for driving Mickey Langston's daddy's new Mustang to Wrightsville Beach without so much as a learner's permit.

I said, "Yes sir, sheriff, sir," and earned myself a nasty over-the-shoulder glower as he opened Randolph's door.

Left on my own, I paced up and down the hallway, listening to intercom pages, squeaking shoes, and a woman crying in a nearby room.

I wondered if it was Lucille.

"Let's go," Stan growled when he came out, and moved down the hall at a such a rapid pace that I had to almost run to keep up with him. We passed two visitors, who stared in dismay at Stan's size, inching close to the wall to give him plenty of room.

"Now, look, Stan..." I tried again.

He held up his hand for silence, flashing me a glare that clearly said, *not here, not now.* I held my tongue. The only thing missing was the handcuffs.

We must have been a sight, rushing through the corridors like a freight train with a caboose. I wasn't so far gone I couldn't see the humor in the situation. We went back through the emergency room and out the entrance to his car parked by the curb.

"Get in," said Stan.

I got in, slamming the door with too much intensity, and sat without speaking while Stan drew one deep breath, then a second one.

He said, "Are you trying to get yourself killed, girl?"

"By you, Stan?"

"Don't you get smart-mouthed with me, missy. As if you don't know what I'm talking about. Running around the countryside asking questions of every Tom, Dick and Harry, just looking to get yourself killed. I'm telling you right here, right now, to cut it out. I ain't putting you in a body bag like I did your daddy."

"That's a low blow, Stan."

"I'm not finished..."

"Well," I flared, "I've got a few damned questions of my own."

"And don't you cuss at me. You got any idea what it would do to your grandma if something happened to you? Now, Eddie was bad enough, but Eleanor thinks the sun rises and sets in you—while you're snooping around the likes of Dog Fowler and getting yourself beat up. Did you take a good look at your face?"

"I've seen it Stan, and your point is well taken. How did you find out about Randolph? Did Lucille call you?"

"Seems like I heard from half the county, including the

mayor. Lucille called Opal looking for me just before I got home for lunch. Then the office called, the hospital called, Mayor Howe called. I guess Opal phoned Lucille back after she left for the hospital."

"And Gran answered the phone?"

"Yeah. Opal didn't know she wasn't supposed to tell."

"Stan, let me ask you a question."

He huffed, "It better be a good one."

"Who the devil is Dog Fowler, and who says I've been asking him questions? I don't even know the name, much less how to talk to him."

"Detective Paige said..."

I made a rude, unladylike, snorting sound. "How would he...?"

"Paige said you went to see Dog this morning out Middle Sound Loop Road."

"*That* was Dog Fowler? Well, I can see how he got the name. What I don't see is how Paige knew I'd been there."

"Plus," Stan went on, "Paige had a few other choice words to describe your attitude, not a single one of them flattering. And he said you never stuck around this morning to talk to the Wilmington detectives. Seemed to think that you either misinterpreted the situation or made the whole thing up. You got something to say about that, Ms. Davenport?"

"Yes," I said. "Your Detective Paige is a first-class jerk."

Stan scratched his chin. "Well, hell, I know that. Tell me something I don't know—starting with this morning and working your way right up to now."

Fifteen minutes later, I had told him everything I could

remember, from the first instant I laid eyes on the man who tried to smother Alex, until we arrived in the ambulance with Randolph. He was brutal with his questions. And before he would let me out of the car, he extracted a promise that I would make myself available to the Wilmington Police as soon as possible and to be damned sure I cooperated fully, whether I liked it or not. He then launched into a lecture about personal safety in general and contributory stupidity in particular. Only a bad four-car pileup on I-40 saved me from complete and total castigation.

He put me out on the curb like a sack of potatoes. No Jeep, no purse, not even a credit card. I waited for him to drive away.

Stan leaned across the seat and powered down the passenger window. "One last thing. Ben Satterwhite is gonna hang around. Don't give him a rough time."

"What does that...?"

The window rolled upward. The car began to move.

"Stan! You better not mean what I think. Stan, you come back here. You can't... Wait a minute, damn it."

All in all, it wasn't the best time for me to spot Ben Satterwhite behind the wheel of my Jeep, waiting two cars back along the curb.

I stood there and stared, counted to ten, long and slow, swearing under my breath, until I felt confident that I wouldn't slap anyone within reaching distance, especially one with the surname of Satterwhite. I told myself several things in the process. That he was an injured man who had just brought my Jeep when I most needed it, that it wasn't his fault Stan wanted to play the heavy father hand, and that I really had to work harder to hold onto my temper.

But it was going to be a bitch being controlled by the two of them.

I stalked back to the jeep and jerked open the door, muttering a less-than-gracious thanks for picking me up.

"Is everything all right, Davenport?" he said.

I sighed, deflated. "Not really, but I should get there by around this time next year. How about you?"

"I've been better. Of course, I can't remember when exactly, but I've been better." He fingered the keys in the ignition, then dropped his hand. "How is the patient?"

"Better than I expected. Awake a couple of times, but drifting in and out. In ICU with a concussion and a broken arm."

"I'm betting he wakes up with a hell of a sore head."

In a tartish voice, I said, "I'm betting I will, too, the way things are going."

He looked straight ahead and out the windshield. "Stan talk to you?"

"Oh, he did that all right. What in particular did he have in mind? Like maybe how you're supposed to keep me out of trouble when you can barely stand up yourself? Or doesn't he know you're on medical leave?"

His jaw tightened.

Bingo!

Satterwhite said, "What he *knows* is that there's a lunatic or two running around killing, beating, and burning. Could be he's worried about you being in the wrong place with the wrong people, so why don't you just cooperate like a good girl?"

I thought I might have to slap him after all, but what I said was, "Tell you what I'm going to do for you, Satterwhite. I'm going to let you buy me lunch before I starve to death, and after that, I'm going home to clean up spaghetti sauce from my kitchen floor before I attack the rest. And when I can't move another step, I'm going to set the burglar alarm and sleep around the clock like I've been promising myself for days."

"Sounds like a reasonable plan."

I went on, "And *if* and *when* I think I need a guard dog, I'll call a kennel and hire one. I don't mean to be rude, but do I make myself clear?"

When the engine fired, he said, "We'll start with the lunch."

In Romanelli's parking lot, he put a hand out and touched my swollen face. "You're going to have quite a bruise. I thought you might need this." He pulled my handbag from the back floorboard.

I flipped the visor mirror down and took a good look at my aching jaw. At least, I thought, it was the same side that Bitsy had clobbered. "I can't imagine why you'd think that, but thanks." I did the best I could with lipstick and hairbrush, and afterward, instead of looking like I'd been run over by a tractor trailer, I only resembled a prostitute who'd been beaten by her pimp. If that earned Mr. Benjamin Satterwhite some dirty looks, so much the better.

We sat in a back booth, ate pizza, and made the kind of

small talk two people make when they're wary of one another. After Daniel, I'd had more than enough of self-assured men, sex appeal or no sex appeal, and avoided involvement with them like a sensible person avoids smallpox. Satterwhite had a placidity about him that I suspected came in handy in interrogations, and it briefly crossed my mind that he could be sitting there wondering if I was a murderess without a trace of suspicion on his face.

We paid the bill and continued to sit. He spoke with ease and affection about growing up between four sisters in Camden, Maine. We talked about wandering feet, the stock market, politics, and sailing.

He was a Republican. I was a Democrat.

Wouldn't you know it.

About the stock market, I said, "You don't strike me as a man who would like to gamble."

He laughed. "I work hard, save my money, and put it where it does the most good. The market has done the rest. It's why I have enough flexibility to tell Lorna to stuff her job, and why I know she won't fire me."

"So what kind of boat do you have?"

"A Beneteau. Twenty-five feet of sweet sailing. When Boss Lorna drives me over the brink, I have my eye on a larger one."

"And what will you name this boat?"

He shrugged. "Same as the last two. *The Three Marys*, for Mother Mary, Aunt Mary, and Sister Mary."

"Nice," I said. "Let's see, that would make it *The Three Marys III*. It has a certain ring to it."

"I guess you're right." He grinned.

"It's odd," I said. "For some strange reason, I've traveled all over the world, yet never been north of New York City. I can't think why."

"You'd like Maine. But go soon before it's too late—before the tourists ruin it forever. In the high season, you can have a hard time walking down the streets of coastal towns, and it drives my mother crazy that tourists lean over the fence and pick her roses."

"Sounds a lot like Wilmington."

He shook his head. "It's a fifth the size of Wilmington, and in the off- season, even less than that."

A heavy hand descended on my shoulder. I looked up at Goldie's ex-husband.

Richard Howe said, "Mind if I join you for a minute?"

There were few things I could imagine liking less, but well-brought-up southern ladies don't necessarily show it. Goldie had told me details that, a hundred years ago, would have gotten him tarred, feathered, and run out of town on a rail.

Too bad we had become so civilized.

Howe ran a manicured hand over perfectly cut and styled hair that was graying around the temples. Very distinguished. But good-looking men who fuss over their appearance have never appealed to me. I moved over and he slid into my side of the booth.

I said, "Hello, Richard. Satterwhite, I don't believe you've met our mayor, Richard Howe." The two shook hands.

He straightened the creases in his trousers. "Someone I

was supposed to meet isn't going to show up, apparently. I was just about to leave when I spotted you back here. I just wanted to tell you again how sorry we all are about Eddie. How is your grandmother taking it?"

"As well as possible, thank you," I said.

"And Alex? It's a damned shame about the baby. Tragic, positively tragic."

"I'll tell her you sent your regards."

"I'd like to tell her in person if you think she's up to a caller. Just for a few minutes, of course. I always had a high regard for Eddie's family."

I shook my head. "Not yet, Richard. She's not up to it physically or emotionally. Give her some time."

"We'll see, we'll see," he murmured, taking my hand in both of his. "And you, my dear?" He looked at the side of my face. "How awful that you'd have your house broken into and destroyed like that. The criminal element in this county needs a firmer hand than it's getting, I'll tell you that, and I'm eager to do my part when I become Lieutenant Governor. We'll have to go out together when your face heals, maybe a concert in Raleigh, to help you get over all this wretched business."

Shit. He couldn't be flirting with me. Surely. His hands on mine were making revulsion goose-bumps pop out on my forearms. I knew about his abuse of Goldie, his women, his over-the-edge business deals. Not in a million years would I be going out with him. I would have sooner gone out with Dog Fowler.

I pulled my hand away, shifted a fraction of an inch toward the wall. "Thank you, Richard. You're very kind."

"I'm just so concerned about all of you."

He was feeling our pain. How very nice.

"Thank you," I said again.

He turned his attention across the table. "Are you new in town, Satterwhite? I'm sorry, I don't believe I caught your first name."

"Ben. Ben Satterwhite. No, I'm vacationing here. Just passing through, you might say."

"You look familiar. Have we met before?"

"No," Satterwhite said. "I would have remembered."

I shuffled my silverware. "Richard is running for Lieutenant Governor and not doing badly, from what I've been hearing."

Howe preened. That was the only word to describe it. "All of it is true, as a matter of fact, but let's don't talk about the campaign when such terrible things have been happening. I must admit to a good deal of curiosity about the details. What does the sheriff have to say? Do they have suspects? And I just have to ask if Eddie was into drugs with that reprehensible Dennis Mason."

I stiffened. "Richard, you know as much as we do. Since you're the mayor, you might have more pull with Sheriff Council than anyone. This much I can say, though. Eddie was not into drugs in any way, and you're welcome to spread that around town."

I reached for my water glass in front of him, sorry that we had finished the pizza.

He went on. "Still, I don't see how you can be certain.

How can any of us know everything about the private lives of friends and family? Are you sure Eddie didn't say anything to you or your black handyman the night he was killed?"

The full glass clattered sideways, tipping the whole contents straight into his lap. He jumped out of the booth, a thunderous look on his face.

"Oh, I *am* sorry, Richard," I said. "What a perfect klutz I've been all day long. It must be the lack of sleep."

He was standing in the aisle by then, mopping at his thousand-dollar suit, scowling like the real Richard. A waitress appeared with a clean napkin. He jerked it out of her hand.

I saw my opportunity and grabbed it. "Will you look at the time! You'll have to excuse us, Richard. We should have been across town fifteen minutes ago."

Satterwhite clapped him on the back, a real grin on his face. "Good luck with the campaign, Mayor."

We made a fast break for the exit, and halfway out the door, Satterwhite said, "Remind me not to get on your shit list, Davenport."

I tossed him the keys. "Too late. You're already near the top. Think you can drive this thing a little longer while I make some calls?"

His reaction speed was good. He caught the keys in his left hand and, with his right, pulled a yellow folded bill out of his jacket pocket and held it out.

"You owe me, Davenport."

"So you said before."

"Yeah, but this one a poor little rich girl can handle—to the tune of four-hundred sixty-five dollars and thirty-seven cents. Hanover Tire called about the repaired Jeep ten minutes after you left in the ambulance. Too bad, really. I was just about to hotwire the Jag."

Chapter Twelve

On the way out of town, I put my cell phone to good use. Detective Wiley of the Wilmington Police Department wasn't in, so I left my home number and a brief message. That was as much as they were going to get from me the rest of the day unless they chased me down. I called my answering machine and jotted down the messages, half a dozen of which were condolence calls about Eddie, and another message from my former father-in-law, Sam Vitelli, in New York. Isabella, his wife, was dying of lung cancer in the slowest and worst way possible. I suspected the call might not be a welcome one. The last message was from Ramon at the Figure Eight Club.

I checked in with Jinks first.

He answered fast. "We drove your grandma and Lucille home. I'm sitting outside her house right now waiting for Davis. He says he's gonna spend the night guarding Randolph's place, but just between the two of us, I think he's scared spitless. You want me to hang with him for the night?"

"Thanks," I said. "That'll be the best solution all around. Besides which, I'll sleep better knowing there's someone else on the property when it gets dark."

"Something else you ought to know. A guy named Pace, Pearce—something like that—from the Sheriff's Department, came by the job this morning, grilling Davis."

"Was it Detective Paige?"

"Yeah, that's the name."

"What was he grilling him about?"

"About where he was Sunday night. Stuff like that. Came right out and asked him if he killed Eddie in a robbery attempt. Shit, he even asked if you and Randolph were covering up for Davis, and if maybe you hired Davis to kill Eddie. I tell you this—when he left, Davis seemed mighty spooked about something. You think he's not telling it straight about being in bed asleep at Randolph's Sunday night?"

I said, "Almost anything is possible with Davis, but not murder. Detective Paige likes to throw a lot of stuff against the wall to see if any of it sticks. That way, he saves himself the trouble of thinking. But you better see what you can find out from Davis. If he'll tell anyone the truth about where he was, it will be you, Jinks. And if he's lying, we can all fry his hide."

"Here he comes now. You need to speak to him?"

"Not if you're going straight to the house. I'll be there myself before long. And Jinks, if he gives you a hard time about keeping him company, tell him I'm paying both of you double-time to guard the place tonight and straighten up a little at Randolph's."

"Gotcha."

I said, "One more thing..."

"Yeah?"

"Any word from Duane?"

"Shit no. Excuse me. I did some calling around, but nobody has seen hair, hide, guts or feathers of him. I'm thinking Tiffany had it right when she said he'd high-tailed it to Tennessee or someplace."

I disconnected, frowning.

Satterwhite said, "Trouble?"

"Who knows. The missing supervisor who hasn't been around since early Sunday is still unaccounted for. The girl-friend thinks he ran out on her and headed to Memphis, where his mother just moved. If he's holed up drunk somewhere, I'm going to fire his sorry bones for sure."

My last call was to Eddie's house. Goldie answered, her voice sounding pinched.

"How is Alex doing? I asked.

"Resting a lot. Better, now that she has Tully where she can keep an eye on her, although I don't know how she can rest with the phone ringing off the hook. She looks better anyway, or she did until Sheriff Council called a few minutes ago to say they found Eddie's truck in an empty garage on Figure Eight Island. And Simpson has finally gotten the fu-neral set up for Thursday morning at eleven. That's as much as she can handle right now."

"Can she make it through the funeral? Physically, I mean?"

Goldie lowered her voice to a whisper. "She says so. And who knows? Perhaps it's better to get it over with sooner rather than later. She also wants friends and family to come back to the house afterwards, and I can't seem to talk her out of the idea."

"Don't try," I said. "She may find it comforting. Anyway, friends and neighbors will bring enough food for an army,

and we can call Betsy Rickall to see if she'll help with her ca-
tering crew."

"I did that, but the food has started arriving already. I
can't imagine where we're going to put it all. By the way, Alex
wants to talk to you at some point. Are you coming back by
the house?"

I told her about Randolph and the break-ins. "I'm going
to try to get by there early this evening, maybe sevenish, so
tell her to expect me. What about Bobby Valentine? Is he still
there? And did the nurse arrive?"

"Wait, give me a second to catch up," she said. "My quiet
little southern town has suddenly turned into Amityville."

"Goldie?"

"What?"

"I need you. Don't freak out on me." God, I was beginning to sound like Satterwhite.

There was a snap in her voice. "I'm not freaking. I'm
just trying to deal with this crap. You're way ahead of me in
experience, so I can't be blamed if my response mechanism
isn't working as well as yours. I'm right here, ready to do
whatever I can."

"Good, Goldie, because we can't do without you. Now,
what about Valentine and the nurse?"

I could almost hear her shifting mental gears. "Valentine
says he'll be here until three o'clock when his replacement
arrives. The nurse seems to have a good grasp of the situation, which at least makes me feel better."

"You're a rock, Goldie. I promise I'll get there by seven
to help out."

"You worry too much," she said. "We're doing fine. I've moved in, and even Simpson is taking some time off."

"Oh, I see." She picked up on my tone of voice immediately.

"You can hang up now. Goodbye, Carroll."

As soon as I disconnected, I wrote out a check for four-hundred sixty-five dollars and thirty-seven cents and tucked it in Satterwhite's jacket pocket. As I leaned over, I caught a faint whiff of lime-scented shaving lotion in the close confines of the Jeep.

"Thanks," I said. "I mean that."

His sideways glance was unreadable. "You're welcome."

"But..."

"Uh oh. But what?" he said.

I gave him a look. "But, now you're going home."

"Home?"

We were beginning to sound like two parrots learning to read in the first grade.

"Well, back to Figure Eight Island anyway."

"Am I?" he said.

"Yes, you are." I was resolved. "You're supposed to be on medical leave, remember. Anyway, with a house full of guns and one in the Jeep, I don't want a bodyguard, no matter what Stan told you." I opened the glove compartment to show him the Glock nine millimeter in its tan leather case. "Plus, Jinks and Davis will be there."

His eyebrows went up. "I hope you have a permit to carry a concealed weapon."

"All nice and legal—and loaded."

With a hint of mockery in his voice, Satterwhite said, "But can you actually shoot anything? That's the real question."

"Jack Davenport made sure his daughter could protect herself," I said lightly. "So far, it's been against beer cans in fast-moving water, but don't tempt me, Satterwhite."

We were stopped at a red light. He turned and looked hard at me for a few seconds, moving with the traffic when the signal turned green.

"I'll say this for you, Davenport. You sure know how to keep a forced vacation from becoming dull."

We rode in silence the rest of the way to Figure Eight Island, where his car was still parked at the Club. When he got out, I slid into the driver's seat.

"By the way," he said, "I let the evidence technicians and a Nationwide adjuster into the house." He paused with the door open. I thought he was going to say something else, but he left it at, "Be careful," and walked away without looking back.

If I had known him longer, I would have realized that he gave in too easily.

An evidence truck was still parked in the driveway by the cottage. I stopped in to ask if they were finished in the main house, and two female deputies said they were just about to wrap it up. I asked them to lock Randolph's door, and went on home, the lack of sleep beginning to catch up with me.

What I really needed was a long nap. Instead, I put on Luciano Pavarotti, cleaned dried spaghetti sauce off my kitchen floor, and in general, tried to put my life back in some kind of order.

There was a six-inch scar in the coffee table, walls that needed to be repainted, broken lamps, shattered china. Making a list for the insurance claim made me feel I was taming the chaos. After three hours of scrubbing fingerprint dust, vacuuming, and putting items back where they belonged, I had made a serious dent in the mess. When I was thoroughly sick of it all, I sat down and dialed Sam Vitelli's private number.

He answered on the second ring.

"Sam, it's Carroll. Is Isabella worse?"

"No, no. Neither worse nor better, just always bad. Fortunately, she is still able to tolerate enough medication to keep her from suffering most of the time."

"I'm glad—for both of you."

He went on. "Time, though, is what we are fast running out of, as she grows weaker by the day. I will tell her you called."

"Please do," I said, "and give her my best."

There was a pause on his end of the line while I waited for him to say why he had left two messages. I pictured him sitting at his massive desk in the dim office, his white head bent somberly over the telephone.

"Forgive me," he said with his customary old-world courtesy, "but Isabella is not the reason I asked you to call. Today I have received information that has made me much concerned for your safety."

I didn't need to ask how he knew what was going on in my life. He possessed long tentacles in many places, and I had for some time suspected that he paid someone in Wilmington to keep him informed. It did not alarm me, because he had never attempted to interfere in my life. From the beginning of my marriage to Daniel and all through the horror that followed, Sam and Isabella had shown me nothing but kindness and love.

"How much have you heard, Sam?"

"That your cousin has been murdered is bad enough, but now that I have been informed that your home has been burglarized..."

"Not burglarized, exactly," I said. "More like torn apart."

"When I first heard, I was deeply concerned that your troubles might be occurring because of, shall we say, a disgruntled business associate of mine, but on closer investigation, I do not find this to be true. Our greatest fear has always been that you will become a target because of my enemies, and that is why we limit our contact with you. But then, you know all of this already. Now I say, do you need my help? I offer it gladly, and you are aware that I have connections who would do this for me."

When I was first married to Daniel, I didn't have a clue about my father-in-law's occupations, and before my suspicions began to form, I had learned to love Sam and Isabella, in part because they stood by me while Daniel behaved like Daniel. But now that I knew what kind of affiliations he had, I could not bring myself to accept his assistance. His love and concern, yes. But not his connections.

"No," I said. "I doubt that I'm in any danger. Thank you for offering, but it's enough that you have Isabella to worry about."

"Isabella is my punishment. *You* were the wife of our only son—the daughter we wished for." He cleared his throat. "We would not want to see you harmed."

"I know that, Sam. You have both been generous with your affections. Believe me when I say that I am strengthened by it."

He hesitated as if he wanted to say something, but he must have reconsidered. "Then sleep well my dear, and with care. Keep my private number with you at all times, and do not think twice about using it."

"I promise," I said. "And you give Isabella my love."

He sighed. "That much, God still allows me to do."

When the line went dead, I sat for minutes with the receiver in my hand. His calls never failed to leave me despondent. It was beyond my abilities to reconcile his devout Catholicism with his occupation. I didn't know his position in the hierarchy, and much preferred to keep it that way. I only knew that he lived opulently on a fenced and guarded twelve-acre estate in Westchester County. It was not the first time I had heard him say that Isabella's cancer was his punishment from God for past sins. Possibly he was right, but for my part, I merely loved them both, and tried not to think about affiliations.

Chapter Thirteen

I showered off the grime and drove back into Wilmington to make my rounds, still feeling disheartened after talking to Sam. In less than forty-eight hours, my life had once again become inundated with death, trauma, and apprehension.

Randolph was fast asleep, with a serious scowl on his familiar face. I knew it was probably caused by pain, but I felt reassured somehow. His expression was the same as when his womenfolk, one of which was me, got on his nerves enough to make him bellow, *Don't all you girls be ganging up on me and telling me how to go about my business.*

According to the head nurse, he had not only regained consciousness, but had eaten a small amount of food. They were checking his vital signs every half hour, she said, and in the process had awakened him twice. I gathered from her tone that he had been less than grateful about the poking and prodding. I left him a large vase of his favorite blue agapanthus and let him sleep.

At Eddie's house on Mimosa Street, all was quiet. Only Goldie and the second-shift guard were awake. Her name was Agnes, and although she had only half of Valentine's muscles, she was clearly no lightweight, and she was not inclined to chit-chat or smile. My guess was that, short of joining the French Foreign Legion, she had chosen an appropriate line of work.

Goldie was exhausted, and I advised her to jump at the opportunity to take the phone off the hook and snatch a quick snooze herself.

Feeling better by the minute, I left them to their slumberland and drove downtown to my grandmother's, figuring I might as well get the lecture over and done with as soon as possible.

Gran's home on the Cape Fear River is as fine an example of nineteenth-century Italianate architecture as you will find west of Italy, complete with belvedere and secret silver room. It was built with cotton money by my great-great grandfather, Henry Carroll, for his bride in 1842. So now you know where I got the male version of the name Carol.

I parked along the side of the house and walked around back, past the garage with its ancient vehicles, Gran's Cadillac and Lucille's navy Lincoln—both as big as houseboats. Between the two of them they could have chauffeured a busload of silver-haired ladies to Sunday School. I found her in a winter coat sitting on the wide back porch, watching the paddleboat, Henrietta II, heading back to port.

I called out, "Is it safe to come up?"

Startled, she peered down the steps. "Lord, you could give me a heart attack sneaking up like that. I was miles and years away in my mind. Of course you can."

I pulled up a matching wicker chair and sat. "Am I forgiven, then?"

"Don't be silly. There's nothing you could do that I

wouldn't forgive. It's only that I get so abominably tired of always being treated like a helpless old woman. And I was sick with dread about Randolph."

"Thank you," I said. "We can now consider that I've been properly reprimanded, and that I promise to watch my manners in the future. I just worry..."

"I know, child."

I laid my hand on her brown, speckled forearm, and we sat there in peace, watching the Henrietta II rolling in the Cape Fear River on a turning tide. A magnificent sunset was about to happen, and the marsh grass and nineteenth-century pilings on the far shore were turning golden pink in the late afternoon light.

She was going to be royally pissed when she found out what else I was keeping from her—the missing guns, Detective Paige's suspicions, the slashed tires, the FBI agent—but I had time enough to worry about that later.

I said, "I can't believe we're going to bury Eddie on Thursday."

She nodded. "Simpson called with the schedule, and I talked to Alex for a few minutes."

"Did you?"

She looked off toward Eagle Island where the willows were topped with a hint of spring green. "I'll tell you what I think about Alex. She's much stronger than she thinks. Oh, it will be hard for her, and it may take a while, but with Tully she'll be all right. And as for financially...well, you know I'll make sure of that."

"You could be right, Gran. For now, I'm just worried

that the funeral might be too much for her."

"You're thinking of the baby."

"Oh, yes," I said. "I'm thinking of the baby."

"Don't underestimate her," Gran said. "We women bear what we can, and the rest we take one day at a time until it finally becomes endurable."

If that was one of the secrets women learn as they grow older, I was not yet a very good student. It seemed to me that many more years would have to pass before I stopped expecting to just turn around and speak to people like my mother and father or Eddie and Daniel.

Well, maybe not Daniel.

He had been waiting outside my apartment six months after I enrolled at Juilliard, at a time when I thought I had everything—youth, beauty, talent—and the world was mine for the taking. Three years later, I left New York with nothing. No, that isn't true. I left with less than nothing. Now, I didn't even open the piano and would never invest that kind of emotion in a relationship again.

I watched a male cardinal land on the feeder, a captivating red in the late winter landscape. "On the bright side, when I ran by the hospital a few minutes ago, I had a chance to talk to the head nurse. She didn't say it in so many words, but I gathered Randolph had been growling like a bear whenever she checked his vital signs."

Gran smiled. "He recognized both of us when we were there. Lucille fed him a little dinner, and when he tried to thank her, she started to cry. Who can explain those two?"

"Where is Lucille, anyway?"

"I sent her down to her sister's. I thought Martha might be able to calm her down some and get her to unwind. Poor Lucille has never learned to bend, not even a little bit, in all the years I've known her."

She shivered, and I said, "We'd better go in. This wind may put us both in the hospital with Randolph." She followed me into the warm kitchen.

I helped her take off her coat. "Are you sure you'll be all right without Lucille?"

Gran gave a chuckle. "The peace and quiet will do me good. My old nerves have been frazzled to the bone the last two days. But don't you worry. A little vodka in my orange juice has helped considerably. Besides, Lucille left me cold turkey and peach pie, and I'll be tucked up in bed by nine. She'll be home by then."

"You promise you'll eat something."

"Carroll. You're doing it again."

I threw up my hands. "I'm out of here, then."

She followed me down the front hallway. In the open door, I paused, my left hand automatically checking to make sure it would lock behind me, worrying as always about two old ladies living alone. Especially now.

For years Gran had kept an ancient German Luger in the antique soup tureen that sat in the middle of the dining room table. Only God knew where she had gotten the ammunition for it, how old the bullets were, or even if it was loaded. I was afraid the gun might explode in her face if she ever tried to fire it, that she would shoot Lucille in the middle of the night, or vice versa. I had nagged her to get rid of it, and it disappeared. She swore she had given it to Stan, but I suspected it could be found somewhere in the hidden silver room where Eddie, at six, had once hidden the cat for two days.

Which reminded me. "By the way, Gran, did Eddie ever ask to borrow money from you?"

She looked me in the eye for a long second. I could be as casual as I liked, but it wouldn't fool her.

"Stan Council asked me the same question, you know. I'll tell you what I told him—just the one time—for part of the down-payment on his house. He said something about not losing interest on his own funds. But he paid back every dollar less than two months later. Now, why would Stan ask such a question? And why would you?"

"Because of Dennis Mason, I guess. The police are trying hard to find a drug connection between the two of them."

She huffed up at that. "Drugs? Eddie? Piffle...just plain piffle. You know he would never have done anything of the sort. He had too much Monroe in him for that kind of self-indulgent trash, even if he needed money in the worst way. Besides, he knew I had one foot in the grave already and all he had to do was wait a short while."

I kissed her lightly on her gnarled cheek, laughing at the expression on her face. "Not even a toe, yet, thank you God. Not even a toe."

She smiled. "Get on out of here, now, so an old woman can get her dinner. Drugs, indeed. I never heard the like."

I let myself out, and went down the front steps in the thickening gloom, thinking how well a good old-fashioned word like *piffle* fit the idea of Eddie and drugs and that it was a good thing I hadn't told her about Detective Paige's accusations. Perhaps that's why I didn't see the pickup truck until the roar was almost on me, bearing down across the liriope and purple tulips. At the last second, I dove headlong into a thicket of azaleas along the foundation.

The pickup skidded sideways on the wet ground, a good seventy feet into the yard, narrowly missing the brick porch and tearing deep furrows in the grass where I had been standing.

Chapter Fourteen

From my prone position among the mulch and azalea branches, I watched in disbelief as a dented, dirty pickup bounced back over the curb and, tires squealing, disappeared around the corner toward Front Street.

The distinctive grinding of his engine evaporated on the night air, and instant tranquility fell once more over the neighborhood. Not a single light came on, no curious faces appeared in windows, no dogs barked. The front door of my grandmother's house remained closed. There was nothing but the faint, distant booming of traffic on the Cape Fear Bridge and the call of a mockingbird. The pounding of my heart.

I pulled pine straw out of my hair and brushed at my filthy jeans. Aside from a smarting ache in my right hip, all that seemed to be damaged was my nerve. Someone, with a great deal of malice and just as much forethought, had tried to run me down. The fleeting possibility of my grandmother finding my bloody body on the front lawn at daybreak was enough to give me the shivers.

The safety of the Jeep had never seemed so precious as I stumbled over the truck ruts to get there. I locked the doors and sat shaking with reaction. In the end, I decided against calling the police. My grandmother had withstood more than enough in the last two days, and I was reluctant to add to her trauma. Also, I couldn't be certain of the color, the make, or even the license plate. Stan Council was sure to say *I told you so*, and I would have to explain what I had done with Satterwhite.

When they woke in the morning, Lucille and Gran would assume a drunken driver had turned the corner too fast and veered across the lawn. Or Lucille would spot the damage when she arrived home. Either way, with one call to a land-scaper, the gouged ruts and broken azaleas would be repaired within a day, while the older generation tutted about the younger and *what the world was coming to.*

Turning in the opposite direction from the truck, I took Third Street down to Market and drove north before I left a message for Stan to call me back. On a Tuesday evening, traf-fic was sparse, but moving like a wounded turtle. At a red light, I leaned forward to turn on the heat, and when I straight-ened, I was blinded by the high beam lights of the car behind. The signal changed, I adjusted the rearview mirror and drove on, pulling into the right lane to avoid his brights. I was do-ing fifty-one miles an hour in a forty-five mile per hour zone with plenty of room ahead and behind when he pulled dan-gerously close to my rear bumper again.

Irritated, I changed lanes twice more. Both times, the high beams closed in behind me. *What the hell?* I sped up to fifty-five, then sixty. And he was still there. A small subdivi-sion was coming up, and I made the abrupt decision to swing right, turning in a wide circle of three different residential blocks before returning to Market Street. The lights fell back, but stayed with me.

The vehicle was a dark mass behind the powerful beams. For all I knew, it was an eighteen-wheeler or a car full of teenagers having a good time, but tonight I was feeling disinclined to take any more chances.

Just before Gordon Road, I pulled a hard right and then a left into McDonald's without giving a turn signal. I heard the screech of brakes, and in front of me, a young mother chased three children across the parking lot. I swerved to avoid them, and by the time I pulled around the building, there were a dozen vehicles bunched together in two lanes at the light. It could have been any one of them. Three were trucks.

At the drive-in window, I ordered a small decaf coffee, unlocked the glove compartment, laid the gun on the seat beside me, and called 911.

For seven-thirty on a Tuesday, the hamburger chain was still busy, the parking lot patrons cheerfully oblivious to anything sinister. The coffee disappeared while I waited impatiently with my emergency blinkers on.

When the Wilmington squad car eased into the space beside me, I got out of the Jeep. The officer was young, maybe twenty-two at the most, but experienced enough to quickly take in my bruised face and dirty clothes.

"You OK, ma'am?"

I brushed dead azalea leaves off my jacket. "More or less, depending on how you want to look at it."

"Ma'am?"

"I'm being followed, by a pick-up truck, maybe dirty

green, possibly the same one that tried to run me down earlier." Even as I spoke, I realized how incoherent I sounded. For all he knew, I was one more hysterical female looking for attention.

He wrote it down, along with my own license plate number. "Ma'am, could you tell if the truck had North Carolina plates?"

"I don't know," I said. "I just got the quick glimpse and don't remember seeing plates at all. I can't even be certain it was a truck that followed me. And he kept his lights on full beam the whole time."

He studied my bruised faced and disheveled hair. "Could there be a domestic situation going on here? Or anything else you'd like to tell me about?"

Yes, I wanted to say. *Have you got an hour to hear it all?* Instead I said. "I wouldn't know where to start. But, you have my word there is no domestic situation, and I never got a look at the person behind the wheel. He changed lanes all the way from College Road to here and followed me through several turns." Even to my own ears, the story became lamer each time I opened my mouth. Lack of sleep was making my brain feel like it was wrapped in seaweed. I wondered if Alzheimer's made you feel the same way.

He should have asked if I'd been drinking, but he didn't.

"Why don't we start with your name..."

I waited for him to finish with another *ma'am*, but he seemed to think better of it.

"Carroll Davenport," I said, and proceeded to give him my address on Bald Eagle Lane and enough background so he would take me seriously.

When I finished, he said, "I want you to wait in your vehicle with the doors locked while I check around the parking lot." He put the green pickup on the radio and cruised around the shopping center. From where I sat, I could see him weaving in and out of rows of cars all the way down to the Harris Teeter until he disappeared around the corner. From start to finish, it took him less than ten minutes.

"Sorry, ma'am. There was nothing resembling your dirty green pickup. That's about all I can do for now, except fall in behind you to make sure you get home safely. We'll keep an eye out for the truck, but it's a real long shot."

Home was at least five miles beyond his jurisdiction, and I wouldn't have thought he was permitted to go that far. If it was the blonde hair and long legs, I wasn't about to argue. I gave him phone numbers, and he followed me all the way home, watching until I was safely inside before driving away. Systematically, I went through each room, including the garage, checking window and door locks and setting the alarm. Charlie was sleepy and irritable, refusing to talk, the same as he usually behaved, but I noticed he hadn't touched his food. I laid the gun on the bathroom counter and locked the door while I showered. The house had never felt more isolated.

Around eight-thirty, it began to rain, pattering on the skylights at first, and then turning into a steady drumbeat that sounded as if it had set in for the night. Randolph's cottage was still dark when I peered out the front curtains, but Max was sitting in the glow of my front floodlights, wet and dejected, staring at the house. I took pity on him. I brought him in, dried him off with an old beach towel, and then warmed him a can of beef stew from my hurricane stores. Dinner for me was a simple toasted cheese sandwich that tasted like cardboard. I ate it anyway, dressed in a worn, green-checked robe and knee socks amid the chaos of the den, which at least had the advantage of a working fireplace.

Max curled up on the rug next to the hearth like he lived there, and I was glad for companionship, even a dog's. Since I was too tired to sleep, I began to straighten my father's scattered files, stacking them in three piles. One to throw out, one to store, and one to keep for my own records.

Soon afterward, I realized that whoever had made the mess had simply pulled out stacks of files and tossed them on the floor, which seemed to say he wasn't actually looking for anything *in* the files. Unless he was throwing things around the room just for the hell of it, it seemed reasonable to assume he had been looking for something in the drawers themselves, underneath the files.

Many of the pages were still tucked far enough into the original file folders so that it was easy to see where they belonged. Any stray papers, I placed in a separate stack to sort through later. For an hour I worked diligently, and found, without much effort, the missing insurance file with its gun collection list. That, too, I set aside.

Around ten-thirty, Max went outside for a few minutes to attend to his doggy needs. I prepared him a bed in the corner of my bedroom, hoping he wasn't the snoring type of male. With clean linens on my own bed, I crawled into it with a faded file marked *Personal* to help put me to sleep.

The remainder of the den mess would have to wait for another day.

The file was an old one, the label peeling with age, and under the light from the beside lamp, I opened it to memories. In my hands, I held a marriage certificate dated two years before I was born. Jackson Paul Davenport married Sylvia Carroll Monroe. There was an eight-by-ten photograph of my father, done a few years before his death, in which he appeared handsome and vital—healthy enough to live another fifty years.

Among the other mishmash were letters of appreciation from several mayors and two Democratic governors for public buildings designs, a Purple Heart from his war days in Vietnam, and a real estate contract with Richard Howe for a tract of land on South College Road.

I fell asleep wondering why this was the first I had heard of any business dealings between the two of them.

Chapter Fifteen

It was well after midnight when I awoke to a strange noise, and in my groggy state, it took me several seconds to realize what I was hearing. If I hadn't known Max was in the same room, I might have guessed the sound was coming from a wild animal five times his size. I had never heard him make such deep, primitive growls.

Rain was still coming down, beating against the sliding glass doors, which meant the wind was blowing in off the water. The drapes were drawn tight, the house dark as a cave, with no sign of the floodlights I had left burning. When I touched the switch, the bedside lamp clicked uselessly. The telephone was dead.

I fumbled for the gun on the bedside table and got to my feet, half afraid I would stumble over the dog in the dark and shoot us both.

"Max?" I whispered, giving a soft whistle. I felt for him with my outstretched hand, following the rumble, wondering if he would bite when I startled him. He was in the center of the room, standing stiff as stone, and his body trembled when I touched him. But he didn't move. I ran my hand up to his collar where the fur at the back of his neck was stiff and vertical.

In the midst of the tension, my grandfather's mantel clock

sounded the half hour. I flinched. But not Max. The last note echoed long in the after-silence.

I thought first of a break-in, but could hear nothing, see nothing, and had no idea whether an intruder was outside or, God forbid, even inside. For that matter, what had happened to my elaborate alarm system that was supposed to guarantee sound sleep for single women? Loosening my hold on the dog's collar, I moved with awkwardness toward the sliding glass doors.

Once, a savvy retired client named Henry Reid gave me a demonstration on how easy it was to crowbar a sliding door out of its track and set it aside without a sound. He had retrieved my car keys from a locked house just that way, and finished by saying *Don't ever trust a simple bar lock*. Remembering gave me goosebumps.

A quick twitch to the drapes showed no movement on the patio and that the door was not only latched, but had its bar locked in place. Max had quieted some, but was still panting, his tail brushing against my leg. I thought for a moment that it meant I might not die in my bed after all. My relief was premature. A fraction of a second later, he renewed his growling, and I thought I glimpsed a pinpoint of light near the north end of the long patio.

To say I trusted Max's instincts at that point would have been an understatement. No raccoon had ever made him sound that way. No raccoon I ever met had carried a flashlight. I felt my way back to the foot of the bed and pulled on my robe. As I was sliding up the low front window of the bedroom, the sound of breaking glass came sharp and clear from the direction of the den.

It was all the encouragement I needed.

With one leg out the window, it occurred to me that I could be making a really big mistake—that there could be another person prowling around outside, just waiting. But what other choice did I have with the phone and alarm both dead, unless I was ready to shoot it out in the dark with a prowler.

I thought not.

A *coward* was not what I wanted to call myself, but in truth, at the last second, it was the remembrance of Eddie in the greenhouse that propelled me out into the elements. I closed the window behind me, leaving a three-legged dog to take care of himself, and had to trust that no intruder would enter a room with a snarling dog behind the door. If I had known what Davis and Jinks would find later, I would have taken him with me, even knowing he might bark and give me away.

A cold rain was falling, sliding like sleety fingers down the back of my neck as I darted away from the dripping roof line. I could see nothing further than the proverbial end of my nose and turned blindly in the direction of Randolph's cottage, feeling my way as fast as possible on icy feet.

To say my heart was pounding with cold and fear would be to trivialize my reaction. My grip on the gun was so rigid I was nervous it would go off in my hand. Every bush, every tree, filled me with a dreadful chicken-hearted apprehension. I passed a cluster of old camellia bushes and a live oak large enough to hide a platoon of killers. I scuttled around them, feeling a huge relief.

A premature relief.

An arm snaked out from its hiding place, grabbing me roughly around the upper body and pinning me tight, as a freezing hand clamped hard over my mouth.

My terror was indescribable.

I forgot about the gun in my hand. I forgot about fighting back. I forgot about everything—except Eddie with his throat slashed. For heart-stopping moments, I froze in abject panic before I began to struggle for my life.

I bit down hard on the hand.

"Shit!" a low voice grated. "It's me, damn it."

"Satterwhite?"

"Be quiet," he said. "There are two of them—one on the right side and one in the back."

"You son-of-a-bitch," I spat. "You scared me half out of my wits."

"Be grateful," he whispered. "It could keep you alive when you're doing something stupid."

I threw his arm off with a violence I couldn't remember feeling toward anybody. My heart was racing like a speedboat, and at that moment, I would have gladly punched him in the mouth. If I had been a man, I might have killed him. Unfortunately, the gun was no longer in my hand, and I had no idea what had become of it.

"Take a look!" he said, his mouth close to my ear. "There." He put his hands on my head and directed my eyes toward a flashlight beam that had appeared near the right rear corner. I could see only the vaguest shadow of the prowler behind it.

From the direction of the flashlight, a voice suddenly shouted, "Don't move! I've got a gun. Put your hands up!"

A shot rang out, then a second one, deafening in the crazy blackness.

"Get down!" Satterwhite threw me face down in the mud and started at a run toward the light, his gun drawn.

Two and two suddenly fused into four as I recognized the voice, and I stumbled over my robe rushing after him. I flung myself on his back like a psychopath.

"No!" I shouted. "It's Davis. Don't shoot!"

I held on to him, a wild person, certain this was the kind of situation anti-gun activists meant when they warned that more family members than burglars are killed with guns. A third shot exploded, and the flashlight rolled across the grass and went out, momentarily illuminating a shadow on the ground.

"Oh, my God...!" I gasped.

Satterwhite made a futile grab for my robe. "You idiot! Get down!"

He was too late. I reached Davis a split second before Satterwhite knocked me flat again, this time pinning me to the ground. As if I hadn't been in the mud enough already. "Stay down," he warned between gritted teeth. "If you move so much as a fraction of an inch, I swear to God I'll belt you one."

"He's hurt, damn it."

"I don't care. You've got to..."

"No, I'm not," Davis whispered.

There was a taut silence, filled with ponderous breathing.

"Too bad," Satterwhite hissed in a low voice. "For a kid with shit for brains, you deserve to have them blown away."

"Satterwhite..." I began.

"Shut up, both of you, and keep your voices down. Give me the gun, kid."

Davis said nothing.

"Come on, I don't have all day."

"I don't have one."

"God in heaven!" Satterwhite sounded like a man choking on his anger. "You mean you thought he was going to throw up both hands and surrender just because you told him to? You have any idea how near you came to dying, a perfect target behind that flashlight? Or how close I came to shooting you myself?" He took a breath. "Which way did he go, kid?"

Through chattering teeth, Davis whispered, "Around the other side, I think. Maybe even inside. I couldn't see much after the gun flashed."

"You're fucking lucky to be seeing anything at all."

I interrupted. "He can't be in the house. Max is there and would be barking his head off. He's how I knew to get out in the first place."

"All right, all right." Satterwhite said. "Was there more than one man? Come on, Davis. He could be drawing down on us right this instant."

"Only one...at least that's all I saw."

"Where the hell is Jinks?" I asked in a low voice.

Davis said, "Out near the road somewhere. He said he

was checking on a pickup parked down near the Harris place."

Satterwhite groaned. "Jesus, I'm surrounded by amateurs. Does this other Rambo have a gun, by any chance?"

"No," I said. "He doesn't believe in guns."

"Yes," said Davis. "He's got Uncle Randolph's old shot-gun."

I could almost hear Satterwhite's teeth grinding. He took my hand in the dark and wrapped it around the gun I had forfeited so quickly in my panic. "Both of you stay put while I check things out. That means you don't so much as twitch a muscle until I get back. If I see something moving out there, I'm going to shoot first and ask questions later, so don't let it be you, kid. I would hate to tell your mother you died because you were too dog-shit dumb to do as you're told. And if you have to shoot anybody, Davenport, for God's sake, don't make it me."

The instant he stopped hissing at us, he was gone, slithering off into the black rain.

We waited, filled with a dreadful anxiety of exposure, while the rain ran in steady rivers into my mouth and ears. No sound came, no movement—only the rain and the darkness. The prowler and his gun could be long gone, or he could be lurking behind the next tree, waiting for us to stand up. The temperature was in the low fifties, and we were shivering with cold. And I gradually became aware that Davis was doing more than that—he was crying.

And why not, I thought. It was a hell of a lot for a fif-teen-year-old to handle. I put my arm around his shoulders. And for the first time in almost a year, he didn't pull away.

When it came, his voice was strangled. "She wouldn't care."

I didn't have to ask who he meant. As long as his mother had a man and a steady supply of crack, she would never care. Until it was too late in every way.

"Maybe," I said, tightening my grip. "Just maybe. But a lot of other people would."

Chapter Sixteen

When Satterwhite returned with Jinks, making just enough racket not to get themselves shot, Davis and I were still sprawled in the grass and mud like wet sheep waiting for slaughter. I could feel the tightness in his shoulders when running feet approached.

I stood up and dragged my sodden, filthy robe around me with as much dignity as possible. "Is he gone?"

"Not one, but two of them," said Jinks. "I couldn't see who was driving the truck, but the one that ran past me was a big motherfucker. He came so close with a gun in his hand, I could have spit on him if I'd had the guts."

"Why didn't you shoot the son-of-a-bitch?" Davis was fast recovering his bravado.

"Yes," said Satterwhite. "Tell us all why."

"I couldn't find Randolph's shotgun shells," he said with a flash of rancor.

"God save me," muttered Satterwhite. He turned to Davis. "Do you feel better, kid, knowing you're not the only fool in town tonight?"

Davis shuffled with embarrassment, staring at the ground, mumbling something I couldn't catch.

"Perhaps," I said in a poisonous tone of voice, "we should get our wet backsides in the house before we all die of hypothermia."

We trooped single file behind Satterwhite's flashlight to the side garage entrance where I kept a key hidden under a paving brick. Two of the group seemed thoroughly chastened, but one of us was getting madder by the minute. Who in the hell did Mr. FBI think he was, anyway?

They took off their muddy shoes and left them in the laundry room when I asked. Maybe *asked* wasn't the way I put it, but even in my rattled state, I wasn't about to clean the kitchen floor more than once in a day.

I flipped the light switch. "Damn it all!" I took a strong light from a cabinet and handed it to Jinks. "See if you can find the master circuit breaker outside."

Satterwhite took the flashlight out of his hand and handed him the smaller one. There was an instant of tense hostility before Jinks let go and the big man in charge turned to Davis. "Come on, son, let's get the power back on." Davis followed him out.

Jinks waited until they were out of earshot before echoing my thoughts. "How much do you know about this guy? And what the hell is his problem?"

"Not much," I said, "except that Sheriff Council trusts him."

"What do you think? Is he really a Fed?"

"I'm afraid so. Supposedly, he's on medical leave."

Jinks said angrily, "He's got one bitch of an attitude."

I passed him a couple of towels from the dryer. "You've got that one right."

He grunted under his breath. "FBI...that explains a lot.

If there had been a shell in this gun, he would have been the one to get blasted to smithereens. He walked right up behind me as big as life and grabbed the barrel. I turned and pulled the trigger, and..."

"And...?" I said.

"Click. And nothing. The son-of-a-bitch never even flinched. It scared the shit out of me, even though I knew it wasn't loaded."

I put the Glock in a drawer before taking the shotgun out of his hands. I broke it open and turned the flashlight beam onto two shiny circles of brass.

"Look again, friend...both barrels. Randolph never fails to keep it loaded. The safety was still on."

The lights came to life, along with the furnace, the refrigerator, and the answering machine. I propped the gun in the corner.

Jinks said, "Jesus, God almighty, and him an FBI agent. I would've been in jail a hundred years." He slumped down into the nearest kitchen chair, a film of sweat on his brow. "Lord, I've always hated guns. I swear to God, I'll never touch another one as long as I live."

I checked on Charlie, hiding safely under his night cover. He wasn't accustomed to so much excitement and could decide not to talk for weeks. On the other hand, he might learn to howl like Max was doing in the bedroom, and a parrot would always win a decibel contest with a dog. It was not an amusing prospect.

I had time to fill the kettle and get down packets of hot cocoa mix, wondering what was taking the other two so long.

The water was hot by the time they returned, talking in low voices. In the bright light, Davis seemed older and straighter. Satterwhite merely looked older, much the way I was feeling myself. I wondered how long he had been waiting out in the cold rain. Like the rest of us, he was wet through to the skin, almost blue around the lips. I experienced a twinge of sympathy until I remembered he knew the prowler was on the premises long before I did. Well, too damn bad for him, I thought, and tossed them both towels.

I said, "If someone will let the dog out of my room before he howls himself into a nervous breakdown, I think I can find enough dry clothes for all of you."

Davis volunteered and followed me down the hall, flipping every light switch we passed. I stood aside judiciously while he opened the door to a snarling Max, who sat back on his haunches, tail wagging, as soon as Davis spoke.

"From now on, Davis, this dog gets filet mignon or anything else he wants." I rubbed Max under the chin enough to make sure he felt appreciated.

Davis grinned.

"Now, let's see if there's something among my father's things that you guys can wear."

We moved two rooms away and pulled out thick flannel shirts, pants, and dry socks, laying them in piles. Each item smelled of must, like long-stored linens at a beach house. There was no scent of Jack Davenport left at all.

I turned back to Davis. "What were you and Satterwhite doing outside so long?"

"Nothing. Just talking."

"Must have been about something important. You looked a lot better when you came back inside."

"Yeah...well, you know. Just...stuff." To his credit, he stopped short of calling it *man stuff*. "He's not such a bad dude after all. He said he was sorry he chewed on me. Said I scared him when he almost shot me."

"Not as much as it scared me."

Davis paused with socks in his hand. "Did you know it was a nine-year-old black kid who shot him?"

"Nine!" I said. "It's hard to believe. The judicial system won't do much to a boy that young."

"Guess not, because Satterwhite killed him."

"What?"

Davis was half out the door. "Said the kid shot him from behind in the dark, and all he saw was the gun flash. And that's why he yelled at me."

All this he had told Davis, in the rain at the panel box, while switching on the electricity.

"How awful!"

"Yeah," he said, and disappeared down the hall.

I shivered and went to my room, the disturbing image fixed in my mind. In spite of the overhead light, my familiar space felt alien and invaded. I could almost feel the presence of the intruder. When I re-locked my escape window, I spotted Max outside in the floodlight streams, zig-zagging across the driveway with his nose to the ground.

I watched him for a further few seconds, until he began to wag his tail and run back toward the front door. I took it as a sign there were no more boogey men to worry about.

In the bathroom mirror I had an opportunity to see what I would look like if I took up mud-wrestling as a career. Some women might actually look good in mud, but I didn't think I was one of them. I took a quick shower and dressed in a sweater, jeans, and warm woolen socks. In spite of a hot shower, my hands remained stiff with cold until I dried my hair.

From two doors away, men's voices rumbled through the walls, and at one point, even laughter. Bonding. One minute they had been ready to fight, and the next minute they were telling jokes. I emerged to find them in the kitchen, having hot chocolate and cookies like schoolboys.

Satterwhite was leaning against the wall, dressed in my father's favorite blue plaid shirt, a phone to his ear. A deluge of old regret and pain swept over me.

I waited until he put the phone down. "Let me guess. You're reporting in to Stan Council."

"Does that bother you?"

"At this point?" I shrugged. "No, I guess not."

He looked at the ceiling. "It gets even worse."

Uh, oh. Here it comes, I thought. "Pray, tell me just how it could possibly get that way."

Jinks and Davis watched, feeling the tension in the air, hearing the shrewish bite to my voice.

Satterwhite grinned. "You're stuck with me for the rest of the night. Maybe even longer."

"Oh, no." I flared. "I don't think so. In fact, I know so. And I have Jinks and Davis to back me up. *They* might not know how to handle a shotgun, but I certainly do."

"Stan said you'd be...difficult, so I'm instructed to advise you that should you call to have me thrown out, no deputies will respond."

Perhaps if he hadn't smiled again—that insufferable, superior male grin that spoke volumes—I wouldn't have suddenly become an acid-tongued bitch.

"Is that right?" I said through clenched teeth. "Well, damn his eyes and yours, too. I already have a guard dog, thank you—one that doesn't hide in the bushes."

His eyes narrowed.

In the long, frostbitten silence that followed, Jinks scraped back his chair. "OK Davis, buddy, this is where we go find the hurricane panels to cover that window." They disappeared into the garage like spooked deer in hunting season.

Satterwhite broke the silence first. "Are you planning to start throwing things?"

"Don't patronize me, you sanctimonious sexist." I tore into the cocoa packet with tight, jerky motions. "So just exactly when were you planning to tell me?"

"Tell you what?"

I motioned with the sugar spoon. "Out there."

"Out there what? I'm lost here."

He had the fake, mystified expression down pat.

"Stop echoing me like the damned parrot. You know exactly what I mean. Precisely at what point in time were you planning to let me know there was a murderer skulking around the house? Me—the one he already tried to kill once tonight."

"What are you...?"

But I was on a roll. "Were you going to hide in the bushes until he knocked on the bedroom door and asked politely if he could come in and slit my throat—or what?"

"There's no reason to get all..."

"Don't you dare say I'm acting like a hysterical female. If you do, I swear I'll have a hard time not slapping you. And don't try to pretend you don't know what I'm talking about."

"I never..."

Suddenly disgusted, I said, "Oh, go to bloody hell," and stalked out of the room.

There was amusement in his voice. "Good night, Davenport. Sleep tight."

Yeah, right. I continued down the hall.

"And Davenport..."

"What is it?" I refused to turn around.

"Try to stay away from the windows."

I gave him a serious bird over my shoulder.

Unfortunately, by throwing a hissy-fit, I missed the report from Jinks and Davis about the five-gallon cans of gasoline just outside the broken window.

Chapter Seventeen

By seven-fifteen Wednesday morning, I was leaning on Goldie's doorbell, and found her not only up and dressed, but with a batch of apple-nut muffins just coming out of the oven.

She shrugged as if every woman in town baked that early. "You know how it is. They're for Alex and Tully."

I didn't, and probably never would. "And not for anyone else? Not even Simpson?" I teased.

She slapped my hand away from the cooling rack. "*You* don't deserve any. Aren't you the one who was supposed to come back last night?"

"Something came up," I said. "Several *somethings*, as a matter of fact. How much time do you have?"

She glanced at me sharply before flipping open a black leather book on the counter and dialing with quick, strong punches.

"Harry? Goldie Goldman here. Listen, I've run into something urgent this morning. Unless it's a great hardship to you, ten o'clock would work much better for me."

I poured coffee for both of us, my mind wandering. The three men had still been sleeping at six o'clock when I dressed and left the house, sauntering into the nearest McDonald's as giddy as an escaped convict. Satterwhite had propped a note on the kitchen table about the gasoline, as if he knew I would sneak out early. I ate scrambled eggs and had coffee refills with abandon, reading the *Morning Star* and taking advantage of the calm. No doubt Satterwhite had long since called Stan Council.

Goldie hung up the phone and sat down across the table from me. "This better be good. We're talking a nine-hundred-thousand dollar listing here, a cool thirty-two thousand dollars in commissions, with a whole lot more from incoming DuPont transfers if this one goes well. If I lose it, you're a dead person."

My coffee went down the wrong way.

Goldie winced. "I can't believe I just said that."

"Never mind," I said. "Just listen up a minute and I guarantee you'll feel even worse."

Her face registered dismay as she listened to the highlights from the night before. "My God, I almost think I need a drink to believe what I'm hearing. You were out in the rain and the dark with this crazed killer? Were you out of your mind?"

"I will be soon if I don't figure out what's going on around here. Besides, what choice did I have?"

"What does Sheriff Council say?"

"Stan is too busy lecturing me and appointing unwanted baby sitters to listen to me. No, that's unfair to Stan. He's doing what he thinks is best, but I'm going wacky trying to figure it all out. The only common denominator I can find in all this is Eddie, and Eddie can't tell us anything."

"What are you going to do?"

I said dryly, "I'm open to ideas, which seem hard to come

by because nobody knows what the hell is behind this. The only thing that makes any sense at all is that Eddie knew something that got him killed, but we've known that much for two days."

Goldie pushed her coffee aside. "And I'm having nightmares that something is going to happen to you or Alex— even Tully."

"You think *you're* frightened? I may never sleep again for wondering if my house will burn down around my ears, or Gran's or Eddie's." A sudden shiver ran up my arms. I had to swallow hard.

"Oh, Carroll..."

"Don't give me a lot of sympathy, please. It would be easy to weep all over your kitchen table, which will happen with the slightest encouragement, but I don't have the time and it wouldn't help anyone." I wiped at my eyes with a napkin.

"Except maybe you," Goldie said, and after a moment repeated, "So, what are you going to do?"

"Something, anything. I don't know what. Maybe the first place to start would be with Alex to see if she can fill in any blanks. You were there all day yesterday. Do you think she's up to it if I promise to tread lightly?"

Goldie frowned. "Maybe. The sheriff spoke with her yesterday for half an hour. She seemed to hold up pretty well, but I don't mind telling you, we're talking right on the edge. And with the funeral coming up tomorrow..."

"Well," I said, "there's only one way to find out."

Eddie's house was in an uproar. We walked into the kitchen to find Detective Paige, pompous and red-faced, threatening to arrest Simpson for interfering with a police officer.

Simpson was shouting. "What the hell does that mean? You think you can come in here and talk to my sister like she's some kind of low-life you're going to haul off to jail? I'll be damned if I'll shut up. I've a good mind to kick your ass from here to Brunswick County."

No one seemed to notice that Goldie and I had entered the room.

Alex was still in her robe, backed against the kitchen counter with Tully clutching her around the knees. Beside the two of them, Valentine stood like a rock, muscled arms across his chest, thunderous and ready to jump into the fray.

Paige was all but frothing at the mouth. "Are you *threatening* a police officer now?"

Simpson was breathing hard, ready for battle. He opened his mouth to answer, but Alex was there first.

"I'm asking you to leave," she said shakily. "This is my house..."

Paige halted her in mid-sentence. "Possibly bought with drug money."

She straightened from the counter and picked up Tully. Her voice strengthened. "You have no right to say such things to me. You've no proof at all, and I want you to leave."

"You heard her. Now get the hell out until you learn some manners," Simpson snapped. He made a slight movement toward Paige, whose hand reached toward his gun.

Valentine stepped quickly between them. "Pardon me, sir," he said to Paige, "but I don't think you want to do that. I'm a witness here, and these people have asked you to leave. It seems to me that unless you have some kind of warrant, you are obligated under the law to leave these people in peace. By not doing so, you could be opening New Hanover County up to a lawsuit. I don't think Sheriff Council would like that."

Paige snarled. "Mind your own goddamn business. You'll be a witness that this man was interfering with a police officer on official business or I'll make sure you never hold any kind of security job in this county again. Now you get the hell out of my way."

Valentine stood his ground. "No sir, I won't. And Mr. Hardwick wasn't threatening you. I would be forced to testify to that in any court of law."

There was a second of silence, into which I slammed the back door with a force that reverberated like dynamite in the tension-filled room.

In a calm voice, I said, "What's going on here? Simpson? Detective Paige?"

"You!" Paige spoke with contempt. "This is none of your business, so you can just turn around and go back out the..."

"Excuse me."

"What?" Paige snapped.

"I want to be sure that Ms. Goldman and I understand thoroughly what's happening here—that you have been asked to leave the premises and have refused for whatever reason. Is that correct?"

He said nothing.

"Alex?" I said.

"Yes," she whispered, cleared her throat and spoke louder. "Yes!"

"Damned right," said Simpson.

"And do I also understand," I said, "that you have no warrant of any kind with which to remain in the house of this grieving widow who has just lost a husband and a baby and been out of the hospital twenty-four hours?"

He sneered, "Well, when did *you* get out of law school? What I have is a truck registered in the name of one Edward Monroe with half a kilo of cocaine buried at the bottom of his tool chest.

Alex flinched as if she had been struck.

Simpson thundered, "That's enough! You're a damned liar!"

"I couldn't have said it better myself," I said.

"Get used to it," Paige snarled.

"Out!" Alex shouted. She was a whirl of action as she handed Tully to Goldie and got in Paige's face. "Get the hell out of my house, *right now*, before I throw you out myself." She was shorter by a good twelve inches and he had seventy-five pounds on her, but she planted her feet squarely in front of him, lowering her voice only a fraction.

Valentine moved to stand beside her. "I don't think that could be much clearer, sir, and in front of no less than six witnesses, too."

"Clear as a church bell," I said.

Simpson jerked his thumb toward the front hall. "The door is that way, asshole, and if you don't leave in a real big hurry, we may just have to help you through it."

You could have heard a feather fall, the room was so still.

Paige cast a last malevolent look around the room, before focusing on me. "Don't think I won't be back with a warrant to tear this house apart. As for you, Sheriff Council may be fooled, but not me," he spat before stomping out, slamming the door behind him.

"And we can hardly wait to see you again," I said under my breath.

Alex collapsed into the wooden kitchen chair, drained, but not so far gone she couldn't gather her daughter in her lap.

Only the adults were at a loss for words.

Tully looked around at the grownups and scolded in a clear, high voice, "You were all saying bad words. You know it's not nice to say bad words."

Wearily, Alex pushed the sleep-tangled curls away from her angel face. "I know, sweetheart, I know."

"And you don't get any ice cream if you say bad words," Tully continued in the perfect imitation of a teacher's voice.

"No," said Alex. "Not a bite."

"OK, then," she pronounced and slid from her mother's lap to wander off into the den.

I had to smile. "So much for severe psychological scarring. I'd forgotten life could be so clear-cut."

Valentine grinned, and even Simpson, who by then had his arm around a speechless Goldie, lost his Cretan scowl. Alex was the one not smiling. I sat down beside her.

Her fists were clenched on the table. "It isn't true!"

"Of course not," I said.

"Why would he say such a thing about Eddie?"

"Detective Paige seems to have a Neanderthal theory that if he throws enough garbage against a wall, some of it is bound to stick. He did the same thing when I went in to give my statement. You've never heard such a load of crap. First he accused me, then Randolph, then even Davis."

She looked up, startled, "Davis?"

"What I'm trying to say is that we all knew Eddie—you best of all. He would never in a million years have been involved in smuggling drugs. No one in this town who really knew him will believe that, so don't even think about it. I'll talk to Stan Council to make sure Paige isn't careless with his accusations."

"He'd better not be," she said. "But if they did find cocaine in Eddie's truck, this isn't going to go away, is it?"

Simpson picked up a cup of coffee. "Maybe we should all calm down a bit here. I, for one, am not in the habit of flying off the handle like that, and I'm worried about you, Alex."

"We're *all* worried about Alex," said Goldie. "But your banker image has been shot to hell, Simpson, and I love you for it. Thank God for Valentine. I forgot to breathe for a few seconds when it looked like Paige would pull his gun on you."

"I've run into him before, Ms. Goldman," said Valentine. "It's my personal opinion that the man isn't quite right in the head, in addition to being a bit of a bully, but I've never seen him this far out of line before. My advice is to avoid him if you can. He won't be a man who takes kindly to being bested."

It was my turn. "At least this encounter with the Barney

Fife from hell has brought a little color back to your cheeks, Alex."

She waved a shaky hand. "I hate violence, but I swear I might have torn his face off if I could have found the energy."

Valentine patted her on the shoulder. "You did OK, Ms. Monroe. Eddie would have been proud."

"Did you know my husband?" she said.

"Everybody knew Eddie," he said gruffly. "That's why you shouldn't worry about what Paige says." He cleared his throat. "And now, if you'll all excuse me, I'd better get back to work before I get fired."

"Not a chance," I said. "A bonus is more likely. But for now, we'll just say thanks for your help. I don't want to even think about what might have happened if you hadn't been here."

"Just doing my job, Ms. Davenport," He left the room, embarrassed by the praise.

Things calmed down after that. Goldie retrieved her muffins by the back door, and we had a quick cup of coffee, pampering Alex for all of ten minutes before Simpson said he had to run to his office for a couple of hours. It was my fourth cup with cream and sugar so far.

Goldie and I followed him down the hallway.

"Before you go, Simpson," I said, "would you mind answering a quick question for me? I know my father used your downtown branch of Wachovia Bank, and I'm wondering if you might remember anything about a development off South College Road that he and Richard Howe were involved in together."

"Sure I do, although there wasn't much activity on my part."

"What do you mean?"

"We denied the loan."

"That surprises me," I said. "Jack Davenport wasn't exactly a poor man. Do you remember why it fell through?"

"I should, since I was in charge of the paperwork, but I'm afraid I can't tell you. If your father's name had been the only one on the loan application, it wouldn't be a problem, but since there were other people involved, I can't divulge the reason."

"I can," said Goldie from behind us. "Wachovia probably figured Richard Howe was a bad risk. Back then he was skating on ice so thin, you could hear it cracking all around him."

"Now, Goldie," Simon said. "You're not exactly an impartial observer."

"Don't *now Goldie* me. Tell me I'm off the mark."

Simpson cleared his throat and looked at his watch.

"See what I mean?" she said in my direction. "Anyway, somehow they did buy the land because Richard later sold the property to Anderson Pharmaceutical."

"George Anderson's company?

She nodded. "He made quite a bundle out of it, too. I remember the figure exactly—three point three million dollars—because my lawyer tried to unearth the details for our divorce settlement. The slime either spent it or hid it, because there was no trace of it anywhere. I figured it was a lot of money to spend on other women, but not beyond Richard's capabilities."

"Hold on a minute," Simpson said. "You're talking about the same man who heads up the United Way Campaign and the Boys Club. I'll admit he sometimes has a way about him, but..."

"So," Goldie said, "it's the bankers who keep voting him in office."

Simpson rolled his eyes and kissed her on the top of her head. "I've got to go. Anything else you need to know, Carroll, just ask Goldie."

As the front door slammed, Goldie caught my arm before I could go back to the kitchen. "Wait up a second. Why do you need to know about the development?"

"I found an old real estate agreement in the files and was curious because I don't remember anything about it in the estate papers. It should have shown up as an asset somewhere."

She frowned. "It would be just like Richard to pull something crooked."

"Not even he would have the gall to steal from a dead man's estate, and wouldn't it have been recorded at the courthouse?"

"It should have been. Don't assume anything where Richard is concerned. I've told you some of the unsavory things about him, but I could tell you others that you would have a hard time believing. There were times when I was convinced he was using drugs, and I seriously questioned his sanity once or twice. After the divorce, I realized that both were probably true."

"You're lucky to be well out of it, Goldie."

"I won't ever be out of it. A part of me will always be

afraid of him."

When we returned to the kitchen, Alex was still sitting at the table where we left her, staring out the window where the sun had come out for the first time in days.

She looked up as we sat down. "I don't know how I'm going to get through this."

"One day at a time," I said. "One day at a time. I know that's a trite old saying, but it's true."

Alex looked from me to Goldie. "Do you know what is tearing me apart? That I was so angry with him when he left that night. He tried to hug me—you know how he was—to kind of jostle me out of being mad." She was still for a moment, seeing pictures out the window. "I'll go to my own grave remembering that I pulled away and turned my back the last time I saw him alive."

"Hey," I said softly. "Don't you doubt for a minute that Eddie knew how much you loved him."

She was close to tears. "I know that. But it doesn't help."

Goldie said, "And don't ever forget how Eddie felt about you."

Alex sighed with exhaustion. "You're right. Of course, you're right. I'm trying, really I am, and I know how much Tully needs me now. It just...seems so hard to make it all come together."

"Did Eddie say where he was going Sunday night or if he was meeting someone?" I asked her.

She shook her head. "No, he just said he had to check on something at the Figure Eight job—something that couldn't wait until Monday morning."

I said, "How about phone calls earlier that day?"

"Sheriff Council asked me all these questions. I think the phone rang about seven o'clock, but Tully was crying and I had just thrown up, so I don't know if I can trust my memory."

"Had he said anything to you recently about problems he was having, or whether anything was worrying him?"

"The sheriff asked me that, too. I could remember only one time about a week ago when I asked him what he was thinking about. He said it was nothing, that he probably had the wrong end of the stick, and made a joke about adding two and two and coming up with ten. I had no idea what he was talking about."

Measuring my words carefully, I said, "I hate to even ask this, but were the two of you having financial trouble?"

She frowned. "I don't think so. At least he never said anything to me. As far as I know, we have very little debt except for this house, unless there was something big he didn't tell me about, and that wouldn't have been like Eddie."

"Had you ever known him to pal around with Dennis Mason—hunting, fishing, partying—anything like that?"

Alex was vehement. "Oh, no. Eddie had strong opinions about Dennis's morals and lifestyle. How he still lived at home, sponging off his mother, and how he never seemed to keep a job." She shrugged. "Everybody knew about Dennis."

Goldie said, "Maybe we should just leave everything to the professionals and concentrate on you, Alex. I suspect you should be resting right now. I'll be back around two o'clock. Can I take Tully then and keep her the rest of the day?"

"No," Alex said. "I mean I'd like it if you both came back

to keep me company, but I need to make myself busy so I won't think so much. That way, too, Tully won't be out of my sight."

"Any way you want it," said Goldie. "I'll be back as soon as I can. Meanwhile, why don't you leave the phone off the hook, take it easy, and let Valentine keep an eye on Tully and anything else that comes up."

"I can be finished and back by about then myself, if you promise to mind your elders and rest like a good girl," I said.

The smile was so small, a near-sighted person would have missed it completely.

Between the two of us, Goldie and I got her up the stairs and back to bed. She collapsed as if she had used her last gram of stamina.

Eddie and drugs! What in God's name would come of it? Sometimes life can be so low-down unmerciful that it almost takes your breath away.

On the way out of the house, we almost stepped on Richard Howe, ready to knock just inside the storm door. Speak of the devil. What a pity we were watching where we were going. We might have run him over like a rat in the road.

Goldie said, "Goddamn it, Richard. I told you not today. She can't deal with the likes of you right now."

He fixed her with a formidable stare and took a half-step closer. "Who are you, besides a harpy ex-wife, to say I can't ring this doorbell. You're not this woman's guardian, and I'll thank you to tend your own business. She won't mind giving me a few minutes to pay my respects."

He was dressed in a different handmade suit that looked

slightly less costly than the Mercedes parked in the driveway. There wasn't a hair out of place, even though the wind was blowing. I couldn't imagine what Goldie ever saw in him.

"She's resting," I said, "and the guard has strict orders not to let anybody in—not the President of the United States, not the Queen of England—nobody." *And especially not you*, I thought.

"Is this your doing, Goldie?"

She was scathing. "Give me a break, Richard. I have better things to do with my time. See you later, Carroll." She hurried across the lawn toward her own house. I watched her skirt around his expensive wheels and without looking around, extend her middle finger behind her back. I made the mistake of smiling.

"Is something amusing you?" His voice had a dangerous edge.

"Why do you think that?"

"Because you just may be laughing at me, when I've come here representing the City of Wilmington."

"Then, please show enough respect to leave Alex in peace for a few more..."

"Good morning, Mayor," Stan Council said behind us. For such a big man, he moved quietly. Neither of us had heard his approach. Once again, he looked as if he hadn't slept.

"Sheriff," Richard nodded. "What brings you here?"

"I need to speak with this little lady about a dog for a few minutes if she doesn't mind."

"What luck," I said dryly. "I was just on my way to see you."

He grasped me by the elbow. "I'll just bet you were. Mayor, if you'll pardon us, I'm pushing a busy schedule here and already running late."

Howe said, "How's the investigation going, Sheriff? Any new developments you need to fill me in on? You must know that these murders are affecting the city in a bad way. We need to do everything possible to find the killer fast."

Stan grunted. "Not that we can disclose at this time, Mr. Mayor. Now, we really do have to get a move on..."

"Then when do you think you *will* give me more information?"

Stan's hand tightened on my elbow. "Mayor, these murders are only two days old. This is a county matter, and we will proceed at the regular county pace while we wait for all the reports to get back to us. In the meantime, we're doing everything we can to keep the citizens safe, and you can furnish that information to the media. Now, I'm afraid we really do have to get a move on. Good day, Mayor."

Halfway to the brown car with its gold lettering, I turned around. "Hold on, Stan. I want to make sure he really does leave."

Howe saw us watching and stalked back to his silver Mercedes.

As he drove away, I said, "Do I detect a spot of friction between you and the mayor?"

"Can't stand the man—never could—from the very first meeting. And as far as I'm concerned, he doesn't wear any better with time. That's not to say I don't appreciate what he does for this town three hundred and sixty five days a year, and so should you. As Lieutenant Governor he'll be able to do a lot more. But that's not why I wanted to talk to you."

"I can guess," I said. "You want a full report on last night."

"I've already had a full report on last night's activities from Ben Satterwhite, thank you, and it's beginning to look like I can trust his version a far sight more than yours. Furthermore..."

He appeared to be searching for the right words.

I leaned against the county car and tried humor. "Furthermore? I always know I'm in trouble when you start throwing *furthermore* at me."

"Your smart mouth is going to get you into big trouble one day, missy. I suspect it already has."

I threw up my hands. "All right, Stan, I know you have my best interests at heart. I just don't much like the remedy, that's all, and neither would you if you were in my shoes."

"Well, he isn't exactly my type, is he, and I'm *not* in your shoes. *Furthermore*, I don't much care whether you like it or not, my girl. There is at least one killer, maybe others, out there, and you've been in the way more than once. I'm not asking anymore, Carroll, I'm telling you. This is serious business. From now on Satterwhite sticks like glue. Where you go, he goes...every hour...every minute. No dodging, no slipping out the side door, no giving him a hard time. He's been good enough to do this as a favor to me, and even if you can't damn well appreciate it, at least cooperate. I am not planning to meet my maker one day believing I didn't do everything I could for Jack Davenport's daughter—whether she wanted it or not."

"You don't have to throw a guilt trip at me, Stan. I appreciate your concern, honestly I do, and I'll hire a private guard within the hour. You have my word."

"No!"

"Be reasonable, Stan."

"Now listen up. I'm gonna say this one time only. Even if you are dumb enough to trust your life to some ten-dollar-an-hour hack, I won't."

"Then someone else, Stan."

"Why the devil not Satterwhite?"

"I don't know why. OK?"

"Not good enough, my girl. This matter is settled, you hear? Settled and done with. Now move your behind away from this vehicle and behave yourself. And no pouting."

"Pouting?"

"Yes, pouting. And you want to know what else I think?" He lowered his voice a few decibels. "I think you're scared. Somebody's gonna take you down a peg or two one of these days, and I think you just might be afraid Satterwhite will be the one to do it."

I laughed. I couldn't help it. "Oh please, Stan. Spare me the male psychology on top of everything else."

He slapped the hood of the car in frustration and said with deep seriousness, "I'm asking you to just do this for me. And if not me, then for your grandma. Eleanor doesn't deserve this kind of worry at her age. She would never ask, but I'll be damned if I can't at least try to safeguard her three last living kin."

He sure knew how to choose his words. I could feel my

principles crumbling. "All right. I'll do it. But I'm warning you, there'll be a limit to how much charm I can muster. And if I strangle Mr. Satterwhite, it will be your fault."

"Atta girl." He patted my head as if I were Tully's age. "I knew you'd come through, out of the sheer goodness of your heart."

I gave a rude, unladylike snort. "And you can wipe that silly grin off your face."

"I intend to. Just as soon as I see you in the same vehicle with Satterwhite."

"He's here?"

"Right across the street."

"Well, shades of déjà vu. I might have known. In that case, I guess I forgot to tell you that I need some favors for doing this." I ticked them off on my fingers. "First, *you* touch base with the city police about the hospital incident. You know as much about it as I do now, and they already have a full description of the guy. Second, call off your crazed Detective Paige. Any man who has to verbally attack a sick woman in front of her child needs another line of work, and the sooner the better. Talk to Simpson Hardwick and a Fidelity guard named Valentine about this morning's little interrogation of Alex."

"I've already done the first, and I'm getting close to doing the second, with or without their testimony. Now cough up the third one."

"I want to know if Eddie's fingerprints are on the cocaine you found in his truck."

"No," he said. "They weren't. And I thought of that one

all by myself, because that's what the job pays me to do."

I felt a load fly off my shoulders. "Thanks, Stan. I knew it wasn't true."

"He isn't in the clear yet, you know. Finding that stash doesn't look good."

I nodded. "But Alex needs that reassurance."

"Are you sure you're finished?"

"I just need to pick your brain for a minute. Dad was involved in a land deal out South College Road with Richard Howe. Do you remember him saying anything about it?"

"Not much. Some office project, I think. Earl McIntyre was involved, too, though I forget just how. It's been a long time. What I do remember is that Earl died of head injuries after an accident on a lonely back road up near Wallace. His blood tested clean for drugs and alcohol, so either he fell asleep at the wheel or he steered his car directly into a big live oak. Not much of an impact, but enough to do the trick. What makes you bring that up? I thought the project fell apart."

"Maybe it did. I found an old agreement between Dad and Howe that made me wonder if it was possible his estate wasn't reimbursed for his share. It all happened shortly before he died, and I don't remember that property in his estate papers. It just set little bells ringing in my head for some reason."

Stan opened his car door. "Girl, if there is one thing you *don't* need, it's more bells in your head. Now go on, get out of here. I've got work to do."

Chapter Eighteen

As I crossed the oak-lined street, Satterwhite got out of the car, went around and opened the passenger door. A nice touch, but wasted.

My grandmother says that if you have to do something anyway, you might as well get through it with grace and good humor. In addition to death, divorce, and hurricanes, I thought this must have been just the kind of situation she had in mind.

After days of rain, a lone mockingbird was singing somewhere close by as if he had discovered paradise. The sun had drifted higher, filtering through the bare branches behind my warden, making me shade my eyes. So if he wore an I-told-you-so smirk, I missed it.

From ten feet away, I flashed him the kind of smile that could knock a lonely sailor off a pier.

He nodded, suspicious, maybe even a bit amused. "Ms. Davenport." He gestured toward the passenger seat. "You look like hell this morning."

I had all but forgotten the bruise on my face, now turning purple and green, and the circles under my eyes. My resolve to make nice slipped a fraction. "Kind of you to remind me." I pointed toward Goldie's driveway. "The Jeep is over there."

He was wary now. "Maybe your vehicle isn't the best way to do this. If we get into a tight situation, I'd feel a lot better if I were behind the wheel."

I am not good with control. I gave him my second brightest smile, which was a long way from the first. "The funny thing is, so would I, and I have the advantage of knowing every alley and side street in town." I shrugged. "Take it or leave it. I have a lot to do this morning."

To his credit, he simply flicked the power locks and slammed the Buick's door. "Lead the way, lady."

A few blocks away in Forest Hills, I found Jinks and Davis hard at work in breathing masks and safety goggles, tearing out a plaster wall between the living and dining rooms.

I long ago determined that there are certain jobs only men are genetically programmed to do with enthusiasm—plaster demolition being one of them. The air was choked with a gummy white dust that stuck tight to hair and eyebrows. In spite of the goggles, their eyes were red with irritation. From a dusty boom box on the hearth, reggae music poured out the windows like a fraternity house. The neighbors must have loved it.

"Break time, guys," I said, turning down the music.

Jinks laid his crowbar down and led the way under plastic and into the next room where we could breathe. He removed his mask and glanced at Satterwhite, who had wandered over to talk to Davis.

"How's it going, Jinks?" I asked.

"Pretty easy so far," he said, one eye on the other two. "No unexpected wires or pipes. We've got it moving good right now, but we'd sure make better time if that damned Duane would show up."

I shrugged. "Looks like we may well have lost him, but I'd rather not replace him quite yet. You know Duane. He's liable to stroll in tomorrow with a cock-and-bull story we'll half believe and never be able to disprove."

He rolled his bloodshot eyes. "Yeah...like maybe being kidnapped by aliens. More like alien motorcycle chicks in Daytona Beach, knowing Duane. You think he could have skedaddled because he had something to do with Eddie's murder? I can't see it, but who knows what anybody will do when they're on drugs."

"Was he?"

"If he was, I never recognized it when he was on the job. A couple of times I wondered when I saw him around on weekends. But, you know how Duane can be high on life one minute and down the next, swearing he's moving to California or Alaska, falling in love with an engineer a week before he settles for Tiffany. Who can figure him?"

"He was seen on the island late Sunday afternoon, and Tiffany said she thought he was going to meet Eddie. I'd hate to think we've been searching all over town for a murderer."

Jinks shook his head. "If I'm any judge of character, it isn't Duane we need to worry about, but if he doesn't show up today or tomorrow, we may need to hire a couple of temps from the labor pool to get this debris hauled out to the dumpster and a few other jobs. We've still got the three bathrooms and sunroom to go before the painters come in, and we may need to hustle along a little. I can hire some extra help first thing in the morning." He glanced at his watch. "Won't be any good workers left this late in the morning."

"Make it Friday," I said. "The funeral is at eleven tomorrow, and I know Eddie would have wanted his troops there."

"Shit, I almost forgot...excuse me. You bet, we'll both be there."

"Forget about the job for tomorrow. We wouldn't get any work done. And by the way, Alex asked me to especially invite you and Davis back to the house after the graveside services. I don't suppose there's a chance in hell that Duane will show up between now and eleven o'clock tomorrow, but if you can find him, he'll want to be there."

Jinks grinned. "Duane will have himself a right fine old hangover when he does drag his tail back here."

"Serve him right," I said. "Let's hope it's a doozy."

Looking over my shoulder, Jinks said, "Did you get a make on the tag?"

"What tag?"

From behind me Satterwhite said, "You left us too early last night. He's talking about the truck parked down the street. Jinks was smart enough to rub the mud off and read the numbers, and we found it was registered to AGHR Corporation. Either one of you ever heard of it?"

"Not me," I said. "I assume you tried the phone book?" He nodded. "And nothing turned up in the computers. I'm waiting for word from the secretary of state's office."

"What about the other tag?" I asked. "The one from the hospital. There can't be many North Carolina plates beginning with RLT on a burgundy Mustang."

"Stolen, both of them. The tag from a middle-aged woman a month ago, and the car from Myrtle Beach last Saturday."

I glanced up at Davis, who was back on the ladder. Young gangs were stealing cars in Wilmington, sometimes as many as ten a night. He held my gaze for a fraction of a second before he looked away.

By the time I was ready to leave, Satterwhite had gone back to the Jeep, waiting patiently, as a cat does for a mouse. He handed me a scrap of paper with a phone number. "I answered your mobile phone. A Ms. Anderson wants you to call her. I think she may have recognized my voice, which didn't improve her mood any. I would have thought she was too far gone Monday night to remember anything."

I groaned. Bitsy Anderson was the last person I wanted to deal with at the moment. "Did she say what she wanted?"

"Not to me. She must have assumed I wasn't your regular assistant."

I said, "That isn't such a bad idea. If I'm going to be stuck with you for God knows how long, I might as well make it worth my while. You could tag along behind and take notes."

He handed me the phone. "Right. Just don't hold your breath. And it can't be longer than a few more days, Davenport. Have a little patience. I might grow on you."

Ah, but that's what I was afraid of.

Bitsy answered on the second ring.

"It's Carroll Davenport," I said. "You wanted to speak with me?"

"It galls me, but yes."

Here we go, I thought. Even at nine-thirty on a Wednesday morning, her voice was slurred.

"George called your lawyer this morning and told him...told him we wanted out of the contract for the house. There's no way I'm going to wait another year for you to mess everything up again, and our own lawyer says you can't make us go through with it."

"I wouldn't even try, Bitsy. You'll have your deposit back as soon as you notify me in writing and I can get a check in the return mail." Without the fire, the house would have been finished within the contract period, but I wasn't about to argue the point. Instead, I would count my blessings and try not to jump up and down with glee that none of us would ever have to work with Bitsy again.

"Anyway," she went on, "with all of your problems, I'd probably have nightmares about faulty wiring and fire the rest of my life. I still think one of your men left a cigarette..." Her tone said she was annoyed that I wasn't making an effort to dissuade her. But then, there was never a time when she wasn't pissed about something.

"Bitsy, listen to me. The fire marshal said it was a clear case of arson. Do you understand? Someone poured gasoline all around inside the house, opened every window and door to a thirty-five knot wind, and deliberately burned your house to ashes."

"What are you talking about?"

"Arson." I wondered if I should spell it for her.

"I don't believe you."

At that moment, I didn't give a tinker's damn whether she believed me or not, but there was zip to be gained by telling her so. I didn't need the aggravation of a revenge lawsuit.

"Whatever you say, Bitsy. Was that all you wanted to tell me?"

There was a long pause on the other end of the line, making me wonder if she had put the phone down and wandered off to fix herself another drink.

"Are you still there, Bitsy?"

She was. Lucky me. "I thought I heard someone at the back door. Don't be so impatient, Miss Old Money, always looking down your nose at me. You and Eddie both."

I was fast running out of patience. "You know that..."

"If you could stop interrupting me, there is something else, but now I don't know if I want to tell you or not."

I said, "It's strictly up to you."

"Yes, it is, isn't it..."

She was giving me a giant headache. "Just spit it out, Bitsy." I would never be able to get along with this woman. I'd stopped trying.

"Not over the telephone. You'll have to meet me somewhere."

I could have sworn she was nervous. Not like the Bitsy Anderson we had grown to know and treasure. "After the other night, I can't think that would be a very good idea. What could be so important you have to meet me in person? Why can't you tell me now?"

There was a clicking over the airwaves, one of the never-ending quirks of mobile and cell phones. Her voice now sounded further away, a tunnel in satellite space, or the way a phone sounds when someone picks up an extension. She whispered something that I couldn't catch.

"What did you say?"

"I said my phone may be bugged."

I glanced at Satterwhite. "What makes you think your phone might be bugged?"

Ice tinkled in the background. "That is for me to know and for you to find out."

"We're picking up interference, that's all you're hearing." A mistake on my part. I was a slow learner.

She flared. "Don't tell me what I'm hearing. You don't know everything there is to know, not by a long shot—like Eddie and the drugs—like who killed your damned nosy cousin, for instance. You don't have any choice, now do you? Or are you happy that he's dead, so you can have a bigger share of old granny's money?"

Enough was enough. "Listen carefully, Bitsy. If you know anything about Eddie's murder, which I very much doubt, call the sheriff's office. They need all the help they can get, but for God's sake, sober up first."

There was a sound of glass breaking. She said in a razor voice, "You'll meet me, or I'll make a call all right, but it won't be to the police. It will be to the newspaper. I'll swear I saw you light the fire that burned down my house—saw you with my own two eyes—then we'll see how you like being in the hot seat. By the time I'm finished, you'll stink so bad they won't even wrap dead fish in the same newspaper."

"Bitsy..."

"Just shut up with the lectures and meet me under the parking deck behind Wachovia Bank at eleven sharp. Stand me up, and I guarantee you'll wish you had never heard of Bitsy Anderson."

For the last eight months, I'd been wishing that very thing—along with my crew and probably half of Wilmington. What I said was, "You wouldn't dare."

"Just watch me." The line went dead.

"Bitsy...? Damn it, she hung up on me. I swear somebody will strangle that woman one day. I only hope it won't be me."

"What was that all about?" Satterwhite asked.

"Trouble," I said.

And all things considered, if I had known how accurate I was, I would have let my new assistant handle the matter.

Chapter Nineteen

There are many different roads to hell, most of which are paved with good intentions. I'd driven on some of those roads, but for the last six years, it had been my policy to stay out of conflicts with the Bitsy Andersons of this world.

Unfortunately, I found myself finished with legal and insurance matters at precisely three minutes before eleven—only two blocks from the Water Street parking deck.

I swear I had no intention of meeting Bitsy. I was more than glad to be shed of our business involvement, even though it looked as if any payoff from Nationwide would be slow in coming. Payton Gray, my agent, rolled his eyes and shrugged his good-old-boy shoulders not once, but twice—always a bad omen when money is involved.

"Ordinarily," he hemmed and hawed, "when arson is involved, our policy holders don't suffer long if we can prove there's no financial reason for them to burn the damn place down. In your case, we can't find a money problem, but a murdered co-owner complicates things all to hell and back. Now we're talking investigations up the old wazoo; three, maybe four investigations, because Eddie had life insurance, too. And nobody, but nobody is gonna pay a dime until the sheriff, the fire marshal, Nationwide, and the life policy boys all finish consulting with each other until the damn cows come home."

I asked him what kind of time frame he was talking about, but got only a third shrug of the shoulders and the kind of *don't worry your pretty little head* platitudes that southern women have to endure.

I left his office feeling that fate was worse than a fickle taskmaster, which must have been why my steering wheel seemed to turn of its own accord down Princess Street toward the river.

Also, I was uneasily curious about what Bitsy had to say. I couldn't be a thousand percent certain that Eddie wasn't involved with drugs in some way, and I wanted to hear what was important enough to bring her seventeen miles to tell me about it.

Water Street wasn't exactly deserted during weekday office hours. After sundown the lower level of the parking deck became a very different kind of place, but in broad daylight, people came and went with regularity.

Supported by decaying concrete supports, the deck was an ugly, two-story structure, open along three sides of a city block. It was a gloomy place to meet, even on a sunny day, with barely enough light to check the hands on my watch. Fifty feet into the cavernous street level, the Jeep scattered a small flock of roosting pigeons in a flurry of feathered panic. There were maybe twenty scattered cars parked in the whole lower level.

I pulled into a vacant space six or seven cars away from Bitsy's baby-blue Mercedes. Satterwhite put his hand on the door handle.

I said, "Where do you think you're going? She'll have a conniption fit if she spots your face. I'm having enough fun as it is, thanks."

"Forget it. You could hide a dozen snipers in here. Try to use your head."

"Satterwhite, damn it..."

"All right, all right," he said. "I'll be behind the nearest car, but that's as far as I go." He opened the glove compartment and took out the Glock. "Put this in your pocket."

He was really going to have to learn not to hand me a gun when he said things like *use your head.* "Come on," I said. "I'm just planning to talk to her, not shoot her. Put it back. Besides which," I said sarcastically, "I'm sure you're armed enough for the two of us." To make my point, I flipped open his jacket, just to be sure he hadn't forgotten he was wearing a gun.

His sudden grip on my wrist was steel, his tone cool and inflexible, which gave me a quick glimpse of what he was like when he wasn't moonlighting as my assistant. "Take it," he said, thrusting the gun into my hand, "or I'm going with you every step of the way."

"For God's sake..."

He let go of the wrist.

I put the gun in my pocket and flounced—there's no other word for it—out of the Jeep, slamming the door with force enough to break the power window mechanism. I heard his own door open, but I didn't look around.

Bitsy's car was pulled head-first into a parking space along the last row, closest to Front Street and the old back wall, so that I was approaching the car from the rear. That far away from the entrance, there was even less light, but enough to see the passenger door standing open. From ten feet away, there was no sign of Bitsy.

It wasn't until I reached the driver's window that I spotted her sprawled across the front seat. Irritated, I tapped on the tinted glass. It seemed logical to assume she had passed out.

I grabbed the rear door handle and wrenched it open. "Bitsy..."

My head and shoulders were inside; one foot was on the rear floorboard. I froze. A full second before I saw blood smeared on the pale leather seats, the smell hit me—a thick, unmistakable, never-to-be-forgotten odor of metallic blood mixed with bodily waste.

Bitsy lay sideways along the front seat, a bloody hand out the open passenger door, as if seeking help. Blood had spurted across the seat, the console, the steering wheel—even the windshield. I made a strangled, choking sound before backing out so fast I cracked my head on the door frame.

Nausea pulled at the back of my throat. There was a roaring in my ears. I escaped from the car in panic and managed to get as far as the nearest support column before vomiting on the filthy concrete, half-disoriented by the squalid horror of fresh blood and old memories.

I knew that stench.

Something touched me on the shoulder. I twisted away in fear.

Satterwhite said, "It's always bad the first time you see

that much blood."

I found a tissue in my jeans pocket. My hands were shaking. "That's the problem," I said.

"What?"

"It *isn't* the first time." I sank down on my heels, my back propped up by the strength of the column, and asked, "What happened to her?"

He hesitated. "Are you sure you want to know?"

I looked up at him and said, "Yes, damn it."

"Her throat was cut."

"Oh, God!" I closed my eyes. "Was that how Eddie looked? That much blood?"

He stared away toward the returning pigeons. "It was afternoon before I saw Eddie. I'm guessing this happened a few minutes ago. Somebody had a hell of a nerve, in broad daylight with a high-profile vehicle in a public parking lot, not fifty feet from the bank." He looked down at me and reached out a hand. "You going to be OK, Davenport?"

"No," I said. "I don't think so."

Chapter Twenty

I've never liked funerals. I don't handle death well, and I avoid them whenever possible. Beginning with Eddie's parents, killed in a foggy car crash in California when we were both eleven, there have been too many burials. Within three years, I had to cope with my mother's, and in due course, Daniel's and my father's, although I wasn't present for the last two.

There's something wretchedly sad about inconsolable hearts, premature goodbyes, and the cold, cold earth. This one, I wouldn't have dodged if I had wanted to.

Thursday was bright and clear, the warmest day of the year, and by eleven o'clock, the temperature had risen to seventy-three degrees. It was the kind of early spring day we're famous for in Wilmington—but too beautiful for a burial. A Mother Nature kind of sick joke.

In the side parking lot of St. James Church, Goldie summed it up well. "For this kind of day, I want lightning and thunder and enough noise to hide my anger at God." Amen to that. Instead, we got sunshine and her ex-husband holding court with Channel Three.

It surprised no one that the church was overflowing. Like I said before, the Monroes have been in Wilmington since forever. In addition to the mayor, I spotted city councilwomen, county commissioners, legislators, and more than one judge. Gran would have said it was ungracious of me to suspect some had attended out of curiosity, as if Eddie might suddenly bolt upright in his casket and admit to being a low-life drug smuggler. To be fair, the back wall was lined with friends Eddie's age, dressed in dark suits for the occasion, and staring everywhere except at the closed mahogany casket.

I sat between Gran and Alex on the front row of the hard pews. Tully was on Alex's left, beside Simpson, intent on the organ playing old hymns—*Rock of Ages, Amazing Grace, I Come to the Garden Alone*—chosen, I suspected, by my grandmother. Rays of sunshine streamed through the stained glass windows and touched the side of my bruised face like a laying-on of hands.

In his booming Scottish brogue, Reverend Thompson reflected on the goodness of Edward Carroll Monroe, who greatly loved his wife and daughter, on the godliness of families and friendships, on the sometime suddenness of life and death.

I had a quick-flash memory of Eddie holding my hand in this same church while we wept together for his favorite aunt and my mother.

I couldn't look at Alex's tear-streaked face or I would have broken down. Tully sat quietly, affected by the mood of the crowd, although I doubted she really understood the somber finality involved.

Alex's hand was colder than my grandmother's, but not by much. One woman was certain that few things in life would ever cause her so much anguish. The other, stiffened and frail, had already buried most of the people she had loved. Gran glanced up at me. I knew what she was thinking—only one grandchild and one great-grandchild left. I swore to myself, in church then and there, that I would move heaven and earth to make some son-of-a-bitch pay for their suffering.

The ceremony was mercifully brief.

On the way to the cemetery, Simpson said to Alex, "Not much longer now. Hang on just a little bit more."

"God help me get through this hardest part," she said and started to cry again. Simpson drew her head down onto his shoulder as Tully began to whimper.

More than a hundred mourners followed us to the cemetery. As we filed into the seats beside the grave, I glanced over the crowd and spotted Satterwhite and Stan Council near the back edge. Further away from the cluster of somber faces, I counted at least four uniformed deputies, spaced and alert around the perimeter. Where had I read that the murderer is almost always somewhere among the mourners?

Twenty feet out into the lake, a noisy cluster of mallards swam toward shore. When the ceremony began, they paddled in place, close together, as silent as churchgoers.

Reverend Thompson remarked on the beauty of that special knoll, the gentle breeze drifting in from the sea, and then he placed his hand upon the casket, calling him at last by the name his daughter knew best, saying *"Eddie, I commend you now to the loving care of God the Heavenly Father..."*

And Tully cried out, "I want my daddy!"

Chapter Twenty-one

Eddie's house was filled with noisy people consuming enormous quantities of food piled into Alex's kitchen by friends from all over town. Goldie called it funeral cuisine.

I've never been able to understand why mourners laugh and joke after funerals, or why they can't see the obvious— that too much good humor is often painful to the next of kin.

When I couldn't stand it any longer, I wandered out into the rear yard, drink in hand, and began to swing back and forth on Tully's blue and red swing with my back turned to the house, in the hope it would discourage any additional well-wishers. At last check, my grandmother, Alex, and Tully were napping in peace upstairs, worn out in both body and spirit by the funeral and its immediate aftermath.

I knew how they felt.

Goldie joined me there, her face flushed from directing half a dozen women, including Lucille, in the kitchen—the kind of women who have efficiently cemented the fabric of the South for generations of funerals, who always step forward knowing just what to do when life deals its nasty little shocks.

"Take a load off, Goldie." I gestured toward the other swing with my glass. "You've been running this feast since dawn."

She eyed the plastic seat. "With our combined weight, we'll probably break the whole thing down."

"What the hell," I said. "We can buy Tully a new one—or anything else her little heart desires. Maybe a dog would be a good idea. What do you think?"

"Oh, no. Better a hamster or a pony."

I shook my head. "I vote for a goat." After two Bloody Marys, even I could be a poet.

"A goat?" Goldie eyed the drink in my hand, the slump in my shoulders. "I think you've had too much beverage, my friend."

"Don't I wish," I said. "A miniature goat. No child can stay sad with a goat. I'm thinking of getting one myself. Or maybe a Ferrari."

"A Ferrari?"

"For Tully."

She raised an eyebrow.

"I'm punchy," I said, "but not from the punch." I wasn't drunk, far from it, just numb from the day.

"Oh, hon. I wish there was something I could do."

We settled into a rhythm, our feet dragging the grass, swinging in harmony like two children made placid by the simple motion and the self-made breeze. The sun warmed my shoulders through the black funeral dress.

"How are you holding up?" Goldie said.

"I've had worse days, but when they get this bad, who's measuring? A feeling has settled in my stomach like I've been kicked by a mule who's coming right back to do it again. Something even more vile is about to happen, Goldie. I can feel it."

She said, "I'm not sure you're even thinking straight. This is not a good day for making obscure and gloomy predictions. Forgive me for saying so, but you're looking almost as bad as Alex. And black isn't your color when it matches the bruises on your face. Shouldn't you be home in bed or something? Or do you just need to go kick the brick wall and scream?"

"Better not encourage me to whine, Goldie. I might not stop. God only knows how many years this has taken off my grandmother's life. And with Alex in a state of collapse and Tully fatherless, I might just babble on for hours. I'm hanging by my fingernails, but I'll tell you one thing for certain. Some maniac or maniacs unknown have put a serious hurt on the people I love, and the worst part is, they can't fight back."

"Oh, yes we can," said a determined voice behind us.

Alex was still dressed in a dark green dress and pearls, wraith-like, the red hair contrasting like a beacon.

"We thought you were still sleeping," said Goldie.

Alex said, "Sleep? I've slept enough to last me a year. No, I was watching the two of you from the upstairs window and avoiding all the commiseration and pity. I don't think I can stand any more. Carroll is right. It's time I started doing something."

I said gently, "It doesn't have to be today, Alex." I gave her my swing and watched her settle her scant frame. She sounded a little better, but she still had the same stunned expression in her eyes.

"Yes, it does," she said. "For Tully's sake and for my own. Things are bad enough for her without having to watch her mother hide away in bed all day. As soon as everyone leaves, I plan to start going through each piece of paper in Eddie's desk and file cabinet. Somewhere, there has to be a clue. I won't rest until I find it."

I exchanged glances with Goldie in silent agreement. Perhaps we shouldn't discourage her. It would keep her mind occupied with something other than the gruesome details. On the other hand, even though I was still ninety-nine percent sure it wasn't true, I didn't want to think about what it would do to her if she found something that connected Eddie with drugs.

"Excuse me, Mrs. Monroe." Valentine had the cat, Lily Puss, draped across his arms like a feline Miss Piggy flirting with Kermit. It all but destroyed his tough-guy image.

"Yes, Valentine. What is it?"

"My favorite bodyguard," I said. "How are you, Valentine?" Since his intervention with Detective Paige on Alex's behalf, I had developed a decided fondness for him and his loyalty. He was money well spent—worth his weight in muscles, so to speak—though I doubted he knew who was paying his salary.

He said, "I can't complain a bit, Ms. Davenport. This job would be a pleasure under other circumstances."

Alex smiled. "He spends half his time teaching Tully games and the other half prowling through the house checking windows and doors. Even the damn cat adores him."

Valentine said, "Agent Satterwhite says you shouldn't be out here, and that the three of you should come inside."

"Oh, he did, did he?" I looked around the back yard enclosed by an eight-foot brick wall. There was nowhere for an assailant to hide. The nearest climbing tree was on the far corner of Goldie's lot, a hundred feet away. The two-story house on the other side was occupied by a sweet old couple who had lived there fifty years.

I said, "We have two deputies, a sheriff, an FBI agent and the world's best bodyguard on the property. What could happen?"

He seemed embarrassed. "Begging your pardon, Ms. Davenport, but Satterwhite and Sheriff Council seemed to think you might take more kindly to the idea if it came from me instead of from either of them."

"How perspicacious of them," I sighed, earning myself another eyebrow from Goldie, who was even more certain I was tipsy. I looked over my shoulder toward the house where Stan and Satterwhite were watching from behind sliding glass doors. Just what did they think they would do if we didn't obey? "All right, Valentine, tell them to be patient. We'll be inside presently."

"Soon," he said. A statement, not a question.

"A few more minutes." Alex took the long-haired cat from his arms, and Lily Puss languidly resettled herself for further adoration.

Coming from Alex, the promise seemed to satisfy Valentine, but he still took up a watchful position halfway to the house, out of earshot.

"Oh, shit," said Goldie.`

We watched the back door close behind him as Richard Howe sauntered across the lawn.

He took Alex's hand. "You were resting earlier, but before I left, I wanted to be sure there was nothing you needed."

The cat gave a drawn-out hiss and shot out of her lap. *Well good for you, Lily Puss, and right when I was thinking you would take up with just anybody.*

"How kind of you to come and ask," Alex murmured in the same barren voice she had used all day. "But there's nothing, thank you. I'm being well cared for by friends and family."

"Thank God for that, but we will all miss Eddie. It's a miserable situation for you and your child. A little girl I believe?"

"Yes."

"A terrible, terrible tragedy."

I had to admit, he handled his consolation role well, from the deep gaze into her eyes to the sincerity of voice and the half smile of shared anguish. With his silver hair glinting in the sun, I thought he had the demeanor of a man destined for lieutenant governor or even governor four years down the road. Sainthood had never been a prerequisite for higher office.

He was still holding her hand. "The city council is more than a little worried about what kind of image this will project about Wilmington. I'm not sure the sheriff even has a suspect. Do you know?"

Goldie made a strangled sound. For once in my life, I kept silent.

"Mayor, surely you would know much more about the investigation than I would," Alex said.

"Not at all. For some reason Sheriff Council is playing this *incident* close to his chest, refusing to cooperate with the city. An ego thing between city and county governments, no doubt, with the elections coming up, but exasperating nonetheless. I thought perhaps he would share his theories with you."

"No," Alex said weakly. "I've been ill, you see, and not up to many questions." She pulled her hand away. "Thank you for your concern, Mayor, and for taking time out of your busy schedule to pay your respects."

I winked at Goldie.

Howe hesitated, not ready to be dismissed, but it was done so sweetly, he was left with no room to maneuver. "Well, then, I'll check back with you soon, but in the meantime, call my office without hesitation if there is *anything* at all I can do, or if you..." He trailed off, possibly because Goldie and I were frowning and shaking our heads.

He cleared his throat. "In any case, I won't intrude on your privacy any longer."

We watched as he detoured by Valentine to slap him on the back before sliding out the side gate.

From out of nowhere, Alex said, "Eddie swore he was sleeping with Bitsy Anderson."

"What?" I said.

Goldie blinked. "Richard?"

"Surely not," I said. "It would have been like trusting the town drunk to keep a secret. That explains why he's worried about what Stan will turn up in his investigation."

Goldie was still skeptical. "I knew he would screw just

about anything in skirts, but...Bitsy Anderson?"

Alex brushed a leaf off her shoulder. "Eddie said he could prove it. I have no idea what he meant."

I thought of the half-page spread about Bitsy's murder in the morning paper, complete with gory pictures, and remembered the startling amount of blood in her car. Discussing her possible infidelity now seemed repugnant and very close to smearing the dead. "Richard deserves his own headlines in the *Morning Star* for adultery, but George Anderson loved Bitsy. I'd hate to have him hurt even more."

"Amen," said Alex.

"You don't think George could have killed her because he found out about the affair?" asked Goldie.

I shook my head. "George is too mild-mannered to kick a rabid dog out of his way. I can't see him hurting anyone." Yet, even as I spoke, I remembered the rage on his face at the Figure Eight fire when Satterwhite pushed Bitsy aside. It was past time for me to change the subject. "By the way, Alex, I meant to tell you the assistant bartender at the Figure Eight Club called to say Eddie left his camera there. I'll try to pick it up tomorrow."

She brightened. "I'd wondered where it went. Stan said it was missing from the truck, and there are some last pictures of Eddie and Tully at the beach that I would hate to lose..." Her voice ran downhill, as if she suddenly remembered that photos and memories were all she had left of Eddie.

I didn't mention the heat-damaged telephoto lens at the fire.

Goldie stood up. "I need to check on Lucille so she won't

clean the whole place up on her own. She was shooing the
church women home when I came out. Besides, we should go
in before the men get the vapors. Come on, Alex, we can sneak
in the back way."

It was past time for my stint at kitchen duty. I found the
room deserted except for an embarrassed Davis, shirtsleeves
rolled up to his elbows, hands plunged in soapy dishwater. I
stood in the doorway and watched him for a moment.

"Hallelujah!" I said. "Slavery is back."

He flashed me the ill-humored teenage eye. "No, ma'am,
it sure is not." The Caribbean dreadlocks added a peculiar
touch to a white shirt and tie. So far on this rotten day, he had
behaved in a way that made us proud, but it never paid to
forget that Davis could be exceptional one minute and intol-
erable the next.

I took off my jacket and nudged him aside with my hip.
"What a good sport you are. Let me wash for a while. You
dry."

He looked a little happier at the suggestion, and we settled
into washing the last of the glasses and coffee cups.

"How did you get stuck with this job in the first place?" I
asked.

"Aunt Lucille," he mumbled. "She went off to see Uncle
Randolph and said if I knew what was good for me, this kitchen
better be cleaned up when she got back. You know how Aunt
Lucille can corner you."

"Do I ever! I grew up with her, too, you know."

"To be honest, she mostly had everything done already

by the time I came in looking for more coconut pie. She's only been gone a few minutes."

"I'm still impressed. Besides, they say dishwashing improves a man's character."

"Who says?"

"Girls, of course. We're not stupid, Davis."

He actually grinned. "I never did get that pie."

I said, "What are you waiting for?"

He cut himself a piece and leaned his back against the counter, the pie in his hand. Between bites, he said, "Can I ask you something?"

"Well, sure."

"Do you think the same man who beat up Uncle Randolph killed Eddie?"

"I think it's very probable, since he appeared to be searching for something in Randolph's house. If we knew what that was, we'd be way ahead in this game, but only your uncle will be able to tell if anything was taken. And since he was driving nurses crazy the last two times I phoned, my guess is he won't be hospitalized much longer. When he comes home, we'll know for sure."

With a worried look, Davis said, "Detective Paige thinks I did it."

"That's ridiculous."

"No, seriously. He thinks I hit Uncle Randolph and killed Eddie, too, and that my old gang was in on it with me."

"Don't let him freak you. I've been on the receiving end of his tactics, myself. Detective Paige is a first-class jerk."

"Yeah, but Sheriff Stan says I gotta go downtown and put

up with his grilling anyway. Calls it an official interview. My question is, do you think I need a lawyer or something?"

I thought about it for a few seconds. "I'm not sure, Davis, but I think without an actual warrant for your arrest, at a minimum they may need permission from a parent or guardian to interview a minor, and you should have the right to have someone accompany you. Let me check with Stan to see if he'll be there."

"He said he wouldn't—that if I was telling the truth, I didn't have nothing to worry about. Besides which, nobody knows where my mama is, and she'll be high as the moon anyway. So that just leaves Randolph or Aunt Lucille, and she's too...too..."

"Excitable?"

"Yeah."

"I see your problem," I smiled. "And while personally I'd love to see Lucille pin Detective Paige's ears back, we can't have your great-aunt getting arrested, now can we? Maybe I'd better have a word with Bill Lee to see if he'll sit through the interview with you. Paige will behave himself with a lawyer present. Would that make you feel better?"

He brightened. "Yeah. That would be great. Mr. Lee's OK."

I assumed *OK* was the highest rating you can get from a teen. Bill Lee had represented him well after the joy-riding episode, so I could understand his relief, but there was something else in his expression that made me ask. "Are you worried about anything in particular, Davis?"

He took his time answering. "What if somebody said they

saw me someplace else the night Eddie got killed?"

I raised my eyebrows. "You mean instead of being home in bed like Randolph said?"

"Just maybe."

"Were you?"

"Was I what?" he said.

I sighed. "Home in bed."

He fiddled with his fork without speaking, finally putting it down with the pie unfinished. I had my answer.

I dried my hands on the dishtowel. "Then I'd say you would have some hard choices to make. I doubt Randoph would be in much trouble. But you, my friend, would have to stand up like a man and explain where you were and why you lied about it. You know it has never crossed our minds that you killed Eddie. It never will. But put yourself in Paige's shoes. He looks at you and he sees a grown man, not a fifteen-year-old, and he'll have your juvenile record right smack in front of him on the interview table."

Long silences were the norm when dealing with Davis. "What if...what if I just don't show up for the interview?"

Lord, the minds of the young. I looked at his bowed head, wondering where the hell he had been to make him lie about it. "Now you answer a question for me. You wouldn't be thinking of doing anything stupid, would you, Davis?"

His head came up like a young tiger, and we were back to sullen and silent again. *I was so good at this.* Too bad I would never get the chance to screw up with my own teenager.

I folded the towel with care, giving him a fair opportunity to come clean, sat down across from him. "Listen, Davis..."

The swinging kitchen door opened with a bang. Stan Council, Jinks and Satterwhite tramped grim-faced into the room.

Stan took one look at Davis, read his body language, and asked me, "Has this young man been pissing and moaning to you about making an official statement tomorrow?"

I said, "Now Stan..."

"He's gonna do what he has to do, whether he likes it or not."

Davis got up from the table, a mulish expression on his face, and started for the door.

Stan barked, "Sit down, young man. You need to hear this, too."

"Go easy, Stan, for heaven's sake," I said. "What's all the commotion about? Hear what?"

His lips tightened. "We've found your missing supervisor."

"Duane?" I had a sudden bad feeling. "Where on earth is he?"

Stan exchanged looks with Satterwhite. "An unfortunate choice of words. You had a bulldozer at the house on Figure Eight this morning?"

"Yes, why? Dan Gilchrist and his boys were there to move some topsoil out of the way before demolition starts. What happened? Is he hurt?"

Satterwhite said, "Worse than hurt. Gilchrist found Duane, along with his motorcycle, buried under several tons of dirt. A good guess is he's been dead four or five days."

Chapter Twenty-two

I rose and walked to the window, feeling a thousand years old. "Tell me what happened?"

Stan shook his head. "We don't know yet, honey. It looks like he got whacked on the head and possibly buried alive. That's all we know so far."

"Oh, God," I said. "Since Monday morning, I've called him every kind of name in the book, even wondered if he murdered Eddie." *Buried alive under ten feet of dirt.* A glass intended for water slipped out of my hand and shattered in the cast-iron sink.

Satterwhite eased me aside. "Go sit with Stan. I'll clean it up."

Jinks and Davis seemed bewildered.

Stan broke the silence. "We'll need his employment information from you so we can notify his next of kin. I hate to ask you now, but the last thing I want is for a mother to hear something like this on the six o'clock news."

I cleared my throat, shook my head. "She just moved back to Memphis. I don't have a new address, but I'll fax her name and whatever else I have in the file as soon as I get home."

"Four murders in as many days," Stan said, stomping back and forth across the kitchen floor, slapping a fist into his palm. "The body count is already as high as all of last year. By God,

I am taking this as a personal insult."

He stopped in mid-stride and looked around the room. "Now where the hell did that boy go?"

"Sit down," I said in exasperation. "You're giving me a crick in the neck stalking around like that. We have bigger problems than one overgrown fifteen- year-old boy. Davis is just a kid, for pity's sake."

"He'd better show up for that interview, or I'm gonna drag him downtown by the ears, and then we'll see whether he's lying to us or not."

"Stan," I said, "he'll be OK, unless you ride him so hard he decides he has no choice except to do something stupid."

He loosened his tie and collapsed in a straight-backed chair that gave an alarming creak. "He's lying about where he was on Sunday night, I'm sure of it."

"So what? You think he killed Duane, too? Get a grip. Didn't you see the expression on his face when you made your announcement? He looked like he'd been hit with a two-by-four. Cool off a little, for God's sake, and try to remember what it was like when you were fifteen."

He ran a hand through his thinning hair. "All right, all right. Then you talk to him and try to find out what he was doing the night Eddie got killed. I'll back off for a couple of days. Does that satisfy you, missy? But, while you're pampering him like a baby, keep in mind that we're in the middle of four goddamned murder investigations."

He hadn't called me missy in years until the last few days. I took it as a sign that he was simmering down. I got up to refill his coffee cup.

He grunted. "Somebody's got to notify Duane's mama. I hate that."

"And Tiffany," I said. "She deserves better than to hear it sensationalized on Channel Three."

He scratched his left ear and stared at me over across his steaming coffee.

I glared right back for a dozen seconds. "Oh, Stan...you aren't going to ask me that."

"She knows you. Even more important, Duane worked for you, and these things are better coming from a woman, aren't they, Satterwhite?"

"Absolutely."

I gave it serious consideration. "All right, I'll do it, but I'm not so sure she's missing him that much. And somebody has to go with me. Dog Fowler was at the trailer my last trip, and I don't relish another encounter on my own. The man has a filthy temper and swampwater eyes that would scare the fleas off a rottweiler."

"How about it, FBI man?" Stan said. "You still on board this boat?"

"Looking forward to it," Satterwhite said dryly.

I sighed a weary breath. "Then let's do it and get it over with. Stan, when you find Duane's mother, tell her to let me know if she needs any help with his funeral expenses. From everything he told me, I got the impression she's a long way from being flush with money."

He said, "I'll get somebody on it right away," and turned with abruptness. Midway through the swinging door, he stopped and looked from me to Satterwhite. "You people stay sharp. We don't need any more bodies. Satterwhite, you know what to do. Hog-tie her if that's what it takes."

After Stan no longer filled the room with his presence, I realized we had given Duane less than two minutes of mourning.

I called Barnaby Bill's and asked for Tiffany, and when they said she hadn't come in to work that day, Satterwhite drove me out to the trailer off Middle Sound Loop Road.

The *Private Road* sign was still in place. Beside it, on a sturdy post, there was a new four-foot square of plywood with *No Trespassing* handpainted in sloppy black letters.

I turned to Satterwhite. "For a change, I'm glad you've tagged along. If one of us gets beaten to a pulp by this guy, I'm kind of hoping it won't be me."

"Relax," he said. "No one is going to get hurt."

"You haven't seen Dog Fowler. He's huge, and he oozes motorcycle mean..." I hesitated, a fuzzy picture flashing in my mind of a green pickup truck parked in the yard the last time I had visited.

"What is it?" he said.

"Probably nothing. Drive around to the water side."

There it sat, muddy and banged up, nose to nose with Tiffany's little navy Nissan. There was no motorcycle in sight. I studied the truck. The rear bumper was backed up to the trailer so we couldn't see the tag, and it was impossible to tell if it was the same one that had tried to run me down in Gran's front yard. It had been too dark, and if the truth be told, I had been too frightened to get a good look. Still, the hairs on my arms were tingling. And I was a firm believer that the mind has a *mind* of its own.

"Speak to me, Davenport."

I shook my head. "Let's get this over with before I lose my nerve. Stay close, Satterwhite."

I climbed the rickety wooden steps to the landing, making sure he was behind me. My heart was thumping. Before I could knock, the door was thrown open with a bellow of bad temper.

"You again! Can't you people read a fucking *No Trespassing* sign? You think I put it up for the fucking fun of it?" His vocabulary remained stuck on a few choice words.

The open front door emitted a stench of foul body odor and beer mixed with another smell that wrinkled my nose. My memory had served me well. He was just as big, ugly, and mean as I remembered...maybe more so.

"I want to talk to Tiffany," I said, determined not to leave until I spoke with her.

"You do, do you? Well, she damned well ain't around, so the two of you get the hell out of here."

I hung in there. "Her car is here."

"So what? You think she can't walk or ride the hog?"

I could feel my temper rising. Just who the hell did he think he was? "I happen to know for a fact that she won't get on a motorcycle. Now we want to speak to Tiffany, and we're not leaving until we do."

"Who gives a double shit what you want? I'm telling you for the last time, Tiffany ain't here. You're trespassing, and you got one minute to get off this goddamned property." He abruptly slammed the door in my face. For the second time.

"I don't believe you," I shouted, my brain shifting into high gear with the sudden recognition of what else I had smelled. "Tiffany! Tiffany!" I kicked the screen door in frustration.

Satterwhite shook my arm. "If she doesn't want to come out, you can't make her. Now, let's go."

I jerked my arm away. "You don't understand. She's in there. I can smell..."

Both doors were thrown open again with violence. "I'm gonna stomp the living shit out of both of you—starting with you, bitch—if you don't get the fuck out of my face." He made a quick lunge in my direction and grabbed me by the wrist with a dirty hand as big as a bear trap. I would have another nasty bruise to add to my collection, assuming he didn't break my wrist first. Or my neck.

"Let go," I said coldly.

His grip intensified. "I gave you your chance to leave, you two-bit bitch. Now you're gonna be sorry you didn't." He raised a huge hand.

I had an instant of pure terror before Satterwhite interrupted. "That's enough," he said, gun drawn and pointed. "Now let her go and move slowly toward the rail. No one has to get hurt here."

"Who the fuck are you?" Dog said.

"FBI. I said let her go and back away."

My arm was abruptly free.

"FBI? What the hell...?" he roared.

Satterwhite said, "Davenport, get down the stairs and in

the car."

"But..."

"Now!"

My mouth dry, I inched around the two of them, expecting Motorcycle Man to lunge again at any second.

As soon as I opened the car door, Satterwhite said to Dog, "Just go back in the trailer. We're not going to have any more trouble here."

"Oh, yeah? That's all the fuck you know."

There was iron in Satterwhite's voice. "We can do this with a bullet in the groin and an assault charge against you, or we can do it peacefully and let you sober up on your own. Your choice."

"You ain't gonna shoot." Dog's eyes were narrow little slits of rattlesnake venom.

"Oh, no? Davenport, call 911 and tell them an FBI agent needs assistance. And tell them to send an ambulance."

As I reached in the car for the phone, I heard the stomp of heavy boots. The screen door crashed back against the wall as the prince of darkness snarled a last warning on his way inside.

"You better get the fuck out of this yard in a damned big hurry." He slammed the door.

As soon as Satterwhite was in the car with the motor started I said, "She's in there; I smelled blood."

"What the hell is the matter with you? Didn't anybody ever teach you not to goad a pissed-off drunk? If I hadn't been there, you would have had the crap beat out of you and maybe worse." His mouth was set in a tight line as he put the

Buick in reverse and began backing up. "Besides, who could smell anything except him? Your imagination is running away with you."

"No, that's not all of it," I ignored his chauvinistic comments. "Call it intuition, imagination, whatever you want. I think he's our man from Randolph's cottage; my nose will all but swear to it, and..."

"Your nose? Isn't it enough that I drew my gun on the man, ready to shoot him for laying a hand on you? Now you try to tell me that, above the reek of God knows what kind of body stench and last month's fish in his beard, your nose tells you he beat up an old man on Tuesday? I'm supposed to shoot him to search the trailer because your *nose* knows?"

"Damn it, don't get sarcastic with me." I folded my arms. "She's in there. I don't care how unreasonable it sounds."

He let his breath out in a huff, his foot jammed the brake. "Let me explain something to you," he said with tooth-grinding patience. "The FBI has no jurisdiction here..."

"Don't patronize me. I know that."

"Just shut up. You seem to have forgotten that we ignored a clear *No Trespassing* sign. Even if the sheriff were dumb enough to respond to your call, just what kind of probable cause would they have to enter the trailer? Your *nose*? Try getting a warrant for that. Do you have any concept of the laughing contest deputies would have once they got a whiff of this guy?"

"I'll take my chances; I've been laughed at before." *And can be as bloody stubborn as the next person.* "So, who makes the call, you or me?"

He heaved a sigh. "You will, by heaven. And anything that comes of this is on your head."

"Just hand me the damned cell phone then."

He picked it up from the left side of the dash and froze. I followed his gaze. Our Hell's Angel was standing in the open screen door, raising what appeared to be a double-barreled shotgun.

"Ah, shit," Satterwhite said in disgust, and threw himself sideways on top of me, just as the gun went off with a sound like a large cannon. The front windshield exploded in a million fragments.

Chapter Twenty-three

To paraphrase an old saying, *he who runs away, lives to fight another day.* And run we did, backwards, as fast as the Buick could tear us out of the yard and down the driveway, ripping into wax myrtles, old camellias, and blackberry brambles as we went. Even the FBI isn't stupid.

I estimated the driveway was fifty yards long, and I hunkered down for every one of them. We slid to a stop halfway into Mason's Landing Road. Satterwhite did a lightning-fast three point turn before he backed onto the unpaved surface of the driveway, facing the road.

I thought he was returning to the trailer and sat upright in my seat. "Are you out of your mind? Where are you going?"

Instead of answering, he stopped the car and got out. Taking up a stance behind the open door, he leveled his gun across the top of the window frame pointing straight down the driveway.

"Find the phone," he said. "Try 911 again and tell them shots have been fired. And keep your head down."

"Are you crazy?"

"We might not have all day, Davenport."

The phone was under my feet, along with my purse that had spilled all over the floorboard. My heart still hammering in my ears, I dialed 911 and gave our location, barely able to hear the dispatcher's questions, much less give answers. My explanation must have been lucid enough because she told me not to hang up and, unbelievably, put me on hold.

I waited. And watched Satterwhite. Who himself waited and watched down the tunnel of rag-tag hedges. The silence was terrible, not even birdsong or squirrel chatter. Nothing moved that I could see, and the trailer itself was out of our range of vision.

The seconds dragged. Where was the dispatcher? Forget the dispatcher. Where the hell was Dog Fowler with his shotgun? We waited more seconds.

Not being able to see was the worst of all. I forced my head high enough to peer cautiously through the serrated hole that once was the passenger window. Nothing, although I could see the dirty rear end of the pickup truck still parked behind the trailer. In the distance beyond the shade of tall pines, sunlight shimmered on water near the south end of Figure Eight Island.

"Don't do that," Satterwhite said in a quiet voice. "You could get your head blown across the road. Is that what you want?"

"What I want," I hissed, "is to get the hell out of here."

"Then maybe you should communicate with the dispatcher."

"What?"

"The phone," he said.

I put it to my ear in time to hear an urgent voice. "Ma'am, are you still there?"

"Yes, I'm here."

"Don't hang up the phone, now. Stay with me till help arrives. Sheriff Council has been notified, and a deputy is two minutes out of your range. Ma'am, do you still have the armed perpetrator in view?"

Armed maniac was more like it.

"He is not in my sight, but I have no reason to believe the situation has changed."

"Have you taken precautionary measures to stay out of his line of fire?"

"That's a matter of opinion," I said.

"Ma'am?"

"We are parked at the entrance to the driveway, fifty yards away." Was the whole damned world destined to call me ma'am?

What was I doing there, a sitting goose for some drunken idiot with a shotgun? We had no way of knowing where he was. He could be running as fast has his boozy legs could carry him or barricaded in the trailer. He could be hiding in the bushes along the drive, just waiting for one of us to stick a nose out. Even now, he might be working his way behind us.

It was so quiet, I could hear the wind humming in the pines.

"Ma'am, are you there?"

"Still here," I said. "Unfortunately."

"Stay on the line, please."

I've never been especially brave. And I have seen first-hand what heavy firepower can do to the human body.

Satterwhite had protection for his mid-section behind the car door, but none at all for his head or his lower legs. No doubt he was confident he would get off the first shot, but the odds weren't anywhere near good enough for me. I wondered if I should remind him that he could possibly miss, and that shotguns seldom do, especially at close range. Anything that went wrong would leave me face to face with Mr. Personality and his twin barrels.

At least I was still dressed for a funeral.

"Satterwhite?" I said.

"Now is not a good time for a heart-to-heart talk, Davenport."

"I don't want to chat. I want to leave. *Like now!*"

"Sorry. You should have thought of that when you picked a fight with a sore-headed bear. The only way you'll get out of here before the sheriff arrives is to walk, and I can't say I advise it. He could be anywhere."

"Tell me about it," I said, heavy on the sarcasm. "And you without eyes in the back of your head."

"Enough," he said. "You can pick a fight later, but for now, don't distract me, please."

Even I could see the wisdom in that, so I kept my head down and tried to think about other things—cheerful things—like whether Tiffany was bleeding to death in the trailer or whether Satterwhite would get his head shot off.

I am such a coward.

Chapter Twenty-four

A lone deputy pulled around the corner, almost ramming us, and came to a gravel-throwing stop mere inches from the Buick's front bumper. He was blocking our escape from the drive, not such a keen idea if we needed to leave in a big hurry, but he had no way of knowing who was who in this fracas. Before his siren died away, he was out of the car with his gun aimed at Satterwhite.

"Sir," he commanded, "put the gun down."

I estimated his age and neck size both around thirty, old enough and tough enough to carry through on anything he started. I thought the *sir* was a nice polite touch.

"Hell and damnation!" said Satterwhite without turning his head. "Didn't they tell you there was an FBI agent on the scene?"

"Yes, sir, but I'll need to see your identification."

"Well then, we may just have a problem besides the son-of-a- bitch with a shotgun, who isn't going to be cowed by either one of us. My badge is not on me, deputy, but Sheriff Council is on his way. He'll vouch for me—Agent Ben Satterwhite out of the Charlotte office, and I'm not taking my eyes off this driveway. I suggest you watch behind you."

This had no effect on the deputy. "Just keep your hands where they are. Do you have any other identification?"

"My driver's license. The girl will bring it to you."

"Me?" I said, reluctant to leave the car. The *girl* comment would be avenged at the first opportunity.

Satterwhite snapped, "Just get the damned wallet out of my back pocket and hand it to him. Can't you see we have a situation here? You want me to get shot?"

"I don't think you want me answer that," I said, sliding across to the driver's side, trying to hunker down at the same time. "Which pocket? I'm only doing this once."

"The right one, Davenport, and try to behave yourself."

I ran my hand into the pocket, warm from his body heat, and pulled out the wallet. You wouldn't believe me if I told you that at that time, in that place, under what any sane person would have called less-than-ideal circumstances, my fingers tingled.

"Now pull out the driver's license."

I did as I was told.

"Ma'am," the deputy said, "will you step out of the car please, keeping both hands where I can see them, and bring me the license?"

"Well, why the hell not?" I muttered under my breath. "Seeing as how I'm wearing a full set of body armor."

Satterwhite said, "What was that, Davenport?"

"Just shut up and keep your eyes peeled," I said. "The *girl* is on her way."

I took a deep breath and got out of the car, feeling exposed and unprotected, a duck at a dove shoot, even with two of America's finest on the scene. I walked the ten feet on unsteady legs and held out the license.

"Hands on the hood, please."

Sighing, I did as I was told, looking over my shoulder all the while.

In the silence, I heard the sudden ear-splitting roar of an outboard motor from the rear yard. It spluttered and died, then revved to life again.

Satterwhite yelled, "He's getting away," and took off at a run down the driveway looking left and right as he went.

Caught off guard, the deputy faltered. His gun wavered back and forth between us before settling on Satterwhite's back. Surely to God he wouldn't shoot.

"Help him," I said quickly. "He's a friend of Stan Council's, and he'll have your job if you screw up."

Who knows what he read in my face, but he hesitated only a fraction of a second longer before sprinting down the drive in Satterwhite's footsteps.

Left on my own, I made a heedless, ill-considered, bee-line for the trailer, stumbling on the stairs before wrenching open the front door. I walked into the chilly, dim interior.

Tiffany was in the only bedroom, laid out on an old chenille bedspread covered with dark smears that I didn't want to think about. At least I assumed it was Tiffany. The room was so dim it bordered on dark twilight. The lamp switch gave me nothing but useless clicks. It could have been anybody's face, swollen and bruised almost black, and caked with dried blood that had run into her hair and eyes.

The stench was unbelievable.

This was what I had gotten a whiff of, the minute Dog first opened the door—blood and urine and death all rolled into one putrid odor. Like Bitsy, like Eddie, like Daniel. I swallowed hard.

A small sound, like a half-dead kitten's mewing, came from the bed. Dear God, I thought, she couldn't be alive. I went closer.

"Tiffany?"

She flinched, but made no further movement. I leaned over her.

Both eyes were swollen to tiny slits, and from the odd angle of her jaw, I presumed it was broken. There was no way to tell how long she had been there. My guess was a couple of days, possibly right after I had seen her last. It was more than likely that Dog had thought she was dead.

I said, "Tiffany, can you hear me? It's Carroll Davenport. Don't try to talk. Just listen. I want you to understand that Dog is gone, that there's a deputy and an FBI agent outside. You're safe now. Do you hear me? You're safe, and I'm going to phone for an ambulance. Just hang on a little bit longer."

I opened a window shade in the bedroom and one in the wrecked kitchen where I finally found the phone. There was no dial tone, which meant I would need to go back to the car.

I picked my way around the debris of the living room. The front door had swung shut, and it was even darker there. To reach the blind I would have needed to climb over the upturned sofa and huge black bags of what smelled like rancid garbage. An empty pizza box lay on top of it all, as if some animal had used the trash pile for a coffee table. My hand was on the front doorknob when a cold muzzle pressed against the side of my head.

I almost had heart failure. Satterwhite had gotten it wrong. Dog had never left, and it had not occurred to me that someone other than Tiffany might still be in the house. My scalp crawled at the thought of what Dog might do. My knees buckled.

"Don't move," said a voice.

A split second passed before I recognized who it was. I could have killed him on the spot with my bare hands.

"You!"

Satterwhite lowered the gun and said between gritted teeth, "Are you out of your fucking mind or do you just have a death wish? What if we'd been wrong in thinking he was leaving and you had walked straight into his hands? I could have shot you myself, you stupid little fool. How would I know you would be dumb enough to run for the trailer as soon as my back was turned? No wonder Stan is worried sick about you. Don't you *ever* stop to think?" Through the tirade his voice had gotten steadily louder.

"That's enough," I said.

"Enough? I don't think it *is* enough, by God."

"Satterwhite, the last time I checked," I said slowly, so he would be sure and understand, "I was not your goddamned property."

"Thank your lucky stars you aren't or I'd be sorely tempted to lock you in the nearest closet every time I left the house."

"Well, hurrah, hurrah! Isn't it nice to know we won't *ever* have that little problem?"

His breathing filled the tiny room.

I took a step backward and came up against the wall.

"When we catch him," he grated, "I'm going to person-ally hand you over to this guy."

I searched for a smart-ass quip and couldn't find one as silence stretched the dimness. Finally, I managed, "Then for now, maybe we could do something helpful. Like call an ambulance for Tiffany. Only if you've finished, of course."

He took a half-step in my direction, gritted something under his breath, and spun toward the bedroom.

I didn't move.

"Jesus!" He was back in a matter of seconds. "Stay with her. And get some light in here."

"And your little dog, too," I said, as he slammed the screen door behind him.

I raised another shade and went back to Tiffany. "Help is on the way," I promised, powerless to do anything but keep her company. I was afraid to touch her. Thick dried blood was caked around her mouth, and something about her still-ness and the way her arms were folded across her midsection made me think of internal injuries.

Weeks from now, someone other than me would have to tell her about Duane.

She struggled to say something, able to open her lips only a sliver.

"Don't try to talk," I said. "An ambulance is on its way, and the bastard who did this is gone. All you have to worry about now is getting well."

Tiffany raised her head an inch off the filthy pillow, agi-tated, trying to speak. I leaned closer.

"How..." she whispered, before her head fell back.

"How? I don't know, Tiffany...I really don't. But they'll catch him, I promise you. And if I can manage it, Dog will never get the chance to do this to another woman again."

"How..." she repeated, and closed her eyes.

Satterwhite and the deputy came back and waited with me. In a little while, Satterwhite laid his hand lightly on the back of my neck.

Chapter Twenty-five

If someone had paid me a hundred dollars for every time I've been wrong in my life, the total amount could have supported the Oxford Orphanage, even without Daniel's insurance money. So I was wrong when I assumed Satterwhite to be the kind of man who would sulk through the night and all the next day. Instead, he slept in the guest room and rose before dawn to make coffee and check on Tiffany's condition.

Or to make sure I didn't sneak out again.

In a civilized manner, we grunted our good-mornings, swapping newspaper sections like an old married couple until the coffeepot was empty. He took cream with two teaspoons of sugar, the same way I did lately, and ate raisin bran with canned milk like a man accustomed to living alone. While shaving, he had nicked a small place along his right jaw, and at six forty-five in the morning, it must have been the measure of my widow's desperation that made him look sleepy-eyed and sexy.

He also looked as if he, too, had slept with one ear alert to every bump, creak or clunk throughout the night. At some point during my tossing and turning, I had gotten over being pissed and decided that anyone who encountered, in his daily profession, the kind of routine violence I'd been seeing lately deserved more respect than they were getting from me. Perhaps even a little more cooperation.

"Listen, Satterwhite..." I began.

"Forget it," he said, without lowering the newspaper between us.

"You have no idea what I was going to say."

"Sure, I do. You were going to apologize for being peabrained and stupid yesterday."

"Apologize? You must be kidding, right?" My good intentions were fast being swept out with the tide.

"Then what?"

"Maybe," I said through my teeth, "I was going to say that I like you better when you aren't being such an egotistical, overbearing son of a..."

He eased the newspaper down just far enough to give me a look over the top edge. "Careful, Davenport, it's a new day. Don't spoil my customary good humor."

"OK, then help me figure out what Eddie, Dennis, Bitsy and Duane had in common that would get them all killed. Is Dog Fowler the connection, and if so, why? I keep thinking about Tiffany asking, '*How*?' There's no way to explain *how* one human being—and I admit it seems a real stretch to use that term with Dog—could do to another what he did to Tiffany."

He ticked through his fingers. "A broken jaw, concussion, dislocated shoulder, three cracked ribs, and a punctured lung. He won't be qualifying for Man of the Year."

I remembered the short moments I had been in Dog Fowler's grasp. If Satterwhite hadn't been with me, I could have wound up in the emergency room with Tiffany—or worse. I shivered.

"It has to be something they all knew," I said.

"Don't leave out yourself and Alex."

"And Randolph," I added.

He nodded. "That's three more people who *could* be dead. You may all know something that you don't think is important."

"I keep telling you, I don't know anything. I've racked my brain and keep coming up with zero, nada, nothing."

"Think harder."

"Damn it," I said. "It's too early to play catch-the-killers. We don't have anything to go on except the possibility of a drug link with Dennis. Mind you, I'm still inclined to believe Eddie was just in the wrong place at the wrong time."

"And Duane? What about drugs on his part?"

I gave the possibility some thought. "Maybe. I don't think so, but it's possible. He had plenty of opportunity for exposure at Barnacle Bill's, but he would have been out on his backside in a hurry if Eddie had spotted any kind of drug use on the job."

"Not all pushers are users," he pointed out.

"But what would Duane have done with the money? He lived from paycheck to paycheck, drove a beat up old Harley, and took pride in not being establishment enough to save for a rainy day. He didn't even own a car, and you saw the trailer he rented. All it has going for it is a great view."

"Location, location," he pointed out. "On the waterway...drugs brought in at night. Easy as pie. You said it yourself."

"Eddie would have guessed."

Satterwhite raised his eyebrows. "Or been a part of it."

"No," I said. "You just didn't know him."

He drummed his fingers on the table. "Eddie was murdered on your property. If I were the killer, my guess would be that Eddie was coming to you, because you already knew whatever Eddie knew."

My head was spinning.

He said, "There's another possibility you have to consider."

"Why do I think I don't want to hear this?"

"That Jinks and Davis also knew. And that Eddie was heading for Randolph's cottage."

"Now you've gone beyond ridiculous. Davis is just a kid and Randolph seventy-five."

Satterwhite pointed out, "Twelve year-old pushers are arrested three-hundred and sixty-five days a year in every major city in the country. Even the senior set has gotten in on the act. Who's going to suspect great-grandpa in his souvenir Hawaiian shirt?"

"Back up the boat," I said, walking to the sink. "You've gone way, way off track."

"All right, let's try it from another direction. Start with Bitsy instead of the others. Start with Bitsy's spouse, since he's the most probable suspect."

"George? I don't think so. He's head of a successful pharmaceutical research company. And he's the most mild-mannered..." My voice trailed off.

Satterwhite said, "What is it?"

"Eddie told Alex that Richard Howe was sleeping with Bitsy."

"Interesting," he said.

"Not really. There are hundreds of other women in town who've been there and done that, both married and unmarried. Our dear mayor doesn't seem to care."

"But not you?"

I glared at him. "He isn't my type."

Satterwhite laughed. "Don't look so insulted. What is your type? Just for the record, of course."

I could give as good as I got. I looked him square in the eye. "If I said *you are*, you'd run like a scared rabbit to catch the next flight back to Charlotte."

Where in the hell had that come from?

Silence stretched out while he folded the sports section with extraordinary care. The sun was just breaking over Rich Inlet, painting the clouds red and the marsh grass pink.

My face was burning. I was eight feet away from him and having trouble breathing.

He looked up, his face unreadable. "Davenport, you're a piece of work."

"Sorry," I fumbled. "It was meant as a joke. I didn't intend..."

"Better leave it, before you get in any deeper."

Mortified, I scraped back my chair. It seemed like an excellent time to leave the room and get dressed. I was saved more embarrassment by the ringing of the doorbell.

He caught me by the wrist as I passed, dropping it as

soon as I resisted. "You might be surprised," he said.

Jinks was at the door. He took one look at my house-coat, my red cheeks, and Satterwhite grinning behind me. Why wouldn't he jump to all the wrong conclusions?

"Davis is gone," he said.

Chapter Twenty-six

For the next six hours, we called everywhere we could think of that a fifteen-year-old, not blessed with the best judgement anyway, might decide to hide. In my mind I held a nightmarish fear that Davis's choice would be a one-way ticket out of state, where he could vanish into the subculture of runaways.

To make matters worse, at one-thirty in the afternoon, we were graced with a visit from Detective Paige, also searching for Davis. He stood on the front porch with an unmistakable smirk on his official face, and informed us that he had talked to Davis by phone at seven-thirty the night before.

"What about?" I said, one hand on the door. He wasn't putting an ugly boot over my doorstep without good reason, and I couldn't think of one short of the opportunity to feed him arsenic. If I had used the peephole, I might not have opened the door at all.

Paige said, "About coming in for questioning this morning. He didn't show up. That tells me he's afraid of something. If he lied about being home on Sunday night, he's probably lying about other things, too—like what he knows about the murders."

"Assuming he knows anything at all," Jinks said.

Paige snorted. "He knows. Else he wouldn't be running."

I hedged. "Maybe he isn't running. He may have just neglected to tell Jinks where he was going. You know how teenagers are."

"I do for a fact. These days they commit the same crimes as thirty-year-olds, and some a whole lot worse. I trust I don't have to explain that you're not doing yourself any favors by hiding him. Accessory to murder and concealing a fugitive are serious offenses. You'd best be remembering that little detail."

Satterwhite said, "Has Davis been charged with something we should know about, Detective?"

"Not yet, but it looks like it may come down to that. We're close—real close."

Exasperated, I said, "About as close as Mars is to Pluto. You're so far off base I'm surprised you manage to get yourself to work every morning. He's just a kid, for God's sake." How often had I said that lately?

Paige's look was sour. "You'd better watch your mouth with me, Ms. Davenport. I've had about all I'm going to take of your uncooperative tongue."

"*Really?*" I said, letting the word hang in the air with some derision of my own.

His eyes narrowed to choleric little slits. "When his fingerprints match up with those in Mason's boat, you're all going to be singing a different tune about this worthless little nigger."

I hadn't heard the word in a long time.

Jinks and Satterwhite stood up at the same time. My hand tightened on the doorknob.

"Now, enough is enough," I said, my blood racing to a fast boil. "No doubt you'll be back to search this place, too, if and when you have an actual warrant. Until then, Detective Paige, I'm going to have to ask you to leave this property and stay away until you've had a mental health check."

His jaw clenched. "Let me remind you that this property is a goddamned crime scene."

"Not the whole property, so I'll thank you to keep your presence confined to the actual scene and not my house." I glanced at Satterwhite, who gave a slight nod of confirmation. That, more than anything, was Paige's undoing.

His face turned redder. "Now, hold it just a goddamn minute..."

"Good day, Detective Paige," I said and shut the door in his face.

I took a deep breath, turned away from the door, and caught one of those maddening, eyebrow-raised male looks between Jinks and Satterwhite. I didn't get it. Six hours before, they had been bristling at each other like male dogs.

"What?" I said.

Jinks cleared his throat once or twice. "Well, the guy appears to have, excuse me, shit for brains, but maybe—just maybe—you shouldn't have done that."

"Paige is a supercilious pig, and I don't mean a law enforcement officer. Neither of you should look so frigging superior. He could be accusing you next, or Gran and Lucille. There's no telling with him. And you," I turned on Satterwhite because he looked like he was trying hard not to laugh, "don't you dare make a single macho statement."

He raised both hands with a shrug. "Not me. I'm just a bit player in this Southern comedy. For the record, though, I'd just like it to be generally recognized that you do have a way with words."

"Just shut up," I snapped.

"Yes, ma'am," they said in unison.

Chapter Twenty-seven

Something picked at the back of my brain, just out of reach, making my skin crawl with an anxiety that in the past had often advised me when something undesirable might be about to happen. As often as not, nothing did, but I had learned to listen with a cautious ear. This time I assumed it had to do with our missing Davis.

We were taking it for granted that he had run away. It was so like him to behave foolishly that it was hard to consider another possibility. But what if he hadn't run away? What if the actual circumstances were different—and even worse?

To be on the safe side, I phoned Alex, who said she and Tully were on their way to tea with Gran and would stay for dinner.

"Be careful," I said. "I've got one of those feelings."

She was silent for a moment before answering. "I lost a husband and a baby all in the same week. What else can be as bad?"

I said, "Just be extra careful, that's all." And I wanted to blurt out, *remember, bad things happen in threes.* But, of course, I couldn't.

"You worry too much," she said. "Besides, Goldie and Valentine will be with us. Tully promised him your grandmother's chocolate cake."

I relaxed a little.

Next on my list was Lucille.

She was snappish and out of breath. "I can't talk now. What do you mean, is your grandmother all right? Of course she is. Why am I breathing hard? Because I'm rushing around getting everything ready for dinner ahead of time so I can pick up Randolph from the hospital. We wanted to bring him home this morning, but he decided to wait until tomorrow. Now he's changed his mind, if you can believe it, and all my scheduling has been thrown out of kilter. It doesn't *help* that I have to keep answering the telephone."

"I hear you're having chocolate cake for tea. That could be the reason Randolph changed his plans."

"My land," she said. "News travels fast. Now what do you want, please? I don't have all day."

"I wanted to know if you had heard from Davis yet."

"Didn't you just call me about that same thing not two hours ago? If he does show up, I'm liable to switch his legs good for worrying everybody, and yours too if you call me again before dinner."

I hung up with that image in my head, since Davis was twice her size already. In spite of her cantankerous nature, I'd never known her to lay a hand or a switch on any child, not even me, and God knows, I had needed it. With Lucille, though, you could never be entirely certain about anything.

Satterwhite was on the phone with his office. From the tic in his jaw, I assumed it was Lorna the witch who could make grown men cringe, and tried not to listen. Whatever she was saying was eliciting chilled responses from his end. Jinks seemed determined to wear the polyurethane off the wooden kitchen floor trying to think of people who would know the whereabouts of our missing juvenile. He said, "Davis will panic and do something stupid. You can bet the bank on it. But we can't let Paige find him first and throw him in jail."

I said, "You've been the one closest to him since he turned into a two-headed chameleon, Jinks. Can't you think of anywhere he might be? Is there even a small possibility he would be at his mother's?"

"Not a chance in hell!"

"Who, then? Does he have a girlfriend? He has to be *somewhere*."

Jinks shook his head. "As far as I can tell, he's still kind of shy around girls. Not that he doesn't notice, but I've never heard him mention any one girl in particular."

Satterwhite was off the phone and watching, his eyes moving back and forth between us, like a cat at a tennis match. "What about his lawyer?"

I stopped in mid-motion. "Good thinking, but Bill Lee is still in Japan with the governor's trade delegation. If he'd been here to talk to Davis, we might not be having to search the whole damn county."

"Well then," Jinks said, "what about the renovation?"

I said, "We can try, but he must know that would be one of the first places we'd look."

Jinks shrugged. "Like I said, he's young and not real hung up on considering long-term consequences. Could be he wants to be found."

I said, "But not stupid enough to be involved with murder, is he, Jinks?"

He was more than irritated. "Hell, no! You can put that idea right out of your head. Davis has had a tough little life so far, but that overnight stint in jail made an impression. I'll bet you a dollar he hasn't told you that two of his best friends recently joined a gang in Brunswick County."

"Oh, God. You don't think..."

He shook his head, defensive. "Davis said no way, and I believe him. You should, too. There's a lot you don't know about him lately. For instance, do you have a clue that he thinks he wants to go to college, maybe engineering or pre-med?"

"Are you sure we're still talking about Davis here?" I said. "He'd have to get back into high school first, wouldn't he?"

There was a real anger in the look Jinks shot me. "Where the hell have you been? Where were you when his buddies gave him a hard time because he wouldn't join the gang? You think that was more than a little pressure on the kid? Their first weekend initiation they decided to hot-wire a car and totaled a sixty-thousand dollar BMW. They're sitting in a cell right now because they can't afford bail. Davis could have been with them, but he wasn't, and he *won't* be in the future, either. You know why?"

"Why?" I asked, feeling like a disloyal, slimy, harbor rat of a friend, and wondering what I had done to make such a loveable kid stop communicating with me almost overnight. Never mind that I had done the same thing to my father and Gran, and then married Daniel in spite of all their warnings that I was making a huge mistake. But that was another story.

Jinks went on, "Because, and I'm quoting here, *They are the first real family I ever had and I'm not gonna let them down again.* Can you guess who he was talking about?"

"Randolph," I said, "and Lucille and Grandmother."

"And you and Eddie and me," Jinks finished.

"You'll have me crying in a minute."

"Serves you right," he said.

"I admit it. I'm rotten family."

"Damn straight you are. Don't you think so, Satterwhite?"

"Whoa!" he said. "I'm just a guy on medical leave, remember? I never stick my nose in family fights, but it might occur to you that you ought to be worried about more than jail. Don't forget Davis may know something that could connect four murders, and we aren't likely to find him like this, are we? It seems to me that the two of you ought to listen to what you're saying."

I turned toward him. "The question is what are *you* saying?"

Satterwhite held up three fingers. "Randolph, Lucille, and your grandmother."

"He's right," said Jinks. "I'm betting that Lucille knows."

I shook my head. "She says not, and Davis would never disappear without checking on Randolph first. I say our best chance would be to start at the hospital and work our way downtown."

The phone rang and Satterwhite picked it up. After listening for a moment, he passed it to me.

"Someone named Sam," he said.

I took the phone and turned my back, stretching the twelve-foot cord as far as it would go. "Good morning, Sam."

"I have an interesting piece of information for you that may be of some assistance. You are not alone, I presume?"

I laughed. "You presume correctly. The room has more men than I quite know what to do with, Sam, one of whom is an FBI agent."

"Ah," he said. "That explains the frosty silence."

"Don't worry about it. He's on medical leave and harmless as a lamb. Tell me about your information."

"My sources in your city tell me that the Cavenaugh brothers have been active in Brunswick County for the last several years. If my map is correct, that is the county immediately to your south, across the river." He paused.

"Yes," I said. "And what else do they tell you?"

"That fish trucks are often seen coming and going during night hours at a certain company in Wilmington."

"Fish trucks?"

Sam said. "I see you are confused. Perhaps I should explain that the Cavenaugh brothers are not the most reputable members of your community. And that their goods are delivered via ingenuous means to your coast."

"What kind of goods, Sam?"

"Cocaine, heroin, whatever is most in demand at the moment."

"I see. Would you know the name of this company? And does it have anything to do with my cousin's death?"

"As for your second question, I cannot be sure. But the answer to the first is Anderson Pharmaceutical Research."

For a moment I didn't know what to say.

"Carroll, are you there?" Sam said.

"Just how reliable are these sources?"

"Extremely," he said. "Or they would not be in my employment."

I was thinking hard. "Am I free to use this information?"

"For the charming Cavenaugh brothers, you may make any use of it you want, so long as you do not connect it with my name. Especially not to your FBI agent. You should also be careful about connecting your own name. I would suggest you repeat this conversation to your very capable Sheriff Council, who will know how to correct the problem. He is the only one to whom you should mention my name."

"You sound like you know him," I said.

"By reputation and one conversation only, I assure you, although it was quite some time ago, but I was impressed with his regard for you."

Suspicious, I said, "Eight years ago?"

Sam chuckled. "That sounds approximately correct. You don't think I would have let my only son marry someone unsuitable in this day and age?"

"You scoundrel," I said. "Those are almost the exact words that my grandmother used."

Sam said, "Please give that delightful lady my best regards. Now, I have talked long enough. Your FBI agent will be more than a little confused."

"Thank you, Sam. And give my love to Isabella."

When I disconnected, Satterwhite said, "That was Sam Vitelli?"

I studied the deep scowl that had been in evidence since he handed over the phone. "Kindly wipe that virtuous, disapproving look off your face. He gave me some important information to pass on to Stan."

"But not to me?"

"No," I said. "You'll find out soon enough, I expect, but I want you to promise not to link my name or Sam's to the information. When this is all over, I don't need any two-bit hoods in my life."

"What is Vitelli, if not a hood?"

"I'll be straight with you. I don't know."

"Or care."

"Of course I care. But it's complicated, and I don't know you well enough to explain."

Jinks said, "I need to get rolling if I'm going to find Davis before dark. We need to split up. I'll check the Forest Hills house, his mother's, and go by the jail to see if they'll let me talk to his friends. You can do the hospital and your grandmother."

"More good thinking." I turned to Satterwhite. "You don't have to come, you know."

He got to his feet. "You're wrong. Stan will kill me if I let you out of my sight again. Besides, I'm waiting for the opportunity to show you what *harmless as a lamb* means."

It was a deadpan comment. No twinkle of the eye, no smirk of amusement. Now how was I supposed to interpret that?

Another look from Jinks.

"Then, let's do it," I said. "Give me a couple of minutes

to grab my cell phone and a jacket."

Sixty seconds tops, I swear, was all I took. But it was time enough for *the boys* to get into mischief. I was halfway back down the hallway when I heard the sounds of scuffling and breaking glass.

Satterwhite had a complete stranger in a hammerlock, up against the front door, patting him down.

"What in heaven...?" I said.

Satterwhite said, "We found him skulking outside the front door with a camera."

"No, I wasn't," the stranger said. Panic with a Central American accent. "I come to see Miss Davenport."

He was not quite my height, dark-haired, dressed in a white shirt, tie, and khaki Dockers, with brand new athletic shoes on his feet. Not your everyday criminal dress code. Jinks pulled a small pocketknife from the right side of his trousers and tossed it onto the side table. The man struggled, and Satterwhite applied enough pressure to make him squeal in fright.

"Let him go," I said. "I think I know who he is. You work at the Yacht Club on Figure Eight Island, don't you?"

Satterwhite released him, and the man backed warily against the closed door.

"Leon send me," he said in a panicky voice.

"Leon who?" Satterwhite took a threatening step toward him. I placed a hand on his arm.

"The bartender at the Club," I said. "Did you leave a message on my answering machine? Are you Ramon?"

His relief was pitiful. The words came pouring out. "Yes,

yes. Leon, he say bring you Mr. Eddie's camera after work last night, but nobody is home so I try again this afternoon. Please...I don't want no trouble. I have a wife and two babies."

"Shit!" Jinks said.

I said slowly, "These two men are watching out for me...after Mr. Eddie. *Comprende?*" I gave him back his pocketknife. "If they apologize for bad manners, will you tell me when you last saw Mr. Eddie?"

Ramon threw a jittery look at Jinks and Satterwhite, who must have seemed less threatening, but I could read in his eyes that he would give a lot for the courage to bolt and run. He swallowed. "Sunday night at the Club. He there when we close. He say he go by boat and too much to drink so maybe he fall in the water, and please will I put the camera in a locker for the night?"

"Did he leave with anyone?" I said.

"If he did, I did not see it. He talk with Mr. Anderson and Leon say the man who drown, and then he leave."

"Mason?"

He shrugged. "I do not know his name. He argue with Mr. Anderson."

I found that interesting, and said, "Did you see Eddie talk with anyone else?"

"Sure. Everybody know Mr. Eddie."

Satterwhite interrupted. "Did he talk to Anderson?"

Ramon wiggled his fingers, imitating chatter. "Everybody at that table talk and drink, talk and drink."

I said, "Who else was at that table? Mr. Anderson's wife?"

"Yes, she very much making eyes with Mr. Eddie and the mayor."

Eddie might not have been off the mark about Bitsy and Richard's affair, but surely he wouldn't have the nerve to carry on in front of George Anderson. Ah, but he didn't say that. He said Bitsy was making eyes.

"Did they all leave together, Ramon?" I said.

"No. Mr. Eddie go out the back way to the boats. The others leave by the front door, I think."

"Who left first?" asked Satterwhite.

Ramon appeared confused. "Mr. Anderson, I think. A very long time before anyone else."

I had to ask. "With Mrs. Anderson?"

"Oh, no. She stay and drink at the bar." Ramon glanced at his watch. "Leon say I must be there by three o'clock."

I took a fifty-dollar bill out of my wallet and tucked it in his shirt pocket.

He shook his head and handed it back. "Mr. Eddie always happy to see me. Not like some people."

"For the babies," I said.

Ramon nodded once and put the money in his pocket, smiling for the first time. "For the babies."

Chapter Twenty-eight

We opened Eddie's camera as soon as Ramon left, expecting to find it loaded with film. Instead, it was empty.

"Why," I said, "would he have the camera with him and ask Ramon to lock it away? Why take it into the clubhouse in the first place if it was useless?"

Satterwhite turned the camera in his hands. "Lots of reasons. Sometimes a camera just hangs around your neck, forgotten until it's inconvenient. Or could be he didn't want it stolen."

"Does it look like the kind of camera someone would steal? That's why he carried this old one under the front seat of his truck, and you *know* what the inside of a contractor's truck looks like. Also, remember it was after dark when he arrived at the club." The camera, still in good condition after twenty-some years, was a beat-up Yashica in a leather case so worn it was literally falling apart. No self-respecting thief would have touched it. A pawn shop would have laughed.

"He may have removed the film at the Club," Satterwhite said. "Or given it to someone."

"Or had it on him."

"That, too," he said. "I'll check with Stan when..."

I finished for him. "When you report in?"

Would I never learn to watch my tongue?

Satterwhite took his time closing the camera and placing it on the counter before he spoke. "I am *not* fighting with you, Davenport. Don't even start with me."

"Well," I said, feeling awkward, "then this might be a good time to drop in on Tiffany and Randolph, if Lucille hasn't taken him home."

Jinks was glad to leave, heading to Forest Hills and to see if Davis had decided to hide out at his mother's. Blood is thicker than water more often than not, but in this instance, I was positive he would avoid her—and the boyfriend—no matter the cost. But Jinks would check it out, anyway, leaving no stone unturned.

The phone rang again as Satterwhite and I were on our way out the door.

Stan Council said, "I got a mug shot I want you to ID that fits the description of your *weasel eyes*."

"My weasel eyes...?"

"The one who tried to smother Alex."

"Oh," I said. "That weasel eyes."

"You got time or are you too busy looking for Davis?"

I watched Satterwhite walk out of the room and down the hallway in the same blue shirt.

"Whatever gave you that idea?" I glanced at the ceiling.

"I know you, girl," Stan laughed.

"Well, you're in a good mood," I said. "Have you and the boys been in the back room working *weasel eyes* over with a baseball bat?"

"Won't be necessary," he said. "We fished him out of the Cape Fear River just after daybreak. If he fell in drunk, he's a candidate for the stupid award, but given the condition of his head, I think he might have had a little help from his friends. Either way, it makes me cheery just to think about it."

"I'll do the mug shot," I said, "as long as you don't make me come in and identify him in person."

"Hah! Ain't nobody doing that after three days in our river."

"How do you know it's him, then?"

"If his wallet hadn't still been buttoned in his rear pocket, I wouldn't be calling you, plus we got a couple of decent fingers left that match up with prints on file. We'll have plenty of time to be sure, though, because this old boy is gonna have to take a little trip up to Chapel Hill to be autopsied."

I swallowed.

"Now, don't go wasting your sympathy. It couldn't have happened to nicer scum. This one has been in and out of town for the last ten years and involved in a lot of dirty stuff around the state—including drugs and murder. We just could never get a good handle on him."

"What time do you want me there?"

Stan said, "I'm way ahead of you. There should be a deputy sitting in your driveway right now. Go take a look-see at this mug shot and tell him to call me with your opinion."

"Wait a second, Stan."

"What is it?"

"I thought you were pulling Detective Paige off the hunt for Davis. He was here earlier and seems hell-bent on pinning this whole mess on a fifteen-year-old boy."

"Now, hold on...hold on..."

I could raise my voice, too. "This time I'm pushing the issue, Stan. The man is bordering on psychotic. He has no business being in law enforcement."

"Like I said, missy, I'm way ahead of you. Sure Paige can be a little erratic..."

"A little erratic? That's what you call it?"

"Let me finish. He's been a good officer for twenty years, whether you like his tactics or not. Also, I'm of a mind to throw a good scare into Davis—enough to straighten him out once and for all. So you just stay out of it, you hear?"

"Seriously," I said. "You're wrong on this one, Stan."

"Now, don't mess with my good mood. I've got every man on duty keeping an eye out for Davis and several of them actively searching for him. When we find the boy, you'll be one of the first to know. Until then, you just stay put and out of the way."

I was silent.

"Are you listening to me?"

"Just trying not to ruin your good humor, Stan. That's the best I can do."

"Well, damn it all," he said. "Put Satterwhite on the phone."

"Not yet. I have some information to pass on to you, which may or may not have something to do with Eddie's murder."

"Spit it out, then."

"I'm supposed to tell you that fish trucks have been seen coming and going after dark at Anderson Pharmaceutical."

There was silence at the other end. "And who exactly might this informant be," said Stan.

"Sam Vitelli, who also mentioned the Cavenaugh brothers and doesn't want you to connect his name to the tip."

"Shit," Stan said in disgust. "My life would be a lot easier if I had your contacts. Anything else? If not, put Satterwhite on."

I called him to the phone, and he watched me out of the corner of his eye as he listened for maybe forty-five seconds. Just before hanging up, he grinned and said, "Right. Stick like glue. I gotcha."

If they just hadn't done that, I would have gotten myself into substantially less trouble. The moment Jinks had closed the front door, I was suddenly certain I knew where Davis was. But I didn't want Stan to find out. And telling Satterwhite was the same as telling Stan. There are some things women just know.

That was the moment I began calculating the ways and means of escaping Satterwhite's clutches.

"As soon as I look at that photo," I said, "let's go check on Tiffany."

Was it just days before that I had sworn off hospitals? Yet I was there again, faithful Tonto at my side, trudging through the hallways searching for Room 622 East. At least on this floor I wouldn't have to deal with Nurse Ratchet.

"First Tiffany, then Randolph," I told Satterwhite.

"You're the boss. Lead on."

At the station, I asked a frazzled young nurse for Tiffany's condition. Her short ponytail had escaped into scraggly poofs of hair hanging down her neck, her cheeks were flushed bright pink, a film of perspiration along her brow. Either she was doing a double shift or it had been a hell of a day. But what did I know? If she had been necking in the storage room, it didn't appear she had enjoyed it overmuch.

"Stabilized and in fair condition," she said, after checking a chart.

"Can she have visitors?"

"For short periods. She had two visitors go in a few minutes ago, so it would be better if you wait. She's still in a lot of pain and not up to much excitement."

"Is she your assignment?"

She pushed stray hair out of her eyes. "For this shift. Are you a good friend?"

"An acquaintance," I said. "Do you know if she needs anything? And have you been able to get in touch with her family?"

"We've been trying to reach her father in Asheville, but so far no one answers the telephone. It would be helpful if we knew where he worked. She tries to tell us when we ask, but with her jaw wired shut and the sedation, we can't seem to get it straight. To be honest, we're not even sure about the Asheville part."

"I don't know the family. What I meant was, does she need a robe, slippers, that kind of thing?"

A look of pity crossed her face. "In a day or two, but right now she isn't even moving around in bed. It's just as well. She won't be eager to look in a mirror any time soon."

Remembering the condition of Tiffany's face, my guess was that she would need a plastic surgeon more than once.

"One last thing," I said. "May I have the name of her doctor?"

"It's Doctor Porter...John Porter, and hold on a second...here we are. The plastic surgeon is Jim Willard."

"Thanks," I said. "I won't keep you any longer."

She glanced at Satterwhite, who smiled at her in a way that made her whole day worthwhile. He knew it, too.

I gave him a thorny look. She was young enough to be his daughter.

We found a seat in a waiting room where we could watch the door to Room 622.

"Looks like we'll be a while," said Satterwhite.

"Unless you have something better to do."

"It depends."

"On what?" I asked.

"Whether I can trust you to stay put long enough for me to...what is it you women say...powder my nose?" He gave me a look that spoke volumes about trust and something else I didn't recognize. But I was equally determined not to fight with him either. He didn't smile.

"Don't be ridiculous," I said. As soon as he was out of sight, I planned to be off like a greyhound after a rabbit.

I would have been, too—the very instant he disappeared around the corner—if the door to Room 622 hadn't opened.

I thought my eyes were playing tricks at first. Richard Howe and Dog Fowler stepped out of Tiffany's room, glanced left and right, then straight at the waiting room.

Together?

Howe's gaze skimmed over me. Did a fast double take. I heard him suck in a sudden breath. Fowler's face turned into an ugly snarl. Howe said something to him in a low voice. They started my way.

I froze.

There was so much primitive menace in their expressions that it scared everything except self-preservation right out of me. There wasn't a soul in sight. No nurses, no doctors or patients. No Satterwhite. I wasted seconds of valuable time wondering if my intuition was working overtime, if Tiffany in her blood-soaked bed had meant *Howe* instead of *how*. All in all, it didn't seem like the right moment to stop and ask.

I bolted for the stairs.

Footsteps thundered behind me.

Dog was bigger than I was, but I hoped not as fast on his feet because of his bulk. I heard him bang through the sixth-floor door and start down the stairs behind me as I passed the fifth floor. Only one set of feet meant one of them had taken the elevator. That one had to be Richard Howe.

How lucky could I get?

Two more flights of stairs. The plaque over the door said *Fourth Floor* and then *Third Floor*, and down another two flights of stairs. He was breathing hard behind me, making grunting animal noises—but gaining all the same. Another set of stairs and he would be almost on me, not to mention that the elevator had long since deposited his partner on the first floor. There were bound to be people in the lobby. What could they do to me in front of dozens of visitors? Or would

Howe try to head me off somewhere on the stairs?

I wasn't about to find out.

My arm slammed the second floor door back so hard I was sure I had cracked the wall. I ran as fast as I had ever run, straight down the hall in the opposite direction, to the side stairs, as if my life depended on it. It probably did.

Dog was fifty feet behind me. So close I thought I could smell him.

I misjudged the top step and slid halfway down, unable to right myself until the turn. If the door at the bottom was locked, I could be a dead woman very quickly. Or wind up like Tiffany. If not, the exit opened onto the back parking lot where the Jeep waited like a getaway car, and no unwashed, beer-bellied, woman-beating son-of-a-bitch in town was going to catch me.

Somewhere on the last set of stairs, a rage settled over me the size of Wrightsville Beach. If I had been a big man, I would have turned and beaten Dog Fowler within an inch of his miserable life.

But I wasn't. And the Glock was in the Jeep.

Sunlight spilled across the concrete landing at the bottom of the stairs, and miracle of miracles, the door was not only unlocked, it was standing wide open, in violation of God only knew how many hospital regulations.

Hurray for smokers.

I hit the parking lot at a dead scramble, my eyes searching frantically for the Jeep. There were literally hundreds of cars parked—too many to find one lonely Jeep in a colossal hurry. Hopelessness almost overwhelmed me when I couldn't find it. I had a sensation of endless wasted seconds, and then I spotted it, half a block away. I chanced a look back at Dog rushing through the doorway.

He was still gaining. Forty feet.

I fumbled in my jacket for the keyless remote, willing my legs to go faster, running like the devil himself was behind me. Maybe he was.

Escape was real. I could taste it.

At fifteen feet I hit the remote, saw the lights blink, and knew I was home free. I jerked the door open and closed, flicked the locks. The key was turning in the ignition when he hit the window with his fist so hard that the vehicle rocked. My arm flew up instinctively. The glass crazed and bent inward. But it held.

It's possible someone screamed. My chest felt like a fire had settled in it. The motor caught, the gear shifted. Dog Fowler drew back his fist for another blow.

I floored it.

Chapter Twenty-nine

On little side street near Greenfield Lake, over a mile from the hospital, I pulled to the curb and rested my head on the steering wheel. My hands were sticky with perspiration.

I dialed 911 on the cell phone and asked to have an emergency check made on the patient in Room 622 East at New Hanover Regional. Then I made a call to the sheriff's office where they promised to find Stan and have him call back. Five minutes. I would wait five minutes.

Soothing classical music was what I expected when I turned on the radio. Instead, WHQR was broadcasting a National Weather Service tornado watch and severe thunderstorm warning. A wide vertical line of strong storms stretched from lower South Carolina to the Virginia line, sweeping eastward with large hail, lightning, and wind gusts to fifty-five miles per hour. Tornadoes had already touched down outside of Camden, South Carolina, killing six people.

Great. Just what I needed. It was early for tornadoes, but not impossible. I could already see the leading edge of the system's gathering clouds on the distant horizon.

From my parking spot under an aging live oak in the middle of the block, I had a clear view of the intersection and main road that circled the lake. Not a green pickup or Mercedes anywhere in sight.

A fat turtle was caught in the roadway, struggling to climb back up the curb to the sidewalk where he would have a straight shot toward the lake. He might not make it, and had probably already realized it didn't pay to wander into dangerous territory. A great blue heron stood motionless near the edge of the lake.

It was as peaceful as Mayberry on a summer afternoon.

I took a deep breath, and the phone rang.

Satterwhite said, "Where the hell are you?"

"Sitting in the..."

"Tell me this, are you in the hospital building?"

"No, because..."

"Damn it, this is not a game, Davenport. Five people are already dead, so if you want to make it six, just keep on playing around."

I said, "Has anyone checked Tiffany's room?"

"I'm standing at the nurses' station, right now, watching the commotion going in 622. *You* are not a part of it."

"Is she all right?"

"I don't know, nor do I know what happened, and as harsh as it may sound to you, she is not my problem. Now where the fuck are *you*?"

I said, "Please be quiet a minute and listen to me. I'm not in the building, but Dog Fowler was in Tiffany's room as of ten minutes ago, and..."

"Shit," he said. "Didn't it occur to you to let me know?"

"Excuse me for wanting to live. Are you interested in hearing the rest or not?"

He said something away from the mouthpiece that I

couldn't catch. There were voices close by his end of the line.

Two houses away, an elderly woman came out her front door, took one look at the shattered glass on my side window, went quickly back inside and closed the door. It was getting to be that kind of neighborhood.

"Satterwhite?"

"Yeah," he said wearily. "I'm still here."

"Listen up. There was someone else with Dog Fowler."

"Who?"

"Richard Howe."

"As in coincidentally with him or..."

"As in leaving Tiffany's room with him, as in conferring with him before sending him to chase me down the stairs and out the building with murderous intent. And as in trying to cut me off at the elevators."

"Davenport..." he said.

"Are you getting the picture?"

"I'm trying, but you're not making it easy. Those are heavy charges to lay on a sitting mayor. Any chance the situation could have been something other than it appeared?"

"I've been accused of many things, Satterwhite, but with a very few exceptions, being stupid wasn't one of them."

"I didn't say you were, but not telling me your location doesn't make you the brightest light on the planet, either."

The turtle flipped over backwards, its legs in the air, struggled to right itself. There was enough traffic on the narrow street to make it a tossup whether he would make it back to the lake without getting squashed.

A headache was building at the base of my skull. "I did

say there were exceptions."

He eased his tone. "Maybe I'm not saying this right, but that doesn't mean I'm any less apprehensive. So give me a break, Davenport. If I have to tell Stan you gave me the slip, he's going to have a heart attack."

That was true.

"Talk to me," he said, in a voice so soft it brought tears to my eyes. "Tell me where you are?"

Instead of answering, I asked, "Have you heard back from the secretary of state's office? Is Richard Howe an officer of AGHR Corporation?"

"No, but AGHR is owned by Anderson Pharmaceutical, and guess who's one of the corporate officers there?"

I fell silent.

"Are you OK, Davenport?"

"I'm trying," I said.

"Why did you ask about AGHR?"

"I just realized the initials read backwards are RHGA— Richard Howe, George Anderson. It seems too simple."

There was a long pause before he said, "I'm beginning to care what happens to you, Davenport. Come back to the hospital. I'll meet you at the front entrance."

"Since when?"

"Since the first meeting, when you tore Paige to shreds, even though you were too tired to stand."

I couldn't think of a thing to say. There was something beyond intimate about sitting in the live oak's shadows, speaking with him by phone. The deep rich voice could have given me goosebumps if I had let it. I closed my eyes to make the moment last and was about to tell him I'd backtrack to the hospital and pick him up.

Then he ruined it by saying, "You know where Davis is hiding, don't you?"

The turtle righted itself, clawed its way to the top of the curb, and promptly fell over again.

I took a deep breath. "I'm sorry. Really I am. It's just that sometimes the ties that bind can be as strong as blood ties."

"You're not going to tell me?"

Again, I said nothing.

His anger was obvious, overlaid with frustration and a hint of disappointment that surprised me. "What if I told you that Tiffany is dead?"

"Please...don't tell me that."

"Does it make any difference to you?"

Everything has made a difference, I wanted to say. Once again, I was on the verge of telling him to meet me at the front hospital doors.

I never got the opportunity.

He took my silence for a negative and, with slow deliberation in each word, said grimly, "If you're still alive when this is over, I'm going to wring your neck."

A green pickup roared through the intersection, heading west toward the river. I disconnected.

Chapter Thirty

Goldie's car was parked on the street. I needed a sounding board in the worst kind of way, someone who knew Richard Howe well enough to tell me if he was capable of murder. And who better than his ex-wife? I pulled around back, thinking that Satterwhite wasn't likely to do more than cruise by looking for the Jeep, assuming he was able to get a car.

No one answered the buzzer. I rang twice more. She could be on the phone with a client, but all our cheeks were going to be red if she was upstairs with Simpson. I had a vague memory of Alex saying something about Goldie and dinner at Gran's, but I hadn't been listening closely enough. It seemed probable that the flight from Dog had scrambled my memory, because none of it had come back to me until just before I reached Mimosa. While I was that close, I figured I might as well check.

I opened the screen and found the door unlocked. She must be there somewhere.

"Goldie?" My voice echoed back with the peculiar vibration of an empty house.

I walked through the kitchen and down the hallway, picking up a small purple sweater with pink roses on the foyer floor, stepped up three stairs and called again.

"Goldie?" I laid the sweater across the banister.

Fading light fell through the side panels of the front door into a cheerful foyer filled with mirrors, prints, and arched doorways to adjacent rooms. Not a place where you could miss a sweater on the floor. I stared at the immaculate rooms. Not a cushion was out of place. Not a speck of dust lay on the wooden tables.

I looked back at the purple sweater. The grandfather clock ticked loud in the empty house. Somewhere over the river, a rumble of thunder rolled across the late afternoon.

There were plenty of reasons why Tully's sweater would be on the foyer floor, the most logical being that Goldie was simply unaware she had dropped it. Still, I felt the hair rise on the back of my neck.

Either I was getting paranoid or my intuition was working in high gear.

I went back out the same way, got the gun out of the glove compartment, and walked across the drive and through the rear hedge to Eddie's house. The yellow tulips were brilliant with color, and a half-dozen fat bumblebees still buzzed around them in the quiet. I tried to tell myself that there was, in all likelihood, nothing wrong. That someone had merely dropped a child's sweater.

But I didn't believe it.

The back door was standing wide open with its jamb splintered, a dirty footprint advertising where it had been kicked.

I didn't have to ask why I chose to check inside. It was the size four purple sweater in my hand, which still smelled of baby shampoo and a faint hint of peanut butter. I couldn't see going back to the Jeep in Goldie's yard to dial 911 and twiddling my thumbs until the police arrived.

The kitchen beckoned like a black hole in front of me. I slid the gun's safety to the off position and walked inside.

In layout, Eddie's house was similar to Goldie's, with a wide center hallway front to back, kitchen and den in the rear, living and dining on either side of the front door, bedrooms upstairs. In the den, toys were scattered about on the rug in front of the cold fireplace—nothing I hadn't seen many times before. I moved around the main level, comforted only a little by the empty feel of the house and the loaded gun in my hand. If there were other things out of place, I couldn't spot them.

Except there was blood on the kitchen countertop.

I flicked on the bright fluorescent lights, and what I had thought was a dish towel turned into Lily Puss, blood matted in her whiskers and champagne-colored fur.

More blood on the white tile of the back splash.

I closed my eyes and images popped up of Tiffany's beaten face and a bloodied Daniel propped up in our bed. I opened them again. No imagination was needed to grasp how much more damage some heartless animal could do to a four-year-old child. The floor was cold under my feet.

I forced myself closer. There was a knife in her side, and from the smears and the strange twist to the head, it appeared the cat had been slammed against the tile—more than once. I shivered.

"Tully?" I shouted. "Alex?"

Nothing came to me but silence as I backed through the rear door, careful to touch nothing on my way, because somewhere in town there was a monstrous son-of-a-bitch who might have left his fingerprints all over the kitchen.

Chapter Thirty-one

For the second time, I was informed by the tart-voiced Janice at the sheriff's department that Stan was still unavailable.

"Look," I said, "it's urgent that you find him—perhaps even a matter of life and death."

By then, she was exasperated. "I'm doing the best I can. He is *not* answering his cellular. Ma'am, I cannot *make* him answer, now can I? It's possible he is in a meeting or doesn't even have his phone with him."

"Who else with authority is available? If you can't find Stan, I need to speak with someone who has enough rank to make a decision."

"Just a minute, I'll find someone." Her tone of voice, with a little interpretation, meant I might get connected to the janitorial department if I wasn't careful.

I had called the sixth floor nurses' station, but they said the FBI man was already gone. If Satterwhite carried a cell phone, I hadn't seen it, and didn't have the number anyway. That would teach me.

I waited through jazzed-up country elevator music about dogs, beer, and wild women, until a familiar voice answered.

"Detective Paige speaking."

My nemesis. Better almost anyone than Paige, but could

beggars be picky at a time like this? Yeah, they could, a little voice said, but at what price in time lost?

"Hello," he said. "Who is this?"

I ignored my misgivings. "It's Carroll Davenport. Stan can't be found and I need your help."

"Well," he said. "Well, well, well. If it ain't the Princess of Bald Eagle Lane actually asking me for assistance."

"Detective, I'm swallowing my pride, eating crow, apologizing to you—whatever it takes." I would even grovel if necessary.

"And just what is this urgent problem Janice pulled me off a break for? You got a hangnail or something, or did all your menfolk get tired of your femi-nazi mouth?"

If I could have reached through the phone lines and wrapped his stained tie around his neck, I would have done so cheerfully. All I could do was hold onto my temper.

A wall of low dark clouds blotted out the light. My headlights switched on automatically. I turned right on Oleander into a long tangle of snarled evening traffic.

"Please listen carefully," I said, and explained what I thought might be happening, as well as it could be explained, in words of few syllables. That something was wrong, that someone had possibly taken four people from a home, or arrived after they left, killed the cat, and then gone after them at my grandmother's. Even to my ears, it sounded like neurotic rambling. Stan himself might have responded the same way.

"A dead cat, huh? That's what you've got? You have any idea how many cats get reported here every month? Runaway cats, dead cats, mangled cats, even horny cats. Bored old ladies believe Satanists get them. If we had to write a report on every dead cat, we couldn't get nothing done. Yellow cats, gray cats, black cats, every kind of colored cat."

I took a weary breath. "Detective..."

"OK, OK!" Resigned. "So which kind of goddamn cat are we describing here?"

Rain began to fall in sudden gusty waves out of the southwest. I turned on the wipers. My jaw was clamped so hard my temples ached. "The Persian," I said, enunciating clearly so even he would understand. "The one with the ten-inch butcher knife still in her side, at Eddie Monroe's widow's house, where the back door was kicked in."

God only knew what a titanic effort it must have been for him, but there was a long silence on the other end of the line.

I hoped it meant he was thinking.

"And what makes you so sure they're all at your grandma's house?"

"No one answers the phone," I said.

The heavy sigh was of thespian quality. "So maybe they went somewhere. Did you think of that? And you just put two and two together and came up with what, twenty?"

"Detective, they are all supposed to be there for dinner. I'm all but begging, because something is very wrong there. I'll admit I don't know for sure what that is..."

"Begging makes a nice change."

When I repeated this conversation to Stan, he was going to tear this man's tongue out. If I didn't do it myself.

"Just check it out." I urged, resorting to the time-tested

remedy for Southern women—a soft voice, a sweet nature, a little wheedling. "Please."

"Now that's a little more like it. Tell you what I'll do. Give me your grandma's phone number, and I'll check the lines and call you back. There's just one little thing, though. You're going to have to cough up Davis Taylor."

Like when Greenfield Lake froze solid, when cows came home to roost, when Paige himself walked on water. "When I find him, you'll be the first to know," I promised, and gave him Gran's phone number and my own. It was the best offer I was going to get.

"What's your location right now?"

"Forest Hills, heading in their direction."

"Oh, no you ain't," he said, suddenly decisive and crisp. "Pull over to the curb right now and wait until I call you back."

"Right," I said, "but please hurry."

Like hell I would.

The Jeep was a quarter of the way downtown, waiting in a long line of traffic stalled by the rain, before Paige called back. Long minutes in which I had time to imagine every gruesome thing that could possibly happen. I pulled to the curb across the street from Bernie's Grocery, where bored young men stood under the overhang and stared at the Jeep. Paige opened caustically. "I talked to your grandma, Miz Monroe. You think you might just be letting your imagination fly away with you here?"

"What did she say?"

"She said everything was just fine and dandy and that you should come on to dinner and quit worrying so much."

Absorbing relief. The words were so typical of Gran that I could almost hear her voice. Often my intuition was wrong.

But not always.

"Still," I said. "Just in case...I think I'd feel better if you could reach Stan and have him meet me there. Or someone. Anyone."

"Ms. Davenport," he sighed heavily, "you're an almighty pain in the ass. Did you know that?"

"Yes," I said, as mellow as I could manage. Several people had been pointing that out of late.

Another heave of breath. "I'm tired of beating the bushes for that overgrown juvenile delinquent, so I'm gonna find Stan for you. And then I expect you and your family to help me get the boy within the hour. You agree to that or all of a sudden I've got a mountain of forms to fill out—which ain't no lie."

"It's a deal," I said, tempted to cross two fingers on each hand.

"Now, I'm serious here. Are you?"

"Absolutely!" A jagged bolt of lightning struck nearby, illuminating the landscape. I flinched. The traffic light in front of me went out.

Paige seemed not to notice. "Then I'm springing into action. Stan is somewhere in the building doing paperwork. I'll find him," he said, and hung up.

Intuition is a fickle soulmate. Like I've said before, sometimes it works; sometimes it doesn't, but wise women learn to be respectful. The sense of danger lingered, fresh and sharp.

I pulled back into the street in a literal torrent of rain,

heading downtown toward Gran's. I was now no more than a mile and a half away.

As always when you're in a tearing hurry, bumper to bumper traffic was at a standstill, the street lined with cars that had pulled over until the rain let up. I knew Wilmington was a fast-growing tourist town, but it was only early March. Where in the hell had all the cars come from lately? Traffic began to inch its way. I turned right and wound my way laboriously down side streets. Half of Wilmington seemed to have taken the same route. The slowness was like a pain in my throat.

At last, with swear words to spare, I turned onto Gran's street and made a drive-by first.

There were no strange vehicles or dirty green pick-up trucks. Not a single car was parked on the street or in the driveway. Only a small green and white helicopter down near the ramp at the base of the bridge. The bridge was old and inspected frequently. I gave the chopper no more than a glance.

No blood dripping down the front steps.

If I had made a fool out of myself by overreacting, why was I still feeling such a sense of urgency?

I parked by the curb and walked around back where, in spite of my admonitions, I knew the door was almost always unlocked. The same two ancient vehicles were in the garage.

The rain had let up a little, and every detail of my surroundings stood out sharp and clear. I could see the tanker, *Cristobal*, easing under the bridge, headed down-river, the white background of the Panamanian flag crisp and new in contrast to the ship's rusty hull. The Cape Fear itself rolled swiftly toward the Atlantic on a falling tide, wide and dark and forty feet deep.

As my right foot touched the bottom porch step I stopped. Better to be safe than sorry with one last insurance policy. I dialed 911 on the cell phone, gave the address and disconnected. There was a strong likelihood that I was going to be more than embarrassed before this incident was over, or fined a hefty sum for falsifying a 911 call.

I sometimes imagine I might have changed the final outcome that night had I simply waited for help. On the other hand, things might have turned out far worse. But at the time, I chose to continue up the stairs, across the porch, and through the unlocked door in an ordinary manner, as if every nerve in my system was not crying out for me to turn around and go in the opposite direction.

"Hello!" I called. "Gran? Lucille? Anybody home?"

The house smelled of fried chicken and chocolate, overlaid with the scent of wood smoke from a fireplace. I passed through the kitchen where steam rose from an open pot on the stove and glanced quickly into the dining room. The long table was set for ten.

Where were they?

In the archway to the living room, I hesitated a fraction of a second before walking through it. To the right of the massive fireplace my eyes found a frozen tableau of four people, so still and anxious they might have been mistaken for figures in a wax museum. The dominating figure of a fierce Lucille stood guard over my grandmother in her favor-

ite stuffed chair, red yarn from the knitting basket in her lap.
At her feet, the lost Davis sat cross-legged with his arms around
Tully.

Four little Indians.

"We've been waiting for you," said Richard Howe, his gun
pointed my way.

And then there were five.

From some primitive place deep inside came the unan-
ticipated urge to run, to weep, to pray. But one look at their
paralyzed faces and my fate was sealed with theirs. I would
not, could not leave them. Those eyes would have haunted
me forever.

"I thought you might be," I said.

Chapter Thirty-two

The room was filled with the presence of evil, recognizable by the sight, sound, and smell of it standing on the far side of the room—Richard Howe, George Anderson, and Dog Fowler.

Anderson also held a gun firmly in his right hand, one with an odd-shaped cylinder on the end, which I assumed was a silencer.

The smell was radiating from Dog.

My four innocents came to life. Tully began to struggle with Davis, whimpering, "Let me go, let me go. I want Auntie Carroll...now." He held her tighter, which only increased her agitation.

"Gran," I said, "are you all right?"

"I have had more enjoyable afternoons," she said with a hint of abhorrence in her voice.

"Haven't we all. Davis? Lucille?" They nodded in unison, without speaking. There was tangible fear in the women's expressions, bordering on panic, and in Davis's face, an anger beyond his years mixed with the same kind of dread.

Lucille, still in her apron, said, "What are they going to do to us?"

"Nothing," I said, after promising myself, just three days before, that I would never lie to her again.

Tully gave another high-pitched squeal of protest and renewed her efforts to pull free of Davis.

Howe raised his voice in a snarl. "Shut the kid up before I have to do it myself."

I said, "That may be easier said than done. Lucille, can you take her?" The gun was burning a hole in my pocket. If he touched Tully, I would kill him.

"Come here to Lucille, angel child. Let's see what your great-grandma has for you to play with." She knelt beside the chair and began to rummage through the knitting basket, pulling out ribbons and different colored yarn with shaking hands. I saw Davis give his aunt a swift glance. She had called him the same name when he was small.

I cleared my throat. "Gentlemen, I think we have a problem here."

Howe stared at me with what Goldie had called his needle eyes. "*You* have the problem. *We* have what they call a situation that needs to be resolved in an expedient manner."

I looked at my watch. "You don't have that long. The sheriff is on his way by now, and I would venture to guess you have as little as three minutes to think of a good excuse for holding two old women, a teenager, and a four-year old child at gunpoint."

George Anderson went pale; his gun hand wavered. "I told you we shouldn't..."

Howe interrupted as if he hadn't spoken. "Wrong. We have more recent information that the sheriff is *not* on his way and won't be coming at all. It is you who have a limited amount of time. So give me the film before we begin eliminating additional members of this family."

"What film?" Something in his voice made me do a double-take. "And what do you mean by additional? Gran, where's Alex?"

"Gone with Valentine and Goldie to get Randolph," she said.

"The film, Carroll." Howe held out his hand. Unlike George Anderson's, it was steady, as if he had been in similar situations before. "As you said, we don't have all day to resolve this problem."

"That might be possible if I knew what film you're talking about. Why don't you enlighten me?"

Anderson found his voice again. "Don't play games with us."

I said to Howe, "Four more people will be arriving soon. Four plus five makes nine witnesses or nine bodies. You can't afford either option, especially now that the sheriff knows you killed Tiffany. You took quite a chance going to the hospital yourself. Now, at least three people know you were in her room just before she died."

"You can't believe we would fall for that, so stop stalling. She agreed to leave town as soon as possible with twenty thousand cash in an envelope in the drawer. Unfortunately, she saw Dog and panicked. He merely placed his hand over her mouth and nose until she passed out. She knows what will happen to her if she talks."

"She's dead."

"Bullshit. You're lying. But, either way, it doesn't make any difference."

"Except for your fingerprints on the envelope."

There was a flicker of rage on his face, and then it was gone. "If you won't give us the film, then we will simply have to wait for the mother of this extremely whiny brat."

"Alex doesn't have it or she would have told me. I don't even know what film you're talking about, much less what could be on it." But it didn't take a nuclear physicist to figure out he meant the missing film from Eddie's camera.

"And you don't need to know," Howe said. "Eddie gave it to one of you, and believe me when I say it will be in the best interest of all of you to return it...especially the child."

"We don't have it," I said. "Nor did we ever have it, or see it, or touch it. None of us. Do you think I'm stupid? We can't give you what we never had in the first place."

George Anderson was growing more agitated. "You said you were just going to scare Tiffany, and I told you this wasn't going to work. We need to get out of here, right now, without letting another minute go by. The company jet is waiting at the airport. I, for one, intend to be on it when it takes off."

"George, George..." Howe said. "Try to be a man for once. First of all, I'm sure it will come as no surprise to Carroll that Detective Paige, being a well-paid and valuable employee, will not be riding to the rescue with the sheriff. Secondly, the plane will not leave without us. Thirdly, we can't afford to leave a single witness—not even the child."

The only sound in the room was a soft gasp from Lucille. I forced myself to breath. "Paige has given an award-winning performance for the last few days. Perhaps they'll deliver his Oscar in Central Prison." I wasn't greatly surprised. It explained Paige's behavior and the differences between Stan's opinion of him and mine. What I didn't know was whether he could have instructed the Emergency Center to ignore 911 calls from this address. If so, we were in hot water indeed—water that would soon be boiling.

"Not the child," Anderson said. "We agreed."

"We agreed to nothing," Howe snapped.

"Excuse me," I interrupted. "Did I neglect to mention that the FBI is also on the way? If you leave now, you still have time to get away." How I expected Satterwhite to guess my location was a puzzle. It all depended on whether he was disgusted enough to go back to the island and prop his feet up on the deck, or mad enough to find Stan and start searching. I had known him less than five days and I was ready to bet all our lives that he was the kind of man who wouldn't walk away.

Howe laughed out loud. "An innovative try...but not one that will get you anywhere. It takes days, sometimes weeks to activate the FBI. By then we'll be safely out of the country, and it won't matter either way to you."

I shrugged and attempted to lie like an expert. "They're already in town. I introduced you to one of them at Romanelli's Restaurant, remember? They're here investigating you and George, and of course, the fish trucks at George's company. They're no doubt puzzled about what fish have to do with pharmaceuticals."

Howe looked at George. "I'll kill Paige for not telling us."

I said, "He didn't know," and hoped they would stew about what else Paige didn't know about. "Let me try to guess what was on the film, though, if you won't tell me. You and George? You and George and drugs? You and George and drugs and money? You and George in a compromising position? All of the above?"

He was not amused. "Don't be ridiculous."

My mind suddenly clicked into a sequence of clarity. How could I have been so dim-witted. "You and Bitsy in a compromising position?"

"That's enough!" Howe said.

Anderson stared back and forth between the two us. "You said Dog saw Eddie and Duane taking photos from across the waterway. It's why we're here—why everything is falling apart. What is she talking about?"

And Duane told Tiffany about the pictures, adding one more layer to the tragedies.

"George, she's talking shit, that's all. You have my word that nothing was going on between Bitsy and me except the utmost respect."

Behind me, Dog Fowler snickered.

As soon as the words were out of his mouth, Howe realized it was the wrong thing to say, because even Anderson, who loved Bitsy, recognized that she respected little, and Howe nothing at all, especially not an alcoholic malcontent who couldn't keep her mouth shut. I watched the doubt multiply on George's face.

"He's a liar," I said. "And he probably even killed her, or had it done by Dog. After all, he had just murdered Eddie and Dennis Mason."

"George, don't listen to her any more. Can't you see what

she's attempting to do?" He turned hard eyes my way. "Dog, search her jacket pockets. Make sure she doesn't have a cell phone."

There was a grunt from behind me before Dog grabbed me roughly. His body odor and breath resembled a Duplin County hog lagoon. The mammoth fleshy arm paralyzed both my shoulders as he went slowly through all my pockets.

"You ain't so smart-shit now, are you, bitch." He pulled out the gun. "Well, well. Look what we got here. Just what you think you're gonna be doing with a piece like this? Shoot yourself most likely." For some reason he found it humorous.

"Give it to me." Howe held his hand out for the gun. "Now get on with it, Fowler. See if she has a cell phone."

"This uppity cow treated me like dirt, boss," he said, his filthy sausage fingers patting all my private places, giving him the biggest thrill he'd had since the last time he'd thumbed through *Penthouse Magazine*.

He found the cell phone without effort. I wasn't sure what else he thought might be hiding down the front of my shirt. The film, I suppose. I shivered with revulsion.

Dog kept his hand on my left breast. "Nothing else on her. Want me to search some more?"

Anderson said, "Let her go, Dog. We don't have time for that now."

He looked at Howe. "Boss?"

It was easy to see who was in charge of that particular piece of low-life.

Howe narrowed his eyes. "Do as he says."

Dog squeezed hard, with a hand that could bend steel, before moving away. I had to clench my teeth to keep from screaming in pain. Davis scrambled to his feet and started in Dog's direction.

Howe raised my own gun and warned, "Sit back down, kid, and don't be stupid. He'll take your head off without half trying."

Davis hesitated, indecision written on his face. Gran looked as if she might pass out any moment.

"Jesus, Lord almighty..." Lucille keened. She put a hand to her eyes, started to rise, and sank back to her knees as if her legs wouldn't hold her.

I shook my head at Davis.

He backed up slowly and sat down again, menace in his eyes, his jaw molded in a hard line. I got my first real glimpse of the man Davis would be when he worked out the kinks of growing up. I liked what I saw in his future.

Assuming he had a future. Or any of us, for that matter.

Dog gave a gluttonous grunt of dissatisfaction, no doubt having much less fun than he would have liked. He flexed his fingers in anticipation, took two steps in Davis's direction.

"He stinks," I complained in a loud voice. "Get him away from us, please."

Howe jerked his head to the right. "Get over here, Dog."

Dog shot me a vile look. I breathed easier in more ways than one when he did as he was told, taking up a stance closer to Anderson. Given a choice between George's gun, the Glock, or Dog, I thought I'd rather take my chances with the fire-arms. At least it would be quick.

The phone rang as loud as a smoke alarm in the silence. The room froze as I counted the rings. For some obscure reason, I thought of Lily Tomlin going, *one ringie-dingie, two ringie-dingie, three ringie-dingie.*

I said to Anderson, who was closest to the phone, "If we don't pick up, they'll know something's wrong."

The answering machine kicked in, and the sound of Alex's voice filled the room. "We're on our way with the patient. Do you need us to stop for anything? Lucille? Gran? Anybody? Where is everyone?"

Anderson tossed the portable phone in my direction, pointed his gun at my grandmother's head. "Answer it," he said. "Tell them everything is fine."

"Alex...it's me, Carroll." I took a deep breath. If she lived through it, Gran would never forgive me for taking such a risk with her life. I closed my eyes, unable to watch, and said quickly, "Take Randolph to my house and stay there. Gran changed her mind. He isn't welcome here." She would know. She had to know.

"What are you talking about? What's going..."

Howe jerked the phone out of my hands and punched the off button. He backhanded me across the face, hard enough to send me stumbling back against the wall.

But Anderson didn't shoot.

"Like mother, like daughter." Howe glared with hatred. "Clever, but fatal."

"What does that mean?" I straightened carefully, keeping my distance.

"Give it some thought, why don't you. A calm day, an

experienced sailor, and...*oh dear*...a dreadful accident," he mimicked in a female falsetto voice that sent a chill down my spine.

"What are you talking about?"

Howe motioned toward Gran. "Look at your grand-mother. She's figured it out."

Gran was faster than I was. Her hand moved toward her heart, a look of torment creeping across her face. "I think he's saying that he killed your mother. Am I right, Mayor Howe?"

"What?" I gasped.

"We knew something was wrong when her life jacket was never found in the search. Sylvia sailed alone from the age of ten and *never once* went without a life jacket—until that day— and still we didn't begin to suspect that you were involved. We should have, and I blame myself, because she confided in me that you wouldn't leave her alone."

My mouth was hanging open. I closed it. "But why? *Why would you kill her?*"

"You don't need to know," he said.

"Don't need to know?" I was close to shouting. "We damn well *all* need to know. You casually toss out that you drowned my mother sixteen years ago, and you want us to just drop it?"

A strong gust of wind hit the side of the house with fury, as jagged streaks of lightning lit up the dark sky. The old house trembled. When hail began to drum on the porch roof, a tornado in early March no longer seemed so far-fetched.

Howe didn't seem to notice. "I don't owe you or your family shit. Sylvia was just like you, convinced she was better than the rest of us. You don't match her in looks, not by a long shot. She was the most beautiful woman I had ever seen in my life—beautiful and rich and a goddamned tease. She threatened to tell Jack." He shook his head. "She deserved it."

I was astounded. If he had been giving a synopsis of Wilmington's history, he might have exhibited more feeling. "So you killed her?" I said. "Just like that?"

"More or less." He shrugged again.

Anger rose in me like a hot tide, for the stupidity of the act, for the waste of a woman's life, for the half-child deprived of her mother. I was just a year younger than Davis when I stared down at her crab-eaten face. And all through the in-tervening years, this bastard had served as mayor twice, been married to my best friend, and gotten completely away with my mother's murder.

"You son-of-a-bitch," I said. "You cowardly, murdering, wife-beating, smirking son-of-a-bitch. I hope you rot in eter-nal hell."

His jaw tightened. "Most likely—if there is a hell—for that and more, but you won't be around to see it. And with a little luck, I'll live the good life another fifty years in luxury, far away from the provincial little town of Wilmington, North Carolina."

I shook my head. "It will never happen." If we were go-ing to die, I would make sure this man never slept peacefully again if he lived to be a hundred.

"Richard...?" George Anderson tried to interrupt once again.

Howe smiled a cold hangman's smile. "And why is that,

Sylvia's daughter?"

"Because I had a phone call this afternoon from Sam Vitelli in New York. Do you know who he is? No? George does. I can tell by the look on his face that he knows. I became family to Sam when I married his profligate son, and my point is this: He will never rest until the two of you die the most painful deaths possible. No matter where you run or how much money you take with you, one day you'll be strolling down the avenue in Buenos Aires..."

"Shut up," Howe snapped. "The women in your family do tend to run off at the mouth at the most inopportune times."

If I had expected him to shake in fear, it wasn't going to happen. I didn't know myself what Sam would do. But I could hope.

"I have a question." My grandmother got stiffly to her feet.

"So do I," George Anderson said. "Several questions, as a matter of fact."

"What the hell do *you* want to know?" I wasn't sure whether Howe was asking Gran or George.

Despite her frailty, she didn't shrink from his tone. "Just this—you seem to have killed everyone else. Did you murder my son-in-law, Jack?"

"Oh, my God!" Bile rose in my throat. For almost seven years I had been consumed with anger and guilt because I thought my father had committed suicide while I was indulging in hysterics in a New York psychiatric hospital.

"Did you?" Gran persisted.

"What the fuck difference does it make to an old woman like you?" Howe said. "It's over and done with. Who the hell cares?"

Gran stood straighter. "I care. Before I die, I need to know whether I failed him, too."

Another load of guilt on the wrong person.

Howe curled his lip. "Wouldn't we just hate for you to die unhappy. Jack had it coming. He wanted to pull out of the partnership and blow the whistle on the rest of us. So, yes, I killed him. Is that the right answer? Now sit the hell down before I shoot you on the spot."

Gran sank into the chair slowly.

Howe continued, "Now listen up, everybody. Playtime is over. Your time is up. We need to leave and leave now. Dog, take them to the boat and over to the island. Do what you have to do, and get back across the river as fast as you can. George, give him the gun with the silencer."

"Not yet," George said. "There is one more question that needs to be answered." He raised the gun and pointed it at Howe.

"Goddamn it, George."

"You lied, didn't you? As sure as I'm standing here, you killed Bitsy, or had it done. Who did it? You? Dog? That filthy piece of garbage you blamed it on and dumped in the river? Tell me!"

"You've got it all wrong."

"No. I think I'm right on target. You used my company to make millions off drugs, and then you screwed my wife. I knew something was wrong, but I thought she was dissatisfied with me and the new house, even that she might be meeting someone there when I was out of town. I didn't think it would be you."

"So you burned the house down. Do you think she didn't guess? Oh, it took her a day or two, but when she wasn't drinking, she finally figured it out."

"*You* burned the house, George?" I said, but he neither acknowledged my question or even seemed to hear it.

The gun was still in Howe's hand, hanging loosely at his side. "Your millions, too, George."

"Shut up!" Anderson shouted. "The money wasn't enough for you, was it? You fuck half the women in town, and you couldn't leave my wife alone? And then you killed her...cut her throat...or had Dog do it." He was silent for seconds. There was an enormous bolt of lightning that seemed close enough to have struck the garage, causing the chandeliers to sway. When the repercussion died away, George said in a hard, cold voice, "I, too, just want to hear you admit it."

I like to think we would have warned Anderson, at least given him some small sign, if we had noticed Dog moving into position behind him. But my eyes were fixed on the two guns. I'll never know. Perhaps we wouldn't have.

And then, several things happened almost in unison.

Dog leapt for Anderson and got one arm around his neck and another on his gun hand. Two shots went wild amid women's screams, mine included, straight into great-grandfather Monroe's portrait, before Dog tore the gun out of his grasp. And Davis jumped to his feet, snatched up Tully, and was out of the room like a seasoned Olympic runner.

And then there were three.

A furious Howe raised his gun, pointed it straight at Anderson's heart. "Since you just have to know, George, Bitsy was a sniveling, drunken bitch—not even very good in bed— but you don't need me to tell you that." He nodded once at Dog, who tightened his grip around George's neck.

There was a muffled popping sound and a louder thud as Dog dropped him on the hardwood floor, lifeless, his neck bent at a hopeless angle.

And then he kicked him.

Howe continued in a normal voice as if George could still hear, or ever hear anything again. "I went by that last morning and found her drunk, on the telephone with Carroll, setting up a meeting and promising to tell all. Why wouldn't I listen in? Lucky for us I did, don't you think, George?"

At that moment, I gave up all hope of getting us out of the situation alive.

He snapped at Dog, "Go get the boy and the kid and meet us at the boat. We've wasted enough time."

I pleaded with him. "Leave Tully. How much can a four-year-old describe anyway? Haven't you done enough to this family?"

Grandmother and Lucille were in shock. Neither moved.

"Now!" he howled at them. "Or I'll put a bullet in her brain." He shoved the gun muzzle against my temple so hard I thought I would pass out. With Lucille's help, Gran climbed unsteadily to her feet.

"That's better." Howe was breathing hard. "Now, out the door. Move it. And, to answer your question, no, I've haven't done enough to your family. But this will finish it."

We went out the door onto the back porch in a pitiful cluster, Lucille on one side of Gran, me on the other. Outside, the storm was raging, the late afternoon sky unnaturally dark and split by lightning every few seconds. For once the weatherman had called it correctly. Hail lay scattered on the ground and the wind was gusting to the full fifty-five knots. Surely nobody would walk out into that—not even a madman.

I was wrong. Howe had no fear of lightning. He prodded us down the stairs and across the grass to the water's edge where the boat waited, a shallow johnboat, maybe twelve feet long. We were shaking with fear, cold and panic, holding on to each other to keep the wind from knocking us off our feet.

The river was a rolling mad thing, with waves boiling like pre-hurricane surf in September, a reminder of why it was called the Cape Fear. The small boat would never make it to the far side.

Don't get in the boat, I kept telling myself. No matter what happens, just don't get in the boat. I tried not to think about snakes and alligators on Eagle Island or giant catfish in the river.

They were likely the least of our problems.

Dog reappeared out of the downpour with his gun at the base of Davis's neck. "I couldn't find the kid anywhere. We got to leave her," he yelled. There was blood, mixed with the falling rain, streaming from a cut on Davis's forehead. But at least he was still alive.

"You won't find her," Davis shouted above the rain. "I

hid her in the silver room, and you ain't gonna find it. Not ever."

Richard Howe's expression was pure contorted rage. For the first time, it must have occurred to him that he might not make an easy, clean getaway, and that even a child as young as Tully could put him in the gas chamber. For an endless moment, I thought he would lose control and shoot Dog, Davis, maybe all of us, on the spot.

Even Dog was stiff with tension.

Coming back to life, Howe railed into the storm. "I'll take care of the goddamn kid myself, even if I have to burn the house down. We're running out of time. Now, get them in the boat and over to the island. Shoot them and throw them in the swamp or the river. I don't give a shit which. Then get back here fast."

Chapter Thirty-three

Dog shoved Davis in our direction. "You heard the man. Fun time is over, so get in the fucking boat."

"We'll never make it." I had to shout to make myself heard. "Five of us in a johnboat with an outboard that size? Look at the way the river is running. We'll be swamped in forty feet of water before we've gotten a quarter of the way across. Only a fool would try it."

Awesome, simultaneous bolts of lightning swallowed up Dog's reply. He cast a quick look up the hill, but Howe had disappeared into the wall of rain. Even the lights from the house were barely discernible.

I held my breath.

Dog took two steps, jerked Lucille away from us, and put the gun to her head. "In the boat...every last motherfucking one of you...and do it fast."

We didn't budge.

"Do it!" he bellowed.

My hand on Davis's arm warned me he was about to launch himself at Dog, guaranteeing a bullet in Lucille's head or in his own. Maybe both. I could feel his muscles tighten.

"No, Davis. Do as he says. Please."

He hesitated, then jerked away from me and helped Gran into the boat. I held out my hand to Lucille. She took it, trembling, when Dog let her go. We turned and climbed in the boat ourselves, huddled like lambs waiting for the wolves. Dog climbed in after us.

I shrugged out of my jacket and put it around Gran's shivering shoulders. "I love you," I said close to her ear. "We're going in the water one way or another, so tell Davis to stick with you. Take off your shoes and say a prayer."

It was our only chance. We had to make it. There was no way for Tully to escape from the hidden room unless someone opened it from the outside, and they would assume she was with us in the boat. The thought of Howe setting the house on fire to kill Tully was a pain beyond bearing.

It took a moment for my words to sink in. When they did, she nodded and put a frail, cold, goodbye hand against my cheek for a fragment of time—or all of eternity. I saw her feet move, her toes ease her shoes off. She leaned toward Davis, and his head bent to listen.

He was a strong swimmer. Much better than me. Together they might have a chance, if he didn't lose his head and fight the awful current.

The motor ground twice before it caught, coughed, caught again, and Dog revved it to an ear-shattering roar.

I turned so he wouldn't see my lips move, and said to Lucille, "Take your shoes off and stay with me, no matter what happens." She had never learned to swim, even though she'd lived all her life near deep water, and she was petrified. Her reply was lost in the noise of the engine, but the shake of her head was a clear, emphatic *no*. All in all, it was not the best of times for Lucille to turn stubborn. But I was willing to throw her in the water if necessary, because we damn sure weren't going without her.

Something nudged me along the upper thigh. I put my left hand down and touched Lucille's frigid fingers...and something else. Something heavy and metallic. Where in God's name had she gotten a gun? I fingered it with care.

Two magnificent old ladies had lied to me about the Luger and hidden it in the bottom of the knitting basket.

The boat began to move out into turbulent water, which instantly washed over the side of the low riding craft. Once out in the current, it was even worse than it appeared from shore. To be in the water without a lifejacket was tantamount to suicide. The beach water temperature was still in the fifties, the river water even colder, but in that range of temperatures it didn't matter much. Hypothermia would occur in minutes, especially for Gran and Lucille.

The cold metal in my left hand was useless so long as Dog kept one hand on the tiller and his gun pointed with the other. Beyond searching for the safety with my fingers, my brain didn't know what else to do.

The boat was riding lower and lower, although only seconds had passed since we left the safety of land.

I had never thought much about whether I believed in miracles, but when we needed one the most, there was a sudden decrease in the driving rain. I looked back toward the now visible house. The top of the hill seemed to be filled with flashing blue lights, with more near the water. A movement near the base of the bridge caught my eye—the turning of helicopter blades.

"He's leaving you behind!" I shouted at Dog. "Look at the helicopter!"

Astonished was the only way to describe his look, and it was quickly replaced by bellowing fury. He was a big man, but he released the tiller and stood up, firing in rage at the rising helicopter. The little boat rocked like it was caught in an earthquake.

I had time for only three fast shots before Dog went over backwards, capsizing the boat and plunging us all into the icy, bone-numbing water. I made a wild grab for Lucille before she was swept away, catching her, I'm almost certain, just by the apron strings.

When I looked up, Davis was already yards down river doing a sidestroke at an angle to the shore. I couldn't see Gran's head anywhere.

Of Dog Fowler or the johnboat, there was no sign at all. Looking back, it seemed that we were struggling in the water an endless length of time, but much of the nightmare is vague in my mind. I remember glimpsing the helicopter over Lucille's shoulder, rising toward the bridge supports. Then, whether from pilot inexperience or the strong winds, the propeller appeared to clip the metal understructure. There were sudden fireworks from sparks on steel. For a brief moment, the helicopter seemed to hang in mid-air, before abruptly exploding in a brilliant conflagration of flames so bright I could see the horrified faces in the cars on the bridge.

In slow motion, the ball of fire half-bounced, half-slid, down the abutment into forty feet of water.

Not much is clear after that, except that I remember

thinking it seemed an impossible one hundred feet back to shore with the water raging downstream and my arms already growing numb. Violent waves broke over our heads and rolled us under dark water again and again until it was impossible to breathe. The current swept us almost to the bridge before rescuers formed a human chain out into the cold water. We would not have made it otherwise.

More than a dozen men, mostly from the sheriff's department, were in on the rescue, including Stan, Satterwhite, and Valentine. Except for Davis, who walked ashore with minimal help, we had to be carried to dry land. Neither my legs nor my head seemed to be working properly, but I was aware that Gran and Lucille were being bundled into an ambulance that arrived out of nowhere. God only knew what kind of bacteria had flowed into their aging lungs.

I recall Alex waiting on shore with Goldie and Randolph, in desperate agony because she thought Tully had been with us in the boat, and men racing for the house to make sure Howe hadn't found her.

Of course he hadn't. Our Davis saw to that.

I think I even saw Randolph with his one good arm around Lucille, but after so many years, that may have been wishful thinking.

The rest is blurred, except that I remember the warmth and smell of a leather jacket placed around my shoulders and an attempt to put me in a car. I kept calling for Davis, refusing to leave unless he came, until Satterwhite persuaded me he had gone with Randolph and the women in the ambulance.

I have an obscure memory of someone crying. I think it was me.

Epilogue

I slept for eleven hours straight and was having coffee on Gran's back porch when Stan stopped by around noon the next day. He brought a bottle of quality champagne and a dish of Opal's blackberry cobbler.

"Do you want the good news or the bad news first?" The old wicker rocker creaked alarmingly as he settled his bulk.

I held up my hand, palm out. "No bad news at all, please. You can just take it right back where it came from. But I thank you for the champagne and the cobbler."

He laughed. "Now, when's the last time you saw me go shopping? The champagne is from Satterwhite."

"Couldn't he bring it himself?"

"Well, now we're getting to the part you aren't gonna like. He's gone."

"Gone?" I said, the pit of my stomach cramping. I told myself it was the river water, tried to joke about it. "Just when I was getting used to having him around." The pain was like an open wound.

Stan slapped his knee. "If you could see the look on your face. Didn't I tell you, girl, that Satterwhite was gonna be the one to straighten you out?"

I was tired beyond description. "Be nice, Stan. I'm not in real good fighting form today."

"Then, this ought to cheer you up. We raided George Anderson's company late last night and his house shortly thereafter. So, naturally we had to do the same for Mayor Howe. Ain't it surprising what kind of evidence you can find in computers these days—even stuff people think they've erased forever—including bank account numbers in the Caribbean and a record of some hefty payments to Dennis Mason. Enough, anyway, to close down Anderson Pharmaceutical and indict the Cavenaugh boys, thanks to a long conversation with a friend of yours in New York."

"Sam Vitelli?"

Stan leaned back in the rocker and stared at the porch ceiling. "I declare, isn't that the oddest thing. I can't rightly remember his name. But no self-respecting sheriff would be having a friendly conversation with Sam Vitelli, now would he?"

"Certainly not," I said, "except from a public phone booth."

He got up chuckling. "I've got to get back to work. You think you can behave yourself for a while without me having to worry about you?"

"Count on it. I've had enough excitement to last me a lifetime." The words had a familiar ring.

I fought the urge to ask until he started down the steps. "Wait, Stan. Did you find either one of them?"

"You mean Dog and Howe? We located the mayor, still strapped in what was left of the helicopter. As for the other one—not yet. The river bottom is like black bean soup down there, a risk for my divers every time they go under. One way or another, he'll turn up in a few days, and if not, well...I rather like the idea of Dog becoming fish food."

"My feelings, exactly."

Stan looked away at the river, somberness in his expression. "He killed Eddie, you know. There's no doubt in my mind. Maybe Dog and Snake Eyes did it together, but only Dog had a record of prior knife use. We'll never know everything that happened that night. Perhaps Dennis was doing a little blackmail, or maybe Howe and Anderson were just ready to cut him loose because he was becoming unreliable. I'm betting they followed Dennis and Eddie from the Yacht Club, figuring they'd kill two birds with one stone."

I blinked back tears and couldn't find the energy to agree with him.

"Now, don't let your grandma come home and catch you with a face like that. There's nothing you can do for Eddie now, and everything in the world you can do for the rest of them."

He continued on down the stairs, pausing again to throw a last comment over his shoulder. "I almost forgot. Satterwhite said to tell you he was sent to Idaho for undercover work and for you to keep the champagne cold. Is that good enough?"

For a man with no sleep, there was way, way too much bounce in his step.

The Cape Fear Memorial Bridge was closed three days for repairs.

During the Azalea Festival that April, a barge salvaging

heart of pine logs from the early eighteen hundreds dislodged the remains of Dog Fowler from the muck at the bottom of the Cape Fear River. Back on board the ship, one of the divers turned in his gear and quit on the spot. Later, in a Channel Three interview, Alvin Jenkins swore he'd rather starve than ever dive the river again.

In late June, three weeks before an early hurricane named Elizabeth, Randolph was repotting orchids and found a canister of film buried under a yellow phalaenopsis. When the film was developed, there were telephoto shots of the rear of the house on Figure Eight Island before the fire, taken from somewhere across the waterway. As the only house at the end of a new street, it made a perfect meeting place. There were several clear shots of Bitsy and Richard Howe in the kind of compromising activity that married women are well advised to avoid. There were pictures of Eddie and Tully feeding seagulls on the beach. Treasures of love. And sharp closeups of Richard Howe taking a briefcase from the hands of the older Cavenaugh brother, standing side by side with George Anderson. Enough to kill for.

After the river, Davis confessed to having been with gang friends the Sunday night that Eddie was killed, not knowing they were on their way to make a drug delivery. He was right to keep quiet. The three gang members are now serving jail time. Once again, he was lucky. He enrolled in summer school, and Gran offered to pay for as much college as he wanted—even medical school. Call it a bribe if you like, but we no longer worry about him. The first summer session he earned straight As.

In the aftermath of a Category 4 Elizabeth, we had more immediate concerns, among which was the loss of the land-scaping and the greenhouse, crushed by the owls' four-hun-dred-year-old live oak. Trees and shrubs fortunate enough to survive would take years to recover. Randolph was devas-tated.

We were among the lucky ones.

Between them, Alex and Goldie had thirty-five old trees down on the roof, the brick wall, their cars, and Tully's new swing set. The chaos, surprisingly, seemed to be what Alex needed to get past the shock of Eddie's murder. She threw herself into the clean-up, directing burly out-of-town tree crews, roofers, and stump grinders three times her size. Eddie would have been proud.

What little time she had left over at the end of the day, she put into planning Simpson and Goldie's wedding.

In the meantime, Tully turned five. My remarkable grandmother celebrated her eighty-sixth birthday. Randolph and Lucille, while still not exactly having a kiss-and-make-up relationship, at least had a calmer one. Gran called it hav-ing *less bite to their barbs*.

As for me, life seemed to move forward, backward, and sideways, all at the same time. There were only occasional postcards from different cities around the country. No signature, no return address, no written words—six in all. I didn't know quite what to make of them.

And then, on a steamy Indian summer morning in late September, I carried my coffee along the path toward the new greenhouse. The mist was just rising off the Intracoastal Waterway, with the call of gulls in the calm, and from somewhere close by, the ring of rigging on a sailboat.

My head turned toward the sound and found a dark green vessel, maybe forty feet in length, docked at the end of the pier and bobbing on the falling tide. The name on the side was painted in large gold letters—*The Three Marys III*.

I went back inside for the bottle of champagne before making the journey down the hill.

Wanda Canada

Wanda Canada is an experienced real estate broker, renovator, and master gardener. She lives on the Intracoastal Waterway in Wilmington, NC, with her husband, John. *Island Murders* is her first published novel.